THE SUTBURYS

Other books by Pamela Hill:

My Lady Glamis
Tsar's Woman
The House of Cray
A Place of Ravens
Fire Opal
Daneclere
Stranger's Forest
The Green Salamander
Norah
Whitton's Folly
The Heatherton Heritage
The Malvie Inheritance
The Devil of Aske

THE SUTBURYS

PAMELA HILL

St. Martin's Press
New York

Author's Note

DURING 1832, FIFTY-FOUR BILLS WERE INTRODUCED TO PARLIAMENT
CONVEYING THE OPPOSITION OF THE TURNPIKE TRUSTEES TO
MECHANICALLY PROPELLED ROAD CARRIAGES. IT IS THEREFORE
REASONABLE TO SUPPOSE THAT ONE MIGHT HAVE BEEN ENCOUN-
TERED ON THE ROAD IN 1829.

Library of Congress Cataloging-in-Publication Data

Hill, Pamela.
    The Sutburys.

    I. Title.
PR6058.I446S8 1989   823'.914   88-29915
ISBN 0-312-02648-X

First published in Great Britain by Robert Hale Limited.

First U.S. Edition

10 9 8 7 6 5 4 3 2 1

ONE

Felix Sutbury, second Viscount Harmhill, urged his four-in-hand forward with a speed which owed itself partly to ill-temper, partly because a new horseless carriage, of the kind obnoxiously to be seen on high roads, was having the impertinence not to let him pass; was, in fact, trying to outrace him. The sight of its spiked wheels and metal body, and the tilt of the driver's cap from behind, unfuriated Harmhill, who risked everything, flicked a knowledgeable whip towards the horses, and caught, as they thundered past, the rival driver on the cheek like a gnat. A shout came; the driver was evidently too ill-bred to swear like a gentleman. Harmhill muttered to his tiger Joshua, who was nowadays his valet as well, 'Fling the fellow a couple of guineas; they will pay his toll-fee.' For toll-gate keepers were notoriously disapproving of the iron horse which prevented their making money by feeding and watering. But for Harmhill, as he passed through, there was only a nod and a pulled forelock. It was known that the old Earl, his father, was ill, and that the heir made all speed for Fenfallow.

Harmhill returned his thoughts to that business. His temper sweetened somewhat now the motor-driver was out of the way. His long curious nose, like the proboscis of an ant-eater, sniffed the clean air now town was left behind; his curious eyes, clear as green water except for odd flecks of brown, looked out from beneath his tall yellow plush hat, which he wore with insouciance. He was not in fact thinking

The Sutburys

of his father, whose illness alone would have brought him down into the country at the very start of the London season. He was thinking of his mistress, Tilly Vaux, and wondering what costly mischief she would have got up to as soon as he himself was out of the way. He did not think she was unfaithful, but she took a fancy for things he could not afford. Last time it had been a snuff-box, tooled in elaborate gold, with a rendering in enamels of the Queen of Sheba visiting Solomon, all in powder and last century's dress. 'What good is it to you?' Felix had asked her. 'You don't take snuff.' But it appeared that Randleford's mistress collected the things 'although she don't take the horrid stuff either; but the colours here are pretty, and will match my Paris fan you gave me.' So she had cozened him, and he had bought the box; and as a result had tried to outbid Count D'Orsay last night at Crockford's, and by four in the morning had lost two hundred guineas to him, a sum which might keep that exquisite in gloves for a fortnight, but represented a serious loss to Felix Harmhill, though he had come away brad-faced as everyone did, win or lose.

But it was a disaster; his money was running out, his father's patience exhausted, and the creditors clamorous. Indeed the bailiffs might be waiting at the door in Arlington Street now, the more so if they had heard my lord was ill. He wondered if he dared approach the Earl yet again for rescue from his difficulties. It depended on how ill the old man really was. Guy would be there, no doubt, subtly working against him. Guy wanted to inherit, and could not.

But it was a fine day, at any rate; the night's cobwebs blown away as Harmhill raced along the road, clear of any rival, his fashionably cut curled chestnut hair flying out beneath the plush hat's brim, his caped coat immaculate. Joshua the ex-tiger gazed at him adoringly. Free with his money, the Viscount was, and never mean. Joshua had been born about thirty years ago into a horse-coping family which fed him assiduously on gin when a baby to keep him small; as a result, he had grown less tall than Bonaparte, the required size for carriage-gentlemen: the lean bones strained out of his face as though he were not now well found and as well fed as any. It had been a good day for him when the Viscount took him over from old Lord Cranbury, along with the latter's horses. Otherwise, if anything had gone wrong, it might have been the gutter, especially if one fell ill. 'Can you brush clothes, fellow?' the Viscount had asked, running his speckled gaze idly over the young man who was not, in fact, as young as he looked. Brush clothes? He'd have brushed his fingers off to be able to handle those elegant coats and waistcoats, the plush yellow hat, the buckskins and high boots that had to be cleaned daily with champagne and wax, the snowy cravats to be laundered carefully by the maid while he, Joshua, stood over her. As to the horses, they knew him; he'd worked hard, first of all standing behind his new master in the brougham and now, with this much faster piece of business, seated below him on the step, except when Miss Tilly was there. Lord! that was a piece if you liked, all honey-gold curls and long eyelashes, and a figure to ravish, as the French said. It was easy to see that the Viscount doted on her, and hadn't been pleased to have to leave her to her devices and come down and visit the old Earl at Fenfallow. But the visit, and maybe the funeral, would soon be over and they could go galloping back to Arlington Street, to the elegant little house there and the stables, which Joshua kept clean as any drawing-room. At Fenfallow the grooms were idle with having too little to do, and there might be foul hay; he must inspect it for mould before Peg and the other three beauties got a mouthful, and he'd look in the water-trough for worms; you never knew. This job was too good to lose; if only it lasted!

Felix Harmhill slowed the horses a little as he crossed the shire border and at last began to recognise the great flat plain of his own county, the hedgerows stretching mile on green mile, the land yawning grey into the distance, just out

of sight of the sea. The only slight eminence was Knocking
Hill, where they had once taken a priest and hanged him.
The countryside always stirred boyhood memories in Felix,
of riding out, rambling out, during school vacations or,
further back, when he was small, with his tutor, the curate, a
pallid individual glad of the money but able to leave no
strength of recollection in his pupil's mind. Felix remembered home more clearly; his vague, beautiful, discontented
mother, like a caged animal trapped at Fenfallow, a dull
place; she had relished nothing more than a day out with the
hounds, and this was not hunting country. When Felix was
twelve years old she died, he truly believed, of boredom. He
had not loved her particularly. There had been a quiet,
competent governess in charge of his sister Fanny, a delicate
child addicted to head-colds. When the Countess had died
Felix's father had not dismissed the governess, and within
the month had married her. That accounted for the
existence of his half-brother Guy.

He reined in soon at sight of the house, rising out of the
flatness with its jumbled lack of coherence. It had endured
building on at different periods, depending on whether
the family had money or had not. The last time had been
in his grandfather's day. Felix did not remember the old
gentleman, but there had been a baronetcy and then an
earldom for some signal favour to the senile George II,
deprived of his wife's counsel and of Walpole's. Felix
reflected, not for the first time, that there had been a
history of royal approval from the time of Dutch Billy, but
royal George nowadays did not favour *him*, immured as he
mostly was at Windsor with Lady Conyngham. Felix flung
the thought from him and returned to gazing at Fenfallow,
while Joshua watched him like a dog. The house was
hardly, Felix decided, imposing enough to be called an
earl's seat; perhaps that was why the county had never
taken his family seriously. Nevertheless Fenfallow had its

ghost, a dark-haired young woman who was to be seen at times, searching for her baby. There was also the legend of his Dutch great-grandmother, who had drunk herself to death alone in the tower room. There was a canal which had been built in her time; he turned his head and saw it, not travelled by barges nowadays, overgrown with green duckweed and the old locks rusted with lack of use. Water-meadows stretched about it, having once been drained; when it was dry weather they were grazed occasionally by sheep. The whole place had an air of idleness and decay. He seldom troubled to come here. In any case his father would not welcome him even now; once, on holiday from Harrow, Felix had brought home measles, had himself recovered, but Fanny had caught them from him and it had turned to pneumonia and she had died. Fanny had been her father's favourite, and after her death she had evidently taken on the qualities of an angel. Guy had caught measles also, but had survived. Survival was typical of Guy.

Unwelcome at home, Harmhill had soon begun to seek diversion and friends elsewhere. He had been fairly popular at school and had frequent invitations to stay in the holidays with one or other family of friends; or, and this he liked best, with his Irish godmother, his mother's elder unmarried sister Eileen Clonmagh, at Marishnageen in County Waterford. Eileen loved Felix as she loved almost everybody, and had let him run wild. When he closed his eyes he could still smell the roses in her secluded garden, hear the bees in the limes and savour the dark shadow of monkshood among damp ferns and brighter flowers. The thought of Marishnageen made him feel lazy and happy, even now when his father might be already dead. He recalled the reason for his journey here, and started up the horses, walking them across to Fenfallow.

*

He had come too late. The housekeeper, Mrs Canning, met him at the door, her eyes full of tears; she was a dutiful soul. She had been longer than anyone else in the Earl's service, having begun as kitchenmaid less than a generation after the death of old Judith Ryden in her cups. 'Oh, sir, my lord,' she said, 'he's gone. He died in the night. Mr Guy was with him, and my lady.'

So now he himself was Earl of Fenn, and not rich by any standards; but the will was yet to be read. His father's body lay in the great hall, with silence all about it and old Judith's portrait looking down on it; two alien presences stood in the silence, his father's widow and his half-brother Guy. He spoke to them while looking at the dead face in the coffin.

'Leave me. I would be alone with him for a little while.'

Emily, the governess who had become a Countess, inclined her head in its black veil, and went out with dignity; since her marriage she had performed no single action which was not discreet. The Honourable Guy Sutbury followed her more slowly, lingering to look on their father's face in a manner that made Felix long to thrust him away. Guy was a slight young man with his mother's prim regular features; one might pass him any day in the street without noticing him particularly. He had declined the traditional younger son's portion in the Church or the armed services, and had been entered, with the late Earl's approval, on the board of one of the lesser-known merchant banks. So seldom had Felix encountered him in London that they might have been in separate houses; the hours at which Guy came and went to Arlington Street were quite different from Felix's own. As he passed Guy said softly: 'I would have a word with you when you have the leisure; perhaps after the funeral.' The tones held faint mockery, a reminder that it was he, the younger son, who had taken the trouble to be present at their father's death-throes. Felix gave a curt nod and mother and son went out. Now he and his father were left alone.

He stared down at the long-nosed waxen face, feeling as if he saw himself as he would be when an old man. The hair lay sparse on the balding head, the mouth, with its grey mutton-chop whiskers, thin and indrawn as if lacking the dentures the Earl of Fenn had worn in former years. The disposed lining of the coffin hid the ears. Felix laid the back of his hand on the cold cheek; how cold it was! As always in life, he could think of nothing to say to his father, yet felt as if that spirit lingered near the body still, and would listen. There had always been constraint, even coolness, between them even before Fanny's death. Had the old man in fact ever loved anyone? He had lived out his long life selfishly, showing no open affection to the two women he had married. He had been a careful enough landlord and had treated his tenants fairly; there would be a good attendance at the funeral. He had been Member for the borough for some years, doing everything that was expected of one in that position, but without enthusiasm or flair. Likewise he had had few vices, unless coldness was a vice; did not gamble, womanise or blaspheme or drink heavily. One could not love him; now, in their last time together, Felix felt in himself this lack of love. Could he have done more to gain his father's affection? Could he have toadied, like Guy? He knew that he could not; and there it was.

He turned away, having made no promises to the dead that he would not keep. The title was his, and its responsibilities, at least; the house and estate were entailed since his grandmother's day; she had been an heiress. When the funeral was over the lawyer would read the will, and he himself would not give Guy a hearing until afterwards. Thereafter he must stay here for a few days, as was his duty.

As he left the hall to go to his room he saw Countess Emily come slowly downstairs, her black draperies slipping after her down the steps. She must have been watching to see how long he would stay by the coffin. There was no sign of Guy at her side.

In his room, Joshua had laid out his mourning-clothes, having already seen to the horses which was the first necessity. Felix thought how glad he was of Joshua, almost his only friend here, if one could think so of a servant. He must try to keep the man paid, whatever happened.

The Earl's funeral took place with its full panoply of sable plumes on the horses, the tall black hats of the hired mourners who surrounded the coffin, weepers flapping like bats' wings about their faces in the slight wind. All along the way, and into the church itself, estate workers and tenant farmers stood with their round hats in their hands, the women, in their best dark stuff, bobbing as the hearse went by. The service itself was packed, with county folk at the front in their own pews, and servants at the back. There was a smell of moth-balls. Felix, as the chief mourner, stared at the elaborate bonnets the squires' wives wore, having no doubt seen in the illustrated gazettes the latest fashions from London and Paris and having had these copied, as well as it might be done, by the local milliner. The ladies' husbands nodded over tight-buttoned coats, high cravats supporting their heads with a decent show of black. None of them had been intimate with his father; there had been little hospitality at Fenfallow, no doubt stemming from the lack of social approval among surrounding Jacobites in King Billy's reign; since then, the Fenns had been blacklisted. But the Glorious Revolution was a century and a half ago; why persist in this thou-and-I? He must see; perhaps something might be done, later; a few dinners given to other folk than the parson twice yearly. The latter was earning his stipend now, declaiming over the many virtues of the deceased in a sermon that was much too long.

The new Earl glanced about him. The lawyer Tupman

was here, of course, keeping his unremarkable place in the pew behind the family. His face was not that of a happy man; he had never married. Perhaps it was the gravity of his profession, or the occasion, that had marked deep lines from nose to mouth; afterwards he mingled with the other mourners in the churchyard, to which the women did not come. Felix had found himself wondering if such a man could have any feeling, by now, for death; it must have become a habit, wills, funerals, condolences. As regarded the will itself, that was yet to be read. Felix put it to the back of his mind as they laid the second Earl in the vault occupied also by his recent ancestors; old Judith Ryden, her cousin and husband Maurice, their daughter Margriet who had been very unhappy and was said to haunt the house still. There on a shelf lay the next generation, who had come over from Holland to take final possession of Fenfallow and had produced the heiress who had married a Sutbury. One of the women had been named Geertruy; he read it on the greened copper of the inscription on her coffin. She had been a cousin too; they were all of them as inbred as foxes. Perhaps it accounted for the long sad features he had himself inherited.

They went out again into the wind, from the recital of ashes to ashes and dust to dust; he felt the relief of the coolness in his heavy blacks, although it had been tomb-like in the vault. He heard the clang of the iron-gridded door as it was shut and bolted into place. He himself did not relish the thought of one day lying there. No doubt his father would have said he lacked responsibility; he almost grinned to himself, then caught the gaze of the local ironmonger, and desisted. It was still difficult to think of himself as Earl.

The women were filing out now to curtsey and condole with his stepmother; the men came past one after the other to shake him by the hand. He saw the ladies of the county bow coldly to Emily; her prudent behaviour had never made her one of them. Had that made her bitter, sly? He would try to provide for her, let her live on at Fenfallow. No doubt his father had left her a jointure of her own.

The will was to be read in the library at Fenfallow. The room was full, not now with any strangers but with the domestics, who stayed away from the fire, and the family who sat near it. Tupman the lawyer produced a document and began to read from it in a surprisingly clear and sonorous tenor voice. He could be heard by everyone. Felix sat by the widowed Countess, with Guy on the other side. If the latter had wanted a word with him before now, he had not obtained it.

Perhaps there had been reason for this mutual avoidance of the brothers. In the terms of the will of Algernon William Maurice Gerard, second Earl of Fenn, only the entail was left to the heir, for that could not be avoided. Felix set his lips; everything else, to the last penny, was left partly to Emily but mostly to Guy. Cold anger stiffened the disinherited heir; not a farthing for him! A house to keep up here at Fenfallow which he could not sell because of the entail, a title which he could hardly support, and only a separate income, from his mother at her death, to live on! No doubt his father had supervised the making out of this will with correctitude. It could not be more devilish; what was one to do, except, for the moment, put a good face on it?

He let nothing show in his expression, accordingly, any more than it had done at Crockford's; remaining in his place till every last kitchenmaid had bowed and bobbed her way out of the room. A hundred pounds had been left to Mrs Canning. Felix was glad of that; it was not too much for a lifetime's devotion.

There would be no purpose in trying, he knew, to contest the will. The sums involved would be swallowed up in lawyers' fees, if he did. A small legacy might, somehow, have saved him. Now –

He became aware that Guy had moved silently to stand by his side. For moments Felix could not bring himself to look at this half-brother who had robbed him, insinuated himself into their father's affections with the help of his mother, no doubt, in his own frequent absences. Sick to his very soul, Felix made himself gaze squarely at last on the smooth, prim face. Its blue eyes showed no hint of the triumph Guy Haining Sutbury must assuredly feel. Behind him, Emily placed a black-bordered handkerchief carefully to the corners of her eyes. She was an expressionless as a sphinx. Felix wondered if she had ever had a vestige of feeling for his father.

Guy spoke in his light dry voice. 'I had hoped for a word with you earlier,' he said. 'This must have been a shock to you, Felix.'

'I have been accustomed to find my way about the world.'

'That is well known; perhaps too well?'

'Damn you, I –'

Guy intervened smoothly. 'I can only repeat the intentions of our father before he died, which may be of assistance to you. He was not unaware of your dilemma.'

Felix raised his eyebrows and said nothing; there was no purpose in doing so. He could not call his brother out, or strangle him: that should have been done in the cradle. He might have replied that as the owner of Fenfallow, Guy and Emily could go out of it to hell; but that would be pointless and vindictive. At the same time he realised that even the house at Arlington Street now belonged to his brother. Must he live on there at Guy's whim? A hard knot clenched inside him at the level of his stomach. On no account must he lose control of his temper; no doubt they were hoping for that.

'Perhaps,' he said, 'you will be kind enough to inform me as to my father's intentions, apart from those made clear in the document which has just been read.' Tupman the lawyer, he saw, had gone; slinking out like a stoat, trust him for that.

'That is my purpose,' said Guy gently. 'This is less in the nature of a demand than an entreaty. I know, for the world and our father knew, that your affairs are much embarrassed.'

'He thought you had displayed great folly by your manner of living,' put in Emily, who was still seated in her chair. 'It was the reason why he left all possible matters in the control of your brother. Guy is knowledgeable about money, and –'

'Mother, pray let me speak. I should like – and this may surprise you, but you do not, I think, know of certain investments I have been able to make over the years, all of which our father knew of and approved –'

'And provided the money to start 'em off, no doubt. There is nowhere else it could have come from.'

'What he lent me was repaid in full in many ways. I now propose, with your concurrence, to pay your debts for you under certain agreed conditions.'

'To enable me to sit here, listen to the walls crumbling, unable to repair them, beetles in the wood and the furniture gone to the bailiffs. I am grateful.'

Guy gave his small tight smile. 'It will be ensured that you are left in enough – state, shall I call it? – to maintain your position as Earl of Fenn.'

Felix stared at him; it might have been a man of fifty who spoke. Within himself he was astonished as well as revolted; certainly he had known Guy was said to be doing well in the City, but their paths had crossed so seldom that he had not been in the habit of regarding his young half-brother as having attained any real financial significance. No doubt Guy had his banking connections behind him. It was perhaps worth hearing the offer out while damning the impudence of the speaker.

'What would you have of me?' he said coldly. Countess Emily bridled, opened her mouth as if to speak, then shut it again. Guy was speaking.

'What I ask is as clear as daylight,' he said, 'and the answer will be either yes or no. If it is no, then the bailiffs will have more than the furniture.'

'What is it you want, damn you? Speak out; don't stand there like a damned grocer.'

Guy flushed. 'I believe courtesy would be advisable. What I want, as you put it, is a piece of land not strictly included in the entail; that part of the estate we have always called the water-meadows. As you know an attempt was once made to dig a canal there, but the venture failed. At present it is inhabited by rabbits, moorfowl and the occasional fox.'

'And what would you do with it? Farm it? You'd get foot-rot in your sheep; and it is good for nothing else. You see I am at least being honest with you.' He wondered for a moment about shooting and other sports, which Guy sometimes practised; he had a good marksman's eye.

'Need I give any explanation except that I want to own a strip of land that in its present state is of no use to anyone? If I pay a sum for it that will cancel your debts outright, would that exempt me from further questioning?'

'Your desire for a bog must be great.'

'No; in either case I am my own master. If I have it, no doubt I shall drain it by planting poplars. I had suggested that measure to our father, who was considering it when he died.'

'You have no thoughts of building a rival establishment?' said Felix with sarcasm. 'It would be like Venice, waterlogged from the start.'

'Let us be serious. Fenfallow is isolated enough without adding to its liabilities in such a way.' Guy began to walk up and down on the worn rug before the fire, as if some nervous energy that emanated from him was being wasted. 'Come,' he said, 'will you have your debts paid and live in comfort, or hold on to a boggy strip fit only for foxes?'

'I might do so, and raise a hunt.'

'You have neither the money nor the standing to finance a hunt, and well you know it. Despite your grand four greys in the stables your creditors will lay hands on everything, including those, if you return to London with a title and no money. Such things are quickly known; every servant in the place knows 'em now.'

'Then take the strip, pay me, and to hell with it and you. What is the nature of your second request? You implied that there was more than one. Perhaps you want to dig drains? You have only to ask.'

'That is irresponsible,' said Emily. Felix shrugged his shoulders; on any other occasion he would have enjoyed baiting the pair of them. Whatever the second request was it was a heavy business. Guy's smile had vanished and he stood quite still, beside his mother. Their solemn, similar faces stared at Felix like two cows. Despite her customary care to show no feeling, a pulse beat in the widow's temple. He could tell that this was a moment of tension, of import.

He himself broke it, impatiently. 'I cannot believe that you are doing all this virtually for no return. You have some plan up your sleeve, depend upon it.'

'I have this plan; to become the next Earl of Fenn, if I live, and my heirs after me.'

'Eh?'

Guy was straddling before the fire. 'I want you to attest, in an oath sworn and signed, Felix, that you will never marry.'

The Earl began to laugh. The tension had already broken like an egg. The thought of pretty Tilly came to him and he thought how he would be able to keep her now until he had tired and perhaps found another. He thought of himself as a pleasantly enough confirmed bachelor; domestic life and children held no charms for him. He let the emptied room echo for a moment with his laughter, then said: 'We do not need signatures or deeds, surely; my word is my bond.'

'Then you will swear an oath never to marry?'

The well-tailored shoulders shrugged. 'If you insist on the formalities, why, of course. It is no hardship.'

Guy reached out his hand and after a moment's hesitation, Felix took it. He had a sudden feeling of doubt; but it did not matter.

'You have my solemn curse if you ever break your oath,' said Guy.

Before Earl Felix left again for town, he made one request of Guy and Emily, after dinner which was still eaten in the hall, and following which the Dowager Countess did not retire.

'I should like to have the Clonmagh moss-agate,' he said. 'It is of no great value, and was my mother's.' He refrained from over-praising it lest their greed made them loath to part with it; he remembered it on his mother's breast, pinning her fichu, and her eyes, the speckled Clonmagh eyes he himself had, echoing its bizarre colouring of mingled browns and greens. There was no reason now why anything of hers should mean much to him; he would have no bride to whom to hand it on; but he wanted it, and had waited carefully for the moment when he might mention it. Guy looked at Emily; their eyes met. 'It shall be sent for,' said the Countess, 'after dinner.'

They brought down the jewel-case, which he was grudgingly allowed to examine; there was nothing in it of any great import. The moss-agate was there, set in narrow twisted silver that needed polishing. Family tradition in Ireland had it, or rather Aunt Eileen had it, that it had once lain in a torque. Felix still did not know why he wanted it. It was not beautiful as other jewels are. And he had sworn away any right to inherit tradition.

But he knew he would not give the moss-agate to Tilly. He took it carefully and placed it in his wallet. He made a graceful little speech of thanks to Countess Emily, not meaning a word of it. He had never disliked her more.

Tilly Vaux was in plain fact Matilda Black of Clerkenwell, aged twenty-eight. With regard to the last dire matter, nobody except Tilly troubled themselves or guessed at it, even first thing in the morning when the sunlight poured directly into the room if one had had the maid draw the curtains. Nevertheless Tilly, with the far-sighted prudence which had got her where she was, had lately taken to wearing little pleated caps of lawn, coloured ribbons and lace, of the kind that so greatly became Lady Blessington. There the resemblance ended; Tilly had no pretensions to understand books, writers, artists, or anybody but herself, and herself she knew too well. She sat now in her boudoir in front of the looking-glass, while the French maid, Suzanne, arranged the glorious honey-gold hair. A morning visitor contented himself by gazing on the scene now that Tilly had donned her frilled dressing-gown; he was Sir John Leete, a widower and said to be very rich indeed. He was in the habit of calling when Felix was elsewhere. He had few words, but much expression.

The door was kicked open suddenly. Tilly shrieked; Suzanne dropped the hairbrush then deftly retrieved it again. The new Earl of Fenn stood scowling in the doorway. Tilly promptly recalled herself and blew him a kiss on her small plump hand, revealing by this means an area of milk-white arm below the loose sleeve of the negligee, which had fallen back to the elbow. As for Sir John, he rose to his feet. His dark-green morning coat was immaculate, his figure still good despite overmuch port.

'My lord, may I express my condolences on your recent loss and my congratulations on your attainment of the title?'

'Oh, yes,' fluttered Tilly. 'A real Earl, look at him!'

The Earl was surly in his replies to both sallies, and the widower soon took himself off. 'What was that fellow doing here?' Felix demanded. 'You see too many such.'

Tilly dismissed Suzanne and relapsed into pouting silence. In this state she looked very beautiful and her follies could be forgotten. Felix's heart melted as she had known it would, and he came and sat by her, fingering her ribbons and lace.

'So you will not speak to me,' he told her. 'Was I interrupting an interlude, my puss?' He had written a note to her to say he would call this morning; no doubt she had not read it. He was never quite certain of how she passed her time when he was away.

'You are horrid,' Tilly told him. 'You stay away for weeks and do not expect me to divert myself at all. Sir John was telling me about Paris. Everybody goes there now the war is over, and Brighton is quite deserted, Sir John says.'

Felix smiled; Tilly's confusion of past and present was worse than a gipsy's. 'The war has been over many years now,' he reminded her. He cast his mind back and remembered how society had flocked to the Continent in time for Waterloo, and again after. And what was there to show now for all of it? The great Duke of Wellington was little more than an arid stock, with his whorehouses, politics and Mrs Arbuthnot, glory forgotten. 'I called,' he said to Tilly, 'to ask you if you would enjoy a drive with me round the Park.'

'I want to go to Paris.'

However she turned her dark-blue eyes towards the window, and looked at the fine day. It would be pleasant enough to drive out in the Earl's grand new four-in-hand, but it meant recalling Suzanne and ordering her to set out a different gown, one's tall autumn bonnet and a fur pelisse. 'As you wish,' said Tilly coldly. Then she remembered her vocation and cast her white arms round Felix's neck and kissed him on his long nose. 'I'm glad to see you,' she said roundly. 'That man is a bore.' She played with his coat-buttons. 'My! It will take some living up to to be seen with an Earl.'

'You are living up well enough now,' he told her, aware that presently she would take the opportunity to ask for new gowns, more pin-money. He had come here resolved to be strict with her, but it was of no use; her beauty, as always, unmanned him. He twined one of the shining curls about his finger. 'Paris?' he said. If he did not pamper her others would. She shrieked with joy. 'Paris! You will take me? You are my love, my love, and again my love,' and she kissed his hand, his nose again, his cheeks, his mouth. He laughed at her.

'Have your trunks packed,' he said. 'We will start on Thursday.'

'Oh, we can buy clothes there. I hear the new rolled hems are *à ravir*. You see I know some French already. Oh, Paris! How happy I am!'

Felix disarranged the négligée and then her bed. Possessing her was like plunging into the heart of a rose, and he took his time about withdrawal; Suzanne must wait.

They went out afterwards in the carriage, Tilly's charming face enhanced by the softness of the new furs; they drove three times round the Park, nodding to gentlemen who nodded to them; the ladies, of course, did not. Then Felix tossed the reins to Joshua, bade him take the carriage back, went in and enjoyed a light repast, made love again, then left to go on foot back to Arlington Street. By this time it was twilight, and the faces of passers-by somewhat corpse-like by reason of the new fishtail street-lighting supplied by the London Gaslight and Coke Company. Flambeaux had been more flattering.

In Paris the twilights were much improved, and Tilly found her *rouleau* gown in a shop on the Rue de Rivoli, and a pair of low-heeled slippers to match, and, of course, by then, a great new bonnet topped with dyed plumes in the latest fashion. Her toilette in the mornings accordingly took some hours to complete, and Felix, who preferred walking to riding, would stroll meantime along the Cours la Reine, looking for any acquaintances who might have crossed the Channel to present themselves at the Bourbon Court. To his annoyance, Sir John Leete was among them; at present he himself made no scene with Tilly concerning it; they were enjoying themselves, and as long as he kept her entertained he had no fear of rivals.

He did not trouble the Court at the Tuileries; it was said to be dull. He once had a glimpse of royalty driving to St Cloud, with much escort milling in the narrow streets; in one coach the King, smiling too much, as he had been used to do since he was the Comte d'Artois and abandoned the fighting men of Quiberon. As for Madame Royale, she was smiling not at all; and the sullen crowds muttered: '*A bas les Ultras! A bas Polignac!*', then changed their tune to mild cheers as the young widowed Duchesse de Berri drove past with the fair-haired *enfant du miracle* and his elder sister. There was a restless, unsettled feeling in the air; Charles X had not only lost his popularity, but had stifled the Press. Felix amused himself by reading the English newspapers which were sent to him at his hotel; and one day came upon certain news which was soon confirmed by letter. It surprised, but did not grieve him.

Countess Emily was dead. It appeared black-rimmed in the gazettes; perhaps the only social recognition Emily had ever been permitted to receive. Guy's letter had a black rim likewise; it had been forwarded from London.

My sainted mother passed away suddenly on Monday, as if overcome with grief for our Father whom she has gone to join. Felix permitted himself a sardonic smile. *It seems her heart failed,* Guy continued. *The doctor was called, but came too late. The arrangements for the obsequies are of course in the gazettes, and as a member of the family you are of course welcome.*

He had best go. It would be discourteous not to be present at his stepmother's funeral. If he travelled fast he could arrive in time. Before he left, while his valise was being packed, he received a second letter; he saw to his surprise that it was from Tupman the lawyer. He put it into the pocket of his great-coat to read on the crossing. Tilly of course made a scene at being left behind; but when he said curtly that she might as well come with him, she went into hysterics. Leave Paris, when they had but newly arrived! 'To bring me here, and then abandon me! How am I to go on by myself? Polite females are not seen alone on the streets. Why should you go to her funeral when you never cared for her? I suppose a Countess must have attention even when she is dead, while I, who am nobody, must live as I can. Ah, my lord, how could you do so cruel a thing to me?' She was weeping, but not seriously; the crystal drops of her tears did not disturb the rouge on her cheeks. Seeing the bright hair lit by such sunlight as filtered between the half-drawn blinds, he thought for the first time that it looked brassy. Perhaps the hired maid here was not as good as Suzanne.

He was impatient. 'I am leaving you with every comfort, and you need not go out at all, or if you hire a carriage and take what is her name, Félicité, with you that will be perfectly proper.' He produced a roll of money and left it by her; her glance swept over it, knowing to the last coin what it would contain. Felix took the plump hand and kissed it.

'Believe me, I will return within two or three days,' he promised her. 'Take a drive, if you will; it is a fine day.'

She was continuing to buff her nails. 'There will be nothing to be seen but men in these great flopping new topcoats. I wish –' But he had gone, impolitely, and took the stairs two at a time, hurrying out to where the coach waited for Calais.

As he stamped with cold on the boat, he remembered Tupman's letter. Its contents puzzled him.

When you are in the neighbourhood pray call upon me, for I had best not be seen with you at Fenfallow. I have news for you which perhaps should have been told before, but chivalry misled me. He signed himself Felix's humble servant. It was too personal for a lawyer's letter. Felix bit his lip. What was the fellow getting at? It must have some connection, whatever it was, with his stepmother's death. Chivalry indeed!

He disembarked at Dover, hardly seeing the jostling crowd of persons of all classes waiting to make the return crossing to France. He wished Sir John Leete well with Tilly. That had been no coincidence, and at any other time would have made him angry.

Guy had had his mother's body embalmed, which allowed for the few days' delay over the funeral. This was attended by few, and no women. Afterwards Felix, his hat still in his hand, went over to where the lawyer Tupman stood, a forlorn figure; there was something desolate about his appearance, apart from the formal black they all wore.

'Go and wait in my carriage,' Felix murmured. It would save time riding over later to visit the man in his office. They would be as private in the carriage as could be desired; he sent Joshua off in another, back to Fenfallow. After all had left the two men sat alone on the carriage-cushions. It might be easier for Tupman to say whatever it was he had to say if they were moving, and he himself was able to keep his eyes on the reins, and listen without expression.

There was much to hear. 'I have to say,' Tupman began, 'what I could not in honour do until now, when the Countess is dead.'

He smoothed his unwrinkled gloves with a nervous gesture. Felix said nothing, and waited; no news concerning his stepmother would surprise him; so silent and discreet a woman might have much to remember that others had never kept hidden.

'As you know,' said the lawyer, 'my wife was – is an invalid. The Earl's first marriage, with all respect to your lordship's late mother, was not happy. When Emily – when Miss Manfield as she was then, came to look after Miss Fanny your sister, the Earl saw more of her than he did of his own wife.'

I know all that, thought Felix; what else has he got to say to me?

'She also,' said Tupman, 'with my connivance, saw a good deal of myself. In fact – in fact, we were lovers, a circumstance I have not revealed to this day except to yourself, and the Earl.'

'My father knew of it? Then –'

'He knew. He knew also, by the end, that she was expecting my child.'

'You are saying that my brother – that Guy –'

'He is my son. I do not know if his mother told him of it. It is probable that she did not; he was brought up in all ways to believe that he was the late Earl's younger son. It is perhaps difficult for you to understand how this could have occurred. But as you know, Miss Fanny, who died that year, was perhaps the only person for whom the Earl had shown open affection. When she was gone, he was very lonely, but as a proud man did not show it to the world. I have no doubt that Emily – that Miss Manfield had it in her power to comfort him.'

I have no doubt either, thought Felix wryly. The woman must have wormed her way into his father's confidence at the same time that she was entertaining her lover. 'Are you certain,' he asked in a cold voice, 'that the child was yours?'

'I am certain. Unusually, I had a letter from her, which I have kept. I know it by heart. In it she tells me that she is expecting my child, and does not know what will become of her. I was unable to send a reply. It would not have been discreet. In fact I never saw her alone again. The Countess died, and Emily and the Earl became man and wife.'

'And he knew of the pregnancy?'

'He must have known. Before it began to show, he took his bride to a shooting-lodge in Scotland, where the birth eventually took place. It was some months before he and his wife and the child returned to Fenfallow, and by then any gossip about the date of the child's coming would have been stilled, if it ever started; in any case everyone would assume Guy Sutbury to be the Earl's son.'

Felix heard his own voice rise in anger. 'And it is to another man's bastard that he left all he had except the house? I can scarce credit it, even of my father. It was madness, madness!'

'He was a strange man. It is as though he transferred his affection for his dead daughter to his second wife and her son. There is no other explanation that I know of. Naturally, I did not speak of it, or speculate upon it. I tried to put the matter out of my mind and to give my life to my work.'

'And the will – its provision is still valid?'

'It is valid. Guy Sutbury is clearly named as the heir of all the Earl had, except Fenfallow.'

From his greatcoat pocket he drew out a flat package. 'This is the letter,' he said, 'which I will give into your hands. It may be some recompense for the harm that my actions, in effect, have done to you unwittingly. Believe me when I say that I had no notion of the Earl's mind until the making of his will, shortly before his death. He was not in a state of health then to be told anything of a disagreeable nature, and Emily was of course present in the room. I could do nothing but take the instructions I had been given. What good would it have done to say to a dying man: "You are leaving your own heir's money to the son of another man"? Perhaps in fact it gave him a strange pleasure to have me, the rejected lover, draw up his will.'

Felix stared at the package in his hand. He knew a distaste at the touch of it. 'Take this back,' he said to Tupman, whose head was bowed and his eyes fixed on the carriage-floor. It was impossible to visualise him as the physical lover of Emily, and Felix knew an overpowering desire to laugh. He replaced the package in the lawyer's hands. 'I will not read it, or use it,' he said. 'Guy has paid my debts, after all – and desires to inherit the title. I daresay half the nobility of England is so descended, were one to think it out.'

Tupman had not put away the package. 'I will keep this in safety,' he said. 'If the time ever comes when you need it, apply to me.'

'I shall never do so,' promised the Earl of Fenn.

'You have acted most honourably,' replied the lawyer. His face worked for moments, as if he were trying to form an expression to which it was not accustomed; then he fell silent, and the two men parted on their separate ways home.

On returning to the house there was a feeling that Fenfallow lacked a presence, despite the fact that the late Countess had been a negative figure. Felix entered, threw aside his hat, gloves and coat, and picked up the mail that was waiting in the hall. There was a letter addressed to himself in a hand he did not know. He went into the library and opened it.

It was from Sir John Leete, from Paris. After a pompous opening it continued thus:

I trust you will accept, my dear Lord, the action I have taken with regard to the Young Lady until recently under your protection. I have the honourable determination to make her my wife on Tuesday first at the Embassy. It will therefore be unsuitable for you further to communicate with her unless all such missives are addressed to myself. Matilda has asked me to let her write a farewell line below this letter, and so I now do.

I am, my Lord, your very faithful and obedient servant,
                    John Leete

Below the letter were scrawled a few lines in a round childish hand. Felix wondered if the prospective husband had read them.

You see, love, a girl has to look after her old age.

He decided to walk off his anger. He sent for Joshua to fetch his old Inverness cape and shooter's hat, which lay in God knew what cupboard. It had, for the past few days, rained in the mornings, and the ground was fresh. Felix stood for a moment on the top step of the great entry of Fenfallow, like a hound sniffing the air. He descended the steps which had been fashioned in his grandfather's time by a pupil of Vanbrugh, turned suddenly, and looked at his house, the only thing in the world he could evidently call his own.

It was fronted, in a classical style which covered the old Gothic front, with red stone, mellow now with lichen, but the carvings and mock Corinthian capitals could still be seen, their flat ridged shafts reaching from ground to pediment. Beyond, the roof was so low-pitched that from here one could not see it; or, he thought drily, the number of slates that no doubt by now needed renewing. The windows were manifold – it was said there was one for every day in the year – and the few maidservants they had kept of late years struggled vainly to keep all of them clean, in spite of Mrs Canning's scoldings. In the end Felix's father had shut off the east wing with its separate entrance completely, leaving it to moulder and gather dust, and entertain its ghost. That still left the great hall, the rear dais-chamber, and a myriad of smaller rooms facing westward, including the old Earl's study from which he had taken leisure at times to watch the setting sun. His bedroom was nearby, with the great tester over the bed with its embroidered coat of arms; by right Felix slept there now, but in fact he preferred to sleep elsewhere. Next door was a small drawing-room which Felix's mother had used informally but which Emily since then had made little use of; everything was as the first Countess had left it, the blue striped satin on the sofa and gilt chairs beginning to split in places now, the gilt itself peeling. But the great harp Rosaleen Clonmagh had used to play had kept its gilding, if not its broken strings. No one had been allowed to touch it in Felix's childhood; once he had tried to coax a melody out of the few strings remaining, and had been whipped.

But now he, Felix Sutbury, was Earl of Fenn. He could enter any room he chose, strum on the harp if he wished, loiter among his father's guns, take his own time going from passage to passage, stair to stair. One day he would do it all; but today was fine. He set off, whistling to his father's old dog Ludo to come with him; but Ludo was bereft and missed his master. He stayed by the fire, thumping his tail, while

Felix strode out alone. He would, he thought, get himself a younger dog, perhaps a couple; they made a house friendly. Somehow he did not visualise himself as going back at once to London.

He had gone through the wood, walked across the fallow field, and came now to the place from which one could see Guy's precious strip of bog and moss, with its traces of the old canal. To his chagrin Guy was there, still in his mourning, with another; a man who had not been to the funeral and whose city clothes looked garish. At sight of Felix he removed his hat respectfully enough, to reveal a balding head; he might have been about fifty. The young poplars Guy had already planted quivered in the light wind, drying out the soil. It was like Guy to have had them dug in punctually.

Felix hesitated before going forward; but it would be ridiculous to disappear again among the trees, without a word. He did not like the look of Guy's friend; so much he knew already. The two men continued what they were at, pointing out certain sites to one another. Guy stopped and flushed a little as Felix came up. 'Mr Durdan,' he said. 'This is my brother the Earl of Fenn.'

Slight bows were exchanged. Into Felix's quick mind had come the certainty, if his appearance had not already told one, that Durdan could not be a gentleman. Had he been so, Guy would have said: 'My brother Fenn.' Of such distinctions was England made, and in all England there was no bigger snob or opportunist than the Honourable Guy Sutbury. His present company surprised one.

Felix smiled faintly. 'Are you staying long, Mr Durdan? This is not a place to which many come.'

The man answered in an ingratiating way; he came from east of Bow Bells, that was well seen. 'That's what makes it a proposition to me, y'see, your lordship. We don't want to begin to h'operate too near the country seats of folks like yourself; that would be disturbing; and the smoke a

nuisance. In the country our policy –' Mr Durdan swelled
with importance, like a cock-robin – 'is to build the stations a
good carriage-drive away from posh houses and villages and
the like. In h-any case, working it out, to lay the rails rahnd
this strip will cut out Dinswood Corner and Farrow, making
it worth our while, just as we've made it worth your while,
'aven't we, your lordship?' Guy by now was scarlet; a vein
began to throb in Felix's neck. He heard his own voice clear
and cold. 'You mean that you have been prospecting for a
railway here without so much as a by-your-leave from me?'

'Well, your lordship, y'see, *he* said –'

Guy was at ease and smiling now, like a cat that has
swallowed cream. Your permission, my dear brother, it said,
is no longer necessary; and the news has been broken.

Felix put as hard a brake on his temper as he had ever
done in his life; he would not make a further fool of himself
before this city gent and the so-called brother who had
betrayed him. There was an air of thumbed money about
the whole business. Discussion of it could wait till later.

'Noise, smoke and soot not too far off from Fenfallow; that
troubles me less than it might some men.'

'You are hardly ever here.'

'That is not to the point. To have set this on foot by
yourself, silently, telling neither our father, despite what
you said, nor myself; pocketing the takings and then
handing a gracious sum out to me in exchange for the
promise you extracted that I should never marry! Would it
not have been more friendly, more brotherly –' Felix felt the
irony of this statement deep – 'had you discussed it openly
with all of us, and obtained our views, possibly our
agreement? The money could have been divided equally
without conditions; there was no need for notaries. Why go
to so much pother?'

'Because, had I failed to do so, I would have been
compelled to watch you marry some heiress and breed from

her, while I myself would have been forever excluded from the title.'

'The title –' He bit his words back. Now or later, he must never give the blow to Guy which the latter could never parry.

His next words softened Felix's heart. 'If you knew,' said Guy, defenceless for instants, 'how I have dreamed of it from a boy –'

'You were an unnatural boy; you told no one anything, except no doubt your mother. Did she know of this?'

'My mother is dead. I will not discuss her.' Guy turned away, his sleek head bowed. 'I have paid your debts,' he said, 'which were not small. I have left the furniture in Fenfallow as it was, for your use, though I could have made a small fortune in selling it off.'

'Selling it off? You have the soul of a broker. You may be Earl in time – I could die tomorrow – but you will never be a nobleman. Your blood –' He had nearly said that it was that of a governess and a lawyer. Meantime Guy had turned white about the mouth.

'That from you, you whoremaster? Our father despaired of you. You had no affection for him, never visited him on his sickbed, cared nothing when he died. My mother and I were heartbroken.'

'Your mother and you had not a heart between you.'

He turned, strode to the door, went through and slammed it shut. Guy was left alone, again wearing his little habitual smile beneath the neat moustache. He was thinking, first and foremost, of the considerable sum he had been able to extract from the railway company, far in excess of that amount it had taken to pay Felix's debts; and it had taken a mind like his own to foresee what would happen even in this remote part of England. There was a railway line already in the Midlands, and another newly built further south. Felix should have kept his ear to the ground. The time was coming when his famous four-in-hand, like all horse travel, would be superseded; no post-chaises any more, but trains and motors, perhaps flying machines. The world as they had known it was speeding up, and nothing would ever slow it down again. Guy himself felt able to match its speed, to have an eye to the main chance always. In this instance it had paid dividends far beyond his expectations: the next step was obvious: he must marry soon, and get himself an heir.

Felix strode through the house, his fury dulling; but his mind remained bitter. Had he had a sword in his hand, or a pistol, he might have done Guy an injury; by now, it was safe enough. But he needed some way of ridding his anger, some diversion; no longer could he ride off in the carriage to Tilly for comfort, and he was despondent of mounting any new mistress; they cost too much. In fact he was at odds with humanity, men and women alike; but one had to go on living, with an empty title and no wife, no heir, to follow.

As a rule he did not see the servants, for the old Earl had given strict orders that they were to be out of sight when he himself passed by; as his movements had been fairly predictable this had caused small difficulty. But now Felix was in a part of the house seldom troubled by the family; up a half-stair, there was an embrasure with a window, and this window was being cleaned by a scrubbing-maid, her pail on the floor beside her, a cloth in her hands. She was plump, with brown curls partly hidden by a cap. Felix knew a sudden urge; he made no bones about it, but pinched her plump backside. The girl squealed, clapped her hands to her buttocks, spun round, saw who it was and tried to curtsey, but the coil of movement was too much for her; she staggered, and Felix caught her in his arms as she fell. He set her away from him and looked her over, still holding her by the upper arms. She was pretty enough, with a high colour that came and went.

'What is your name, child?' he asked; she might have been

sixteen. She rubbed her hands on the coarse stuff of her scrubbing-apron and said: 'Catherine Maverick, sir, m'lord. They call me Cathy,' and she bowed her head and went on wiping her fingers, which were red with work. Felix slid his grasp down and took her hands; they were cool and still damp. 'How old are you?' he asked. There had been Mavericks about Fenfallow as far back as anyone could remember; cottage folk, although at one time there had been a marriage with a Ryden, last century. This girl would not be of that stock; she had no distinction.

She giggled. 'Sixteen, sir, m'lord.'

'Are you courting, Cathy?'

'I – I'm walking out, sir, m'lord. There's nothing settled yet.'

She was wearing clogs, made of wood and leather, with brass nails fixing the thick soles to the uppers. 'Would you like to have a new pair of shoes, Cathy?'

'Oh, yes, sir, m'lord. I'd like a pair made all of leather. There's a packman comes with 'em, and soon there's the fair, and –'

'And you would like to go to the fair in new shoes and ribbons. If you do as I tell you, you shall have a new gown as well. Come with me; leave your pail.'

He shepherded her, unprotesting, to the room where the great bed was, and as she gave a gasp at sight of it, his fingers fastened the latch. It had come to him that it would assuage his anger to take this girl, this serving-wench, across the old Earl's very bed and in sight of his coat of arms. His own fortunes were become a mockery; very well, some of that mockery should reflect on the one who had from the beginning given rise to it.

'Take off your clogs, Cathy, and your cap. I want to stroke your pretty hair.'

Later he let down the hair, which was soft and pleasant to the touch. It smelled freshly of woodsmoke, her body of soap. She was a clean little creature, pliant and willing except that, as he was taking her maidenhead, she let out a little cry. Felix soothed her, and made her giggle again soon when he told her a true story about an old man in one of the clubs who wore a famous maidenhead on his fingertip till the day of his death. It had been like dried leather from a glove. Soon her laughter turned to the babblings of ecstasy; Felix was an accomplished lover and it pleased him to give her pleasure. The great bed rocked; no doubt, in the room below, they knew it.

'Oh, sir – oh, oh, sir – oh, m'lord –'

This was better than possessing Tilly; he would give this one more to remember, he swore, before surrendering her to the embraces of her rustic swain. Outside careful footsteps, a woman's, no doubt the housekeeper's, passed by the abandoned pail. Their owner must have seen the closed door and known what it meant; hesitated for a moment, and then turned away. The footsteps died. After that episode, Felix would not admit to himself that he was slightly ashamed; and persuaded his conscience that he could not bear to wait to witness the digging and carting involved in Guy's ugly, profitable proceedings over at Fenfallow canal. He took himself, accordingly, to town, idled there a while, then set out, as he had known he would do in the end, to Ireland to visit Aunt Eileen at Marishnageen. As always, she welcomed him as if he had just come in from a day's ride.

'Your room is always ready for you, and I have had them light a fire,' she told him. 'Go you now and have a sleep, and I will get Johnny Daley to bring up your baggage.' He had not brought Joshua on this trip, preferring, in the state of the roads, to travel by hired conveyance. The appalling transport on the journey had jolted him and his clothes were splashed with mud; but that mattered less here, where everyone did as they pleased, than in London.

'Is Johnny still alive?' he asked incredulously. Johnny Daley was an ancient who passed his time in making bog-oak buttons, which he sold for fair sums and spent them on whiskey. Felix when a boy had wondered how he managed to contrive to exist, and was told Johnny managed well enough. 'He has his chickens and his plot, where he grows potatoes, and gets his milk from the dairy here; what more could he want, besides the whiskey?' Eileen Clonmagh had asked reasonably. When Johnny came groaning up with the bags Felix chatted to him while he himself shaved in Irish rainwater soft as velvet, taken from the chipped white-and-gold ewer and jug which stood on the cabinet nearby the bed. The looking-glass was spotted with damp and made his face look like a debauchee's; was he one?

'I am well,' said Johnny in lordly fashion. Like his countrymen he had always this notion of superior eminence, saying however that he was descended not from the High Kings of Tara but from a Frenchman, a Huguenot who had landed on these shores at the time of persecution by the old French King. A colony still existed in the valley from which Johnny's parents had come, and its name had been slurred down from De Heilly to Daley. Perhaps Johnny never knew that he was descended from one of the twenty brothers of Anne de Heilly, Duchesse d'Etampes, but it would not have been too much for him if he had. He emptied, when Felix had finished, the used water and slops into a pail, took it up, and was gone noisily. Felix leaned out of the window and looked at the soft green day. It healed his mind to be here again, even so soon.

Eileen Clonmagh had not her dead sister's beauty, but made up for its lack by an abundant good-nature and charm. Like many Irishwomen of good family she had taken too long to marry ever to have done so. She was tall and thin, dressed always in thick woollen stuff against the damp, and her pepper-and-salt hair was screwed up on top of her head with pins and straggled, vaguely out of curl, down each cheek. Occasionally she would look up from whatever she was doing and would take a duster to the portrait of an ancestor which hung on the wall and would say: 'Well, well, the line ends here.' The portrait was of a Cromwellian officer who, unlike his fellows, had earned the cautious respect of the peasantry on the estate allotted to him and had married the daughter of the old house and taken her name. Since then there had been a history of good and happy relations at Marishnageen, even in the rising of '98. That had resulted in no more than the whipping and sending home of a small boy who had gone out with the rebels. He was considered too young to be hanged like his father and brother. He lived to beget Eileen and Rosaleen. And if Rosaleen had not married Lord Fenn she would be here still, and happy as the day was long, Eileen would be heard to say sadly: in fact the two sisters had never got on.

Felix had brought with him, and retrieved from his baggage now, the great Clonmagh moss-agate, and gave it to Eileen, who at first refused to receive it while gazing at it longingly. 'Keep it for your bride,' she kept saying. 'Keep it for her, and then your sons will have speckled eyes like all the Clonmaghs.'

'I will never marry.'

'Ough, get along, now, that is not for any man to say, least of all yourself. You are a great man for the ladies. It will be a pity if after all of it, there is nobody left at Fenfallow. It is a fine house. I was there once, and you lying kicking on a rug in the garden before you could walk.' She sighed, and fingered the brooch. 'Very well, then, I will take it if you say so, but when you change your mind and marry it shall be my gift to your bride. A pity Valentine is not here; she would do very well for you now.'

Valentine was her god-daughter, whom Felix remembered faintly as a coltish creature with long light-brown hair, whom he had tried to teach to play cricket one summer in the school holidays. He found that he had no idea of what she must look like now. She was in Germany, Eileen went on, as paid companion to an old baroness. 'It will improve her languages, her French is very good as well. And music! Give her a pianoforte and she will play whatever you tell her. It's a gift, that it is. You should marry Valentine.'

Felix immediately determined that he would do no such thing, and was glad the young blue-stocking described was abroad. The role of paid companion was, in England, a dreary enough prospect; perhaps German baronesses were different.

Down the lane at Marishnageen was a field, and in the field a donkey grazed the short rich grass. There had been a donkey there as far back as Felix could remember, and it was always called Rebecca. This Rebecca came at a call, friendly and curious, nuzzling her velvet nose into his hand in expectation of a titbit. She was in foal. Felix remembered a long-ago walk here with Eileen, and every word of what she had said then. 'It's the blessed animals they are, notwithstanding most folk are so cruel to them, beating them and starving them and the like, and letting their feet grow and putting great burdens on their backs. The dear blessed Lord rode one into Jerusalem that last time. Think of it, the colt of a foal no man had yet ridden! It must have known who He was for sure, or He would never have stayed on its back.'

Johnny looked after this donkey and evidently saw to its feet. Felix fondled its nose and regarded the great mark of the cross that grew on the shoulders of all donkeys. He was aware of a gentle relaxing sensation in his innards, a peace from strife; out here, with the sky coming on to rain, he wondered why he had let events at home so upset him. Did it matter, after all, that Guy was making money out of a railroad which should have gone to himself? He should have thought of it first, that was all. He should likewise have been more attentive to their father, and then maybe it would all have been different, and the Earl would never have married the governess out of loneliness and fathered another man's son.

He strolled back to the house presently, and found Eileen polishing mirrors. 'The girls never do them properly, they're busy making great eyes at their own reflections, but it doesn't matter any longer about mine,' she said. Felix kissed her cheek and told her she looked younger than ever. Just then Johnny came in with the mails, his lips pursed in a soundless whistling tune. There were several for Felix, forwarded from Fenfallow and London. He excused himself to Eileen, and opened them.

He was silent for so long that she asked at length, unwilling to hector him or exclaim over bad news, 'Is it all right? Are they all right over there?'

He answered slowly, not looking up from the letters. 'Yes. My brother Guy is to be married.' He did not add that there had been among the rest a letter from the Fenfallow housekeeper, Mrs Canning.

My dear Lord, it read,

I venture to write because Cathy the Second Housemaid is in some trouble, although she blames no one openly. The Young Man with whom she was Walking Out will no longer look at her since it is known she is become what they call a Spoiled Maid, by reason of your Lordship. I hope that your Lordship will forgive an old woman who has known you all your life for writing so, and that something can be done to help her. She is a good obedient Girl and has never caused trouble, and you know her Mother, Hester, who worked her way up to Parlourmaid to her late Ladyship before she married.

Your Lordship's humble servant

Jessie Canning.

Indeed, he had known, if at a slight distance, Cathy's mother Hester, and all the tribe of cottagers, mostly Mavericks, all of whom would by now be buzzing with prurient gossip; he knew very well that he had not got Cathy pregnant, but that would not stop the old women. Felix made a resolve to write to the factor at Fenfallow to give the girl's young man some money: would fifty guineas be enough to sweeten his temper, and maybe a rent-free cottage promised as well, as long as he married Cathy and was good to her? Felix realised that he had forgotten the little housemaid's face by this time; he chiefly recalled the pretty soft hair that had smelled so sweet of woodsmoke.

Guy's marriage was not to be in London, but in Manchester. That fact, and the one that he himself knew nothing of the girl's family – her name was Isabel Manning – made Felix fairly certain that, as usual, Guy had feathered his nest. He decided to attend the wedding, which was in the next month. It did not in fact greatly inconvenience him to do so, except that he would have liked to stay somewhat longer at Marishnageen; but it was not worth while making the return journey twice. In any case he ought to get back to Fenfallow. The reason why this was so urgent was not clear in his mind.

Mrs Canning greeted him with a whisper that all was right now about Cathy and her young man; they were to be married, and would live in one of the cottages. He was amused at her firmness in conveying the news, as though she were telling him, as a child, that he had been a naughty boy but it was all forgiven. He did not come across Cathy in his journeyings about the house, for they were made mostly at night when, candle in hand, he wandered through the uninhabited part of the east wing. Sheeted forms of furniture loomed up at him like ghosts; some of it had not been used for a hundred years. The delicate astragals of the windows, once the architect's pride at the time of rebuilding, were uncurtained and let in the night outside, pressing against the glass as though it had form. There was no sign of Margriet Ryden's ghost; he had never seen it, and knew a mild wish to do so, as if he must sample all forms of experience about his house. In the whole great building everyone but himself slept, the servants tired with their day's work, Mrs Canning at last ceasing to be watchful. Felix felt his own solitude in a way formerly unknown to him. He descended at last to the empty wine-cellars; the great bins were empty and cobwebbed, and the hot wax dropped from the candle and burnt his fingers; he held it at an angle, and the flame sputtered. How pleasant it would be if he could fill the wine-bins with knowledgeably chosen vintages, open up the house, hear the laughter of his children! But all that was a dream, and he himself dreamlike at this hour. At last, he sought his bed.

He had not looked forward to Guy's wedding with any degree of pleasure, and the journey itself was tedious: he had sold the greys. The church, when he reached it from his inn, was no doubt one of the most fashionable in the city; it had a certain pretentiousness, and the rustling skirts of the women, over-bright with the new aniline dyes, had a prosperous satisfied sound. However the assembled relations on the other side – there was no one but himself on Guy's – struck him in themselves as a dull, purse-proud lot. He had been shown a seat where he would obtain a good glimpse of Guy and his groomsman, and the bride when she should come in afterwards. Guy was punctual, dapper in his morning-coat, a flower in his buttonhole, his hair brushed sleek. The groomsman, to Felix's disgust but not surprise, was the man Durdan who had come to Fenfallow to prospect for the future railway. He looked much the same as when he had paced the moss that day for sleepers; florid, overdressed and cocksure. Felix had learned from gossip in the inn parlour that Miss Manning was an orphan, very rich, an heiress; in fact exactly what Guy had wanted, her people having made their fortune last century from coal. When she came at last, she was very plain, and evidently frightened. There were no bridesmaids, but a stout woman with a hooked nose and an incipient moustache stood by her, either as matron of honour or, as it seemed, dragon to ensure that the ceremony took place smoothly. The bride wore a gown of striped silk, chosen for her, with frills beneath the bodice to hide her lack of bosom. She seemed as immature in all ways as a child; Felix was overtaken by a sense of deep pity. What if he should stand up and say, at the proper moment, that there was every reason why this marriage should not take place? He stared at Isabel Manning as she passed by. Her eyes were large, blue he thought, and like the rest of her terrified; her fair hair had been frizzed beneath the fashionable hat. She clutched the tight little bouquet Guy had sent, made her way to the altar, and at last nervously spoke the vows. Guy was confident, his head held back at an angle that was almost as cocky as Durdan's: perhaps it conveyed the fact that he was fortunate in having made one fortune and married another, or perhaps – as the female relatives must have whispered among themselves often – that the girl was fortunate in marrying an Honourable, the brother of an Earl. Perhaps her good fortune would become more apparent to Isabel as time went on, and again perhaps not.

The pair returned after signing the register, the bride's gloved hand laid lightly on Guy's arm. The reception was to be held at an hotel, one of the new buildings springing up like mushrooms briefly to house the men of commerce who came and went, and would not be satisfied with the homely conditions of the old inns. Felix pleaded a prior engagement which did not exist; he lingered on the ostentatious Turkey carpet only long enough to take the bride by her little thin limp hand, and have a word with his brother.

'You must bring your wife to visit Fenfallow soon,' he said. Guy smiled and murmured some correct reply; the bride's scared gaze flickered upwards for a moment to dwell on Felix's singular face, and the corners of her mouth turned timidly upwards. It was, he was certain, the first time she had smiled all through the ceremony. The stout hooknosed matron he had already observed bustled forward; evidently she was Isabel's aunt by marriage, and delighted to make his Lordship's acquaintance. Her name was Mrs Malvina Burridge. Felix decided that it suited her.

He left, settled his bill at the inn, drank some wine and had a meal, and travelled back to London as fast as he might. He felt that, on this particular night, he could not endure the silences of Fenfallow. Instead he betook himself to a theatre, and watched a play whose name he could never afterwards remember; then he went to Crockford's, got drunk and even won a little money; he hardly recalled returning to Arlington Street afterward to sleep the victory off.

In the morning he for some reason thought of the hook-nosed Mrs Burridge again. Clearly, he remembered her bringing forward her own daughter, widow Lilian, who for the occasion had worn half-mourning. She had been handsome, with a brassy voice; he had disliked her. The deceased husband had been, one understood, a merchant of foreign goods. Why should he remember the two Burridge women so clearly? It was as though two peacocks had strutted beside a little peahen, poor Isabel.

Felix spent a few more days in London, saw his barber and his dentist, and last of all his bankers, who were more welcoming than formerly. Lacking Tilly, he was spending less money. He decided, whimsically, to pay a visit to Paris, in which city Sir John and Lady Leete no longer resided, having betaken themselves home to Sir John's very dull place in Yorkshire. Felix made a leisurely journey, tarried for some days at a whitewashed inn where the food was good and the wine better, and the surrounding fields lavender with flax. On arrival at last in the capital, he decided to avoid his usual haunts and go to different ones. He went in fact to a half-known world within a world, of which he had heard; he wandered about the steep hill of Montmartre, where pine martens had once bred wild among the trees, soon, after a war and siege, to be felled in readiness to build a great new church in honour of the new devotion to the Sacred Heart.

When it was completed it would be visible from every part of Paris. But that was not yet; meantime, there were painters at work on easels in the sharply rising street, with completed canvases for sale standing by them. Most of these Felix thought ridiculous, but were no doubt the newest thing; as the days passed he got to know some of the painters slightly, and enjoyed drinking Alsace *bière* with them in the old tavern on the cobbles. He gained a little knowledge of art thereby, and much of life. There was one painter, Arnot, bearded like most and dressed in paint-stained flannel; for some reason Felix was invited soon to visit his *atelier*.

Accordingly, one morning he thrust his way through the cluttered narrow ways of the quarter, with great bunches of onions and cloves of garlic hanging in the grocers' shops; and at last, by dint of asking, found the place he was looking for, up precipitous stairs which smelled less of paint than of urine. Arnot was already working from the life amid a shambles of beer-bottles and cigarette-stubs, but the part of the floor surrounding his easel was clear. The model was a startlingly ugly, skinny woman with a saddle nose, not young; she lay half recumbent, half sitting, on a dais. Felix's presence did not appear to trouble her, and he went round to watch Arnot at work; and stood amazed. The figure on the canvas had been transformed into undreamed-of beauty, with a spectrum of colours Felix would not hitherto have thought of as belonging to flesh. The face was brushed in by a blur of colour only. The painting had a tremendous power. Felix asked Arnot how much it would cost, and was given a curt estimate; the man was still intent on his work. The model laughed, showing stained teeth. It was time for her rest and she came down, having flung a soiled blue robe about her body.

'Do not pay him yet,' she said. 'He will go out and get drunk with the money, and the work will never be finished.'

She came to the canvas, and regarded it with the air of a connoisseur; no doubt she had been painted many times in many poses. But Felix nevertheless paid for the painting as it was and ordered that it be brought when dry back to his inn. He would take it to London, have it framed and later hang it in his bedroom at Fenfallow. It would be the one piece of furniture he did not owe to Guy. He could see in his mind the place where it would hang; the thought of Mrs Canning's face when she should notice it amused him.

Later that day he strolled down to the Tuileries, staring at the prim bright flowerbeds, the families out walking in the late afternoon sun; the men in tall wide hats, the women in round narrow skirts and lapped lace headgear, or bonnets, their children well behaved, bowling hoops or listening to the barrel-organ which a man played, while the monkey in a red jacket collected coins. Now and again there would be, scrawled on a wall, the head of King Louis Philippe shaped like a pear in caricature. It amazed Felix to think that since he had last been here there was a new reign after revolution and that the new ruler had already lost his popularity in the same way as Charles X had done: the Press was once more censored in France, there were mutterings again and talk of freedom. He even heard it in the streets. He felt a growing desire to return to England, to accepted freedom and Fenfallow and his painting that he had chosen for himself. It would distract him from too much awareness of the railway line, in existence by now; the trains would soon be running noisily, blackly along the old strip of fallow land and the filled-in canal. Would the smoke and soot erode the stone of his house, turning it to a dirty brown, killing the lichens that grew on the flat Corinthian pillars? He realised that his short holiday among the painters of Montmartre had given him an insight he had not before possessed. He was grateful to them, but he could by now too clearly imagine things as they might in the end become.

He made the crossing safely, with a calm sea; but knew a certain surprise and anger when, waiting for him at Arlington Street, was a letter from Guy, which said that

Isabel had had a miscarriage and that her husband had sent her to Fenfallow to recover her health. *Her maid would not stay in the country, and Canning has found a young woman who will do for the present; I myself am down fairly frequently.*

There was some irony in it, which he recognised; Guy had prevented any hope of his, Felix's, legitimate children, and wanted to ensure issue of his own by inhabiting his, Felix's, house, or rather putting Isabel there. He had no real objection to housing the poor creature; it must be a relief to her to be sometimes free of Guy and the two Burridge women, whom he would not willingly permit to cross the doorstep.

'I believe I shall travel down by steam train, now that the station, as they call it, is finished. And you, Joshua?'

Felix's extraordinary nose quivered with amusement; the little man was making grimaces of obstinacy, like a monkey.

'M'lord, saving your presence, I'd do anything for you, except get into one of them monsters. Twenty miles an hour, and soot in your eye whenever you open a window, that's what they tell me. I hope I don't give your lordship offence, but that is one thing I will not do, not if it costs me my job, which I hope and trust it won't.'

'No, it will not do that; in fact I'd be glad if you brought the baggage down in the small carriage.'

Joshua registered relief. 'Fact is, I'll race your lordship's train. Wager fifty to one I get there before you do, and am waiting with the bags, like one of their porters.'

'You seem to know a great deal about the railways. Don't kill Moll and Toby racing them to beat trains.'

'I'd not do that, but they do say time's lost at them stations getting fancy females on board, an' all their hat-boxes, and the like, an'I can drive straight on, that is if there's no delay at the toll.'

'The toll-officers will be glad to see you these days, I dare say. And I will divert myself with a sight of the fancy females, if I can see them for soot.'

The journey was much as Joshua had predicted, with the tall thin funnel of the train-engine spouting forth a smoke so black that Felix felt dirty almost before the train had hissed its intention to start; when it began to move he felt a pleasant anticipation, for the speed they gained was more than the carriage ever had done, or even the four-in-hand. But it was less diverting, and challenged a man in no way, except to keep himself free of smuts; and being summer the carriage was incredibly stuffy, and no one dared open the window. Twice or three times they stopped at the brash new stations, and saw both females and gentlemen shepherded into the first-class carriages, or the third-class with their wooden seats, where the common people were herded much like cattle at a market and were exposed to the open air. Ladies could, if unescorted, occupy a Ladies Only carriage, and Felix saw one undoubted chaperone, tight-lipped, in charge of two young girls white with excitement, put into one such with all their baggage. He wondered idly where they were going, and why.

After an hour or so the train stopped at Fenn station, and the Earl emerged, feeling much in need of a bath. He blinked away the grit that in some manner had got into his eyes, and observed Joshua, a grin widening from ear to ear, coming forward to handle his luggage in spite of the obsequious porter, to whom Felix nevertheless tipped sixpence. 'We been here a good quarter-hour, your lordship,' panted Joshua. 'The hosses are in good heart.'

'You are lying, you have not got your own breath back yet. Let us see what pace they make to Fenfallow.'

The train gathered strength, started up again, and clanked away round the curve of track which had helped to make Guy's fortune. Felix saw it go without regret. He did not think he would often use the railway. It was pleasanter to feel the jog, jog of the two bays Toby and Moll, humdrum successors of the grand four greys: and to smell the clean air and horse-sweat, and know oneself to be coming home. The house came in sight and, not for the first time, Felix felt a rising of pride; few men had such a place to which to return, and he was beginning to be drawn to it more and more, and less and less to London. But all he said on alighting was 'Have them draw me a hip-bath; I will take it in my room. Get your breath back, Joshua, and then bring up the baggage.'

He had taken the stairs two at a time and went for a moment to an embrasure where there was a window from which one could see the station, an ugly enough intrusion on the flat summer landscape. He suddenly became aware that someone was behind the curtain; a presence; a cringing young woman. It was Isabel, in pale grey barathea. Felix withdrew courteously, and bowed. She was flustered, apologetic, and still evidently frightened; the fear in her was almost visible, as though she were never rid of it; as though it were a part of her, like her scared child's eyes and thin hands and spindly body.

'I – I heard an arrival: I thought – I thought it was my husband, and I – I –'

'You hid behind a curtain. Are you afraid of him, Isabel?' He spoke gently, as to a child. Was Guy cruel to her? It could be possible; his smugness could cover a good deal. How little one knew about it all, and what was the kindest thing to do?

'I – I am – foolish, I know it. It is only – only –'

He gave her his arm, and led her out of the window-embrasure. 'Come,' he said, 'I will take you to your room, and you shall lie down before dinner. Why, we hardly know each other; I have not seen you since the wedding.' Light, polite talk; to ease the tension, if that were possible. A little colour had come into her cheeks, and she smiled and thanked him.

'I – I do not come down to dinner. I – I have it on a tray in my room. Cathy brings it to me.'

'Cathy?' He felt bewilderment and anger. Perhaps it was a different Cathy, someone she had brought with her. Yet Guy had said that her own maid had gone back to town.

'Yes, she – she is a good girl, and very kind; she does everything I ask of her. I will miss her when – when I go back.'

'That will not be for some time, I hope,' he told her courteously. They were at the door of her room. He opened it and saw, from within the firelit space, Cathy rise from a flowered chair. She was dressed in black under her apron, and seemed thinner than he remembered. She bobbed to him, her colour rising, then came forward to assist Isabel as though he were not there. 'Come away, madam, and sit you down by the fire, for it's cold enough in here although it's summer.'

'I want to lie down,' he heard Isabel say as he closed the door and went off. 'Will you unlace me?'

Afterwards, bathed, shaved and refreshed, he went downstairs, a little frown between his eyebrows above the preternaturally long nose. He was singularly upset by the presence of Cathy as Isabel's maid. He would speak to Mrs Canning and ask how it had come about; though it was too late now to change.

She came and stood before him, and he had a feeling that she knew what he was going to say. In fact she said it for him.

'My lord, I thought you would maybe be angry at Cathy being up there with Mrs Sutbury. But after the accident she was very low, and having lost her baby with the shock and all, I thought the change would do her good, and she makes madam a good maid. I should maybe have written to you, my lord, but there wasn't the time, the other one flounced away so fast, and someone had to attend to her, poor soul.'

'What shock? What accident?' he asked, thinking as though on two levels; the life he himself led, and the other which went on like a stream, in spite of him, at Fenfallow.

'Why, sir, Joe – he was a good enough husband to her, but he liked his drop of drink – Joe was killed, coming back from the Swan it was, and Cathy was upset –'

'Killed? How was he killed?' He remembered Joe Hendry, a sound farm-worker, a trifle sullen perhaps, with the narrow mind that had at first rejected Cathy, then agreed to take her for money and no rent.

'Why, on the railway, my lord. The train ran right over him. They found him on the rails, all blood he was. Likely enough he never knew what hit him, but it was nasty for Cathy. That was a month ago.'

Felix knew great regret and sympathy for Cathy, and no longer resented her presence about his sister-in-law. In fact, he made her the ambassador for better relations; it was not good for Isabel to pine always in her room, and at first she had refused to come down for any meals; gradually he persuaded her, and when she sat at last, shyly, at his table, suggested they should go out for a carriage-drive next day, taking Cathy with them.

'It will be a diversion for you and for her. The weather is fine and I will show you some of the country; the roads are dusty, so wear a veil.'

They came out, the pair of them, in veiled bonnets, Cathy walking behind like the good servant she had always been, and Isabel staring at the well-groomed horses with a child's pleasure. He helped her up beside him while Cathy sat in the back. If the equipage were seen by anyone, there could be nothing improper about Lord Fenn's taking two veiled ladies on a drive together. But in fact the nearest neighbours were several miles away; Fenfallow had always been solitary.

They drove gently, and Isabel exclaimed in admiration at the way Felix's long fingers handled the reins. A sigh escaped him, remembering the four-in-hand; that would have been something to show her! But he said aloud: 'I will give you a turn at the reins, if you should care for it.'

She extended her small gloved hands, and with a delight he had not anticipated took a lesson from him in how to control, how to speed up and slow down; Moll and Toby were obedient, and gave no trouble.

'It is like riding,' he said. 'Show the mount he must do as you tell him, and be firm but gentle, not hurting his mouth.'

'I do not know how to ride,' said Isabel sadly. She had always lived in towns, always, with Aunt Malvina Burridge and Cousin Lilian. Lilian had been married four years ago, to a wealthy manufacturer. She was very handsome and knew her mind. Isabel had always been a little afraid of her, and, of course, of Aunt Malvina.

Felix said: 'I will teach you how to ride on Moll. Let us start tomorrow.'

She was flustered at once. 'Oh, but – but I have no habit.'

He laughed. 'What clothes one wears do not matter here. It will only be for a little way, walking beyond the house. You will come to no harm; I will hold the bridle till you are accustomed to it.'

'It – it is very kind of you.' She gave her timid smile; what would Aunt Malvina say? But Aunt Malvina was not here, neither was Guy; she hoped he would not come this week, there had been no letter.

'Then let us go before breakfast. That is the best time to ride.'

Over the next few days Felix was delighted to find that Isabel had physical courage. She was also, now that she had been given the opportunity, a natural rider. They progressed from walking Moll to the trot, then the canter; Felix himself did not think it wise to train his sister-in-law yet to the gallop or jumping. Yet an accident occurred nevertheless; on the fifth day out, one of the girths of the side-saddle, which had been hung up in the stables since his mother's time, broke; the leather was dry. Isabel took a toss to the ground, and lay there helpless for moments, her foot caught in the stirrup.

Mercifully Moll stood quiet. Felix dismounted hastily and
freed the foot, then helped Isabel to her feet. He had
expected trembling and tears – many women would have
indulged in them – but she only smiled radiantly, the fresh
colour brought to her cheeks by the exercise, and the
summer breezes, her lank fair hair loosened from its pins
beneath her hat. He knew a certain pleasure in holding
her. He was profuse in apologies about the girth. 'My man
should have kept them waxed,' he said. 'I'll tell him a thing
or two, you may be assured. You are certain you are not
hurt?'

'Not at all.' She was still smiling; she was like a different
creature from the cowed girl he had found behind the
curtain the other day. 'Will you get on Toby, or shall we
walk?' he suggested, taking the weight of the saddle off
Moll and holding it on his arm, with the reins of both
horses over one and Isabel's light touch on the other. 'Let
us walk,' she said; they were not far from home.

They walked together amicably, the two horses
following still on the rein. Isabel's free hand held up her
skirts; she wore little boots with side-buttons. He realised
that it was a long time since he had found anyone as
restful; most women talked too much. It was almost as if
she had forgotten her fear of Guy and her marriage.

But as they walked round to the house-entrance they
found Guy himself waiting for them, his baggage being
dismantled from the hired chaise the station boasted.

It was evident that he was not pleased. His shrewd
glance took in the horses, the broken saddle, Isabel's
disordered hair. Her pretty colour vanished as he gave her
a light peck on the cheek. 'I am glad to see,' he said drily,
'that you have regained some of your customary health,
my dear.'

'I – I –' She was the stammering, uncertain child again.
Felix made himself speak, not denying that the sight of his
brother was as unwelcome to him as it was to Isabel. They

went into the house and Isabel slipped up to her room. Felix poured wine.

'I must say that I do not approve of my wife's riding,' Guy said, turning his goblet about and savouring the colour and bouquet of the wine. 'It is her duty to bear me an heir, and such exercise is hardly conducive to a happy state; I should have thought that you would know that, familiar as you are with the ways of women.' His eyes glinted with malice. 'In fact, had I known that you were returned from abroad at all, I would not have left Isabel here alone; it is most improper. I now intend to send her aunt down; I can trust Mrs Burridge to see to it that there is full opportunity made for a recovery from the recent affliction. It was a great disappointment to me.' He sounded aggrieved, as if his wife had had her miscarriage on purpose; the heartlessness of his whole speech and manner angered Felix unspeakably.

'Isabel is far happier and in better health than she has been for a long time,' he said roundly. 'Evidently you regard her as a brood-mare –'

'Perhaps we should leave the subject of horseflesh alone. Understand that I expressly forbid Isabel to ride again, and I shall tell her so myself.' He swallowed the rest of his wine, set down the glass, rose and went coolly upstairs. Felix, left alone in the hall, watched him go with open dislike. If only the poor girl could have been free for a little longer! And the company of her aunt, the egregious Mrs Burridge, was hardly such as he, or perhaps Isabel either, could anticipate with pleasure. As he had found in their talks, the girl's parents had died before she was seven, and apparently she had been cowed by this woman ever since; such was his guess, for she had not said so openly. Her fortune, of course, must have been tied up securely: had it not been, she might now be free of Guy.

Guy had been with them only two days when the diligent

Malvina Burridge came down by train. She was duly met by
the carriage, with much fuss over baggage and hat-boxes.
She had brought her maid and her daughter Lilian. Neither
Lilian's spouse nor her own were ever referred to in
conversation, and Felix played in his mind with the idea that
Lilian Packworth had been born by parthenogenesis, like an
aphid. She was, as he admitted, very handsome, and knew it;
her forward manners were put to the greater contrast by
Isabel's shyness, and Felix, accustomed as he was to pursuit
by females, engaged all his defences. However Lilian, in her
mauve gowns and neat-trimmed bonnets, hung firmly on
his arm whenever she could; followed him on his occasional
walks about the estate, and thankfully could not ride or she
would have taken charge of the stables also; and, in whatever
situation, chattered to Felix about matters which only
concerned herself and did not interest him in the least. In
lack of sensitivity she all but outshone her mother, and Felix
increasingly understood how Isabel had grown up like a
wilting lily between two prosperous dahlias.

Guy evidently admired Lilian, however, and addressed
most of his talk to her. She dressed as boldly as her widowed
state allowed, and Guy never failed to comment on her
appearance and how well her mauve-and-black plaids and
lilac bombazines became her. When he was present his eyes
in general followed her, and it was evident that had it not
been for all the money which was Isabel's, Lilian might well
have been the one favoured; but one had to be practical.

'And to think that Guy will inherit all this one day!' had
been Malvina's comment on first beholding Fenfallow in its
seasonal glory. The remark plumbed such depths of
tactlessness that Felix, who was present, began to wish the
lady's visit ended before it had begun. However it was plain
that she had every intention of staying for some time, after
Guy, Lilian and even the maid had gone back to town.
Malvina Burridge then announced that she would move
into Isabel's room and share it with her. Mrs Canning, when

she heard, was outraged. 'There's more than enough rooms at Fenfallow for every guest who comes,' she said roundly. 'Madam should stay where she is, in the blue room; nothing wrong with it, and a fire and all.'

But madam was adamant. 'Mr Guy left orders that I was to look after Mrs Sutbury, who is very nervous,' she insisted. 'She is subject to nightmares from a child, and I know how to deal with them.'

'Perhaps Mrs Sutbury should be consulted as to her own preference,' said Felix coldly. Did Guy perhaps suspect him of nocturnal visits to Isabel? The cure for a nightmare certainly seemed worse than the fact, if fact it was.

'I should – I should prefer –'

'Come, now, child, you know very well that you must obey your husband's wishes,' said Malvina Burridge loudly. And move in she did, and, lacking the presence of the second maid, Cathy had to do the hair of both of them and lace them up in their separate armouries. Later Mrs Canning came to Felix where he sat, trying to subdue his temper, in the library, looking at a book he was not reading. She gave her little formal curtsey, which lightly rattled the bunch of keys at her belt.

'My lord, Cathy came to me to ask if she might have a word with you in private.'

'That was very correct of Cathy. By all means let her do so.'

Cathy, who must have been waiting outside, came in and the housekeeper, discreetly, left. Cathy stood twisting her hands in her apron the way he remembered; but it was a better apron now, as her status had climbed to that of lady's-maid, and the hands were less red.

'What is the matter, Cathy?' Felix said gently. He recalled that he had taken no opportunity of condoling with her over her husband's death, and did so now. She gave a little rueful smile, and folded her hands before her.

'He was a good man to me, my lord, although as you know he drank a good bit. I think the babby might have steadied him. He wanted a boy, and that's what it was – or would have been. It was the sight of the blood done it. Well, it's over. My lord, I hope you won't be offended with what I felt I had to say. It's about Mrs Isabel.' She hung her head somewhat. 'As you may know, my lord, I sleep in her dressing-room, to be near her if she needs me. While he – Mr Guy – was here in her room at nights, I couldn't help hearing certain things, not that I would have listened a-purpose. He was right nasty to her, my lord, and that's the truth. Kept telling her she wasn't up to scratch, whatever that means, and saying how she must give him a child and do it right this time. He isn't good to her, my lord, and she a sweet lady that's no trouble to anyone and never an unkind word from her. That other, Mrs Lilian – well, it's not my place, but I could say a lot.'

Felix was staring at his hands. 'But what can I do about it, Cathy?' he said. 'They are man and wife, and Mrs Isabel has no rights in law; you may not know that a married woman's property is her husband's, no longer her own.'

'That's a wicked law, my lord. There's some would drink it all.'

'And maybe have done, Cathy. Had I known what I know now, I would have prevented the marriage, somehow –'

'How, my lord? You wasn't to know.'

'As you say; I scarcely see and hardly know my half-brother, and only learned of his impending marriage when the invitation came. The bride was no one I knew. Nor did I know her – her family.' He made a wry face.

'That's not family, only an aunt by marriage and a cousin, for what that's worth, and I dare say,' added Cathy, with surprisingly worldly knowledge, 'they've feathered their own nests pretty well out of it all, having had charge of Mrs Isabel from a child. If I was to say what I think would help her, my lord, will you be angry?'

'I could be angry with many people, Cathy, but never with you.' It struck him with refreshment how cleanly their former relationship had been broken off, without scenes or embarrassment. Cathy remained, as long as she chose, his friend as well as his servant.

The clear eyes met his. 'Well, my lord, you taught me something about loving, that can be between a man and a woman. It wasn't the same even with Joe, he hadn't the patience. What you and I had together was as different from ordinary folks as – well, chalk from cheese, as they say. She needs a bit of that, a bit of your kind of loving. Maybe I'm a bad woman to say it, but that's the truth.'

'That aunt is with her night and day.' He surprised himself with the feeling of ease that grew in him since her suggestion. Perhaps it followed the course of his own wishes, after all.

'That old woman sleeps like the dead, I can hear her snoring. I could put something in her bedside jug, if you like. I don't know much, but I know herbs, and there was one my mother used to take when the aches took her something terrible. I could –'

He had begun to laugh. 'Cathy, don't let us have a murder on our hands; she might take too much. Or Mrs Isabel might take it by mistake, and sleep when she wasn't supposed to.'

It was Cathy's turn to laugh; he was glad to see it, having regretted mentioning the word murder after her recent experience. But her determination did not change.

'I meant just enough to put that old bitch to sleep, my lord. But just as you like it. If you say not, I won't do it, trust me not to.'

'We will return to town tomorrow,' announced Malvina Burridge at breakfast. Felix was not present, being out on his ride.

Isabel knew a sinking of the heart. 'But Aunt, why? It is beautiful weather, and – and you have Cathy to attend you.' She put Cathy in as the only bait she could quickly think of; she had grown fond of the maid, and would have liked to

ask her to accompany her when she did go back; it would be a
relief to have – she confessed it to herself – a friend.

'I dislike living the country, and poor Lilian requires my
company. You must not always think only of yourself, my
dear.'

'Then – then go to Lilian, and I will stay on here.'

'That is quite impossible; Guy was right, it is most
improper.' The dark hair on Malvina's upper lip almost
bristled with self-righteousness. She had hoped that the
handsome, though penniless, Earl of Fenn might be taken
with Lilian, but instead he merely looked at Isabel – plain,
meek Isabel – as no gentleman under sixty should look at a
young married female. The sooner it was put a stop to and
Isabel returned to her husband's care, the better. And it was
quite true that Malvina detested the country; smells of cows,
horses and sheep, and rough farm-fellows everywhere, and
that Cathy no better than she should be, as one could in some
way perceive. It was certainly time to be gone.

Isabel sat with her eyes downcast, but inwardly she felt
rebellion. Aunt Malvina had promised that when she was a
married woman she might do as she chose, but there was no
sign of it; taken all in all, it had only made her deeply
unhappy as well as being downtrodden, which last she knew
she had always been. It had been difficult to stand up – in
fact she had never dared to try – to the combined wills of
Aunt Malvina and Lilian, who had been two years older, and
had always been brilliant, handsome, and witty, all the
things Isabel knew she herself was not. All the same – Isabel
allowed the disloyal, wayward thought to enter her mind –
Lilian's assured ways had frightened off young men, and it
had been considered fortunate when at last, at twenty-four,
she ensnared the passive, wealthy widower, Mr Packworth,
who had obligingly died quite soon. Money was so important, evidently, that one should direct all one's behaviour to
acquiring it and keeping it. Yet she herself had never
handled large sums and even her clothes were still chosen
for her by Aunt Malvina, as Isabel had been allowed to

develop no taste of her own. All she had ever wanted, in fact, was to be left in peace, to let the quiet person who was Isabel Manning have space and time to breathe. But it had not worked out like that, not even yet; and she dreaded going back to Guy. Like most brides she had been kept in entire ignorance until the wedding-night, when his cold, competent lovemaking had terrified and hurt her: soon the monthly occasions which must never, never be mentioned to anyone, not even to other young females, except possibly as a headache, stopped, and Aunt Malvina had told Isabel in hushed tones it was because she was to have a baby; the thought had been pleasant, and Guy had left her alone, but she had been sick and out of sorts almost from the beginning and then, for no reason, there had been the miscarriage, which was miserable and she had been ill and Guy very angry, as if it was all her fault. Now everything was supposed, from what Guy had said and done here, to happen again, and the thought made her heart quicken with fear. If only they could have stayed at Fenfallow for a little longer! Felix – he had asked her to call him by his Christian name, which otherwise Isabel would have been hesitant to do – was handsome and kind, the kindest person she had ever met, except perhaps Cathy; but that was different. She raised her head suddenly.

'I am going to ask Lord Fenn if Cathy may come back with me to be my personal maid. She – she suits me very well, and I should like to have her.' It was almost a plea, a request for permission, and as such Malvina treated it.

'She has a great deal to learn before she becomes a proper lady's maid, I can tell you,' she said. 'I do not know if I can be responsible for introducing such a young person into Guy's household.'

'But it is I who will introduce her, Aunt,' said Isabel gently.

*

The twilights were late in summer, making it no longer necessary to light the lamps before the moon rose. Its silver light streamed into Felix's bedchamber, where he lay restlessly, unable to sleep. The painting of the nude he had bought in Montmarte was transformed into purples and browns. He had learned, in course of the day, that Isabel and the aunt were to leave tomorrow; a week ago that news would have pleased him and he would have been glad to be rid of the encumbrance; now, the whole matter troubled his conscience. He had done nothing to follow Cathy's advice because he could not contrive it; the Burridge was everywhere. At this very moment she would be lying by Isabel's side, sleeping noisily, if what Cathy said was true. How was anyone to rescue that poor girl from the double thrall of her dominant aunt and her heartless husband? There was no way he could think of, except to have been as kind to Isabel as might be, and allowing her to take Cathy, as she had asked, back to Manchester. Cathy was pleased to go; he had seen the girl and ascertained as much. 'And remember, if anything goes amiss, your home is at Fenfallow,' he had told her. Cathy had then done a thing which touched him; she had curtseyed, and had taken his hand and kissed it, as though he were a king.

A king. Without money, without power, without the right to make a marriage of his own, let alone an heir. What sort of ruler was he? In what ways could his will, if he had one, be made manifest?

There was a timid scratching at the door. The thought flew into his mind that it must be Cathy, come after all to say farewell in lover's terms, and the thought made him impatient; surely she knew by now that that was ended? It reduced her gesture of the afternoon to the action of a fool.

He got out of bed, went and opened the door; and drew a breath in the silence. Isabel stood there, in her thin nightgown, her hair down about her shoulders, silvered over in the light of the moon. She was like an elfin creature;

and she was shivering, her small bare feet on the cold stones of the passage.

'I – I wanted to come, I – I – she is asleep – Cathy told me where you were. I – I –'

He took her gently by the shoulders, guided her into the room, shut and latched the door, picked her up and carried her light weight to the bed. The moon rose higher in the sky and shone down on their rustlings. There followed a warm silence, presently broken by her moans of pleasure. He laid his mouth over hers and quieted these, but gently; everything he did was gentle. It was dawn before she slipped away.

'Where were you, Isabel? What happened? I woke and you were not there. Where did you go? Why did you not wake me? I called out, but you were not in the room, nor were you on the commode, for I looked behind the screen. Where had you gone?'

Breakfast again; grilled bacon and eggs and kidneys, porridge and kedgeree and cold beef from last night's dinner, and her own mind so filled with glorious happiness that she did not know what she was eating from her plate, or care. She heard Aunt Malvina's customary questioning as if it came from outside a rainbow bubble, in which she, Isabel, lived and would live always. It did not matter what happened now; what had already happened, the having known full, requited happiness and joy and love, was all. Love ... it did not die, as people did. It would be with her always, even if she never met him again.

She heard herself answering lightly, untruthfully; it was the first time she had ever told Aunt Malvina a lie. 'Why, Aunt, I could not sleep for your snoring, so I went and lay down in the blue room, and passed a very comfortable night.'

If Felix had been here they would have passed a twinkling, conspiratorial glance at each other, and no doubt that would have been noted, so it was as well that he was not; as well perhaps that he was out in the saddle, on one of the rides she had so much enjoyed, when for a time, in his company, she had shed the crushed creature she had formerly allowed herself to become, and begun to turn into the whole, contented, joyous person she had been meant to be from the beginning. And that would never leave her; whatever happened now, that would never, never leave her. Last night had been their true farewell; going down the steps into the carriage later today, getting on to the train and being borne away from Fenfallow, seeing his raised hand in farewell, would not count. She had last night to remember always, like a jewel beneath her heart.

Cathy accompanied them on the train, her few belongings clutched in a hamper. She looked forward to seeing Manchester. It would be the first time she had visited a city. And she looked forward to being with Mrs Isabel. After all, they had both known – though one would never mention it – the same love, the same lover. That was a bond between them. As for the rest, it didn't matter.

The hay was ripe for cutting, and with the continuing fine weather Felix went out and worked with the men, taking a scythe in his hands and feeling the strength of his lean body and arms as he made great swathes on his way; it was essential to get the stacks built in time, before the rain, and they were short of a man lacking Cathy's Joe. The women came out in the afternoon and gathered the cut hay into bundles, stacking it to dry; at the same time they brought ale, and the thirsty men drank gratefully. Felix promised them a return drink in the winter. He had long had the notion of pulling out the very old quince trees in the orchard, which for long had borne no fruit, and replacing them with new apple saplings. Now that he had begun to take an interest in the estate ideas came to him daily concerning it. He wondered how he had ever found time for living in town.

He had heard nothing more from his late visitors except for a formal note of thanks from Malvina on behalf of herself, Isabel and Lilian. Cathy must be giving satisfaction, as she was not mentioned. Felix crumpled the missive with its careful precise handwriting and threw it on the fire. The days went on and he forgot it.

The time came to cut down the quinces and pull up the roots with cart-horses and ropes. The horses were great thick-maned heavy-limbed shires, their tremendous strength making their muscles shine with sweat as they heaved; he recalled hearing that they were descended from the destriers of knights in battle. They did battle now with the ancient trees; the old trunks groaned, shifted and finally came away with a rattle of earth and stones, the smell of uprooted moss and grass strong in the one-time orchard. The old wood he gave orders to be stacked in an open field after the stubble was picked over; later, when it had dried out, he would have a bonfire and return the men's hospitality with a roasted sheep or two and the house-ale. The evening came and the great fire was lit, flickering on the expectant faces of men and women alike and roaring upwards; the sparks flew; afterwards there would be a barn-dance. The mutton frizzled on the fire, giving out a tempting smell at last; soon it was ready to cut up, and knives were ready, sharp from much honing. Everyone ate their fill, with home-made bread and the ale, welcome as the nights were already chilly. They cheered Felix and he listened to the shouting, rough and hearty against the firelit dark. 'And to the next squire as well as this,' shouted a voice, and Felix's mood, which had been mellow, plunged again into the old blackness. The next squire would be Guy, not himself; or Guy's son.

Within the next few days there came another letter from

Malvina Burridge, who seemed to have taken upon herself the responsibility of writing to Fenfallow. She said that Isabel was expecting a child, *and we must hope this time for a fortunate outcome, so she is to be kept very quiet, to receive no visitors, and to lie on a sofa for much of the day.* There was an almost vindictive smugness about the words, as though Malvina defied Felix to try to visit them; in fact he had not thought of doing so, and would not now. But he hoped Isabel was in health and spirits, and would fare better than before. There was no word from Guy.

Christmas came, and Felix ate his dinner alone, though the parson and his wife had invited him to dine with them. He felt a growing need for solitude, as though he saw all of life from behind a glass screen. It seemed incredible that he had once been one of the crowd at Crockford's, throwing the dice with D'Orsay and dining often afterwards with Lady Blessington as had been his habit. He heard news now only through the gazettes; and took little heed of it, until a certain day in late February. It was announced in the columns that a daughter had been born prematurely to the Honourable Guy Sutbury and his wife Isabel Manning, but that the mother had not survived the birth.

Felix watched the new young apple-trees dug into the newly turned earth, purified by winter frosts and now raked clean. The thought came to him that he would never see them grow to full maturity; perhaps one day there would be another thick old orchard at Fenfallow where the women would gather fruit in their outstretched aprons while the men shook the harvest down from the trees. When the planting was done he walked among the new saplings, saw that the ground about them was firm, and then went back to the house. He had called for Joshua to pull off his muddy boots and bring his house-shoes, when Mrs Canning came to him, her face without expression. It came to him that she was getting old. She must have been at

Fenfallow forty years, and her seemly brushed hair was white.

'My lord,' she said in a low voice, 'they're in the library. I put them there for quiet.'

'Who are they?' he asked, but she had turned and gone quickly away. He went to the library and opened the door. There among the books sat Cathy, a wrapped bundle in a shawl on her lap. She stood and tried to curtsey, but he prevented her. 'Stay in your chair,' he said. 'What is this?'

'My lord, there's a note. I was to give it to you myself. Mr Guy – he paid our fare here, my lord. He –'

He read the short letter. *This is evidently your daughter. I am accordingly returning her to you with your servant. I take no further responsibility for either.*

Cathy had pulled the shawl gently away from the baby's face. Its eyes stared up towards him, trying to focus. They were speckled green and brown, moss-agate Clonmagh eyes. 'That was when he knew,' said Cathy. 'The first few days they were like all babby's eyes, a blue colour. Then they cleared, and he knew at once. Maybe he'd thought of it before, I don't know. She's at rest at any rate, poor soul.'

'She is at rest,' he echoed quietly. He looked down at the baby. Its skin was like a roseleaf and the fine hair, which the shawl had partly hidden, was like his own, curling chestnut, still close to the scalp. 'What shall we call her?' he said to Cathy.

'My lord – I didn't say anything till now – *she* wanted her called Catherine, after myself. I was the only friend she had there, my lord. He wasn't cruel to her, only kept away after the first, and nobody minded that. He's turned the little thing out like a stray kitten, my lord. I'm glad I was there, to take her with me. I've fed her on cow's milk watered, till now.'

'She is not unlike a kitten,' he said, looking at the child's pointed chin. 'We'll call her Catherine and shorten it to Kate. That suits her.'

*

The small Kate thrived; they found a wet-nurse for her, but Cathy was always in charge. Kate was a lively baby despite her small size, and cheerful; Felix often had her brought to him during the day and put on the heathrug before the fire, to play and prattle until tea. What the servants said, what anyone said, he did not know or care; the only person with whom he discussed the matter, apart from Cathy, was his aunt Eileen Clonmagh, to whom he wrote the whole story. *You must bring Kate here when she is a little older,* the old lady had written at once. *In the meantime, give her my love and Valentine's.*

Guy Sutbury remarried, after a decent interval of about a year. His bride was Lilian Packworth. Felix was not invited to the wedding. After a further year Lilian fulfilled her duty and bore Guy a son, to be called Gerard. He heard of them occasionally and that they had moved to London, taking the bride's mother with them. He seldom thought of any of them and never met them again, except on one occasion.

TWO

Kate, aged six, lay still asleep beside Cathy in the good bed at the inn. He had left orders that they were not to be disturbed until ten o'clock, for the crossing had been stormy. Meanwhile he knew a strong desire to stretch his legs, and would walk to Marishnageen, six miles off. Aunt Eileen expected them at dinner, and there would be plenty of time for the hired coach to follow.

He had put off this visit time and again; unimportant matters had always cropped up, and he could give no reason even now why it had taken so long. As if to make up for his lagging duty, he took great strides along the road, his long legs enjoying the exercise, his mind full of news for Eileen and a pleasant vagueness about the duration of the visit. They could stay as long as they liked, and if Kate was happy that meant several weeks. A great deal had come to depend on Kate; she was by way of being spoilt, and soon now he would have to find a governess strict enough to teach the child manners and stop her running to Cathy for comfort, and understanding enough not to make Kate rebel.

Cathy had been like a mother to the child, despite the other duties that had fallen to her as his housekeeper after the death of Jessie Canning. Fenfallow was well kept; Felix had no complaints, and when he needed his own comfort Cathy had been his willing mistress. He had had her taught to read and write, largely for his own convenience as she could now understand accounts. He would not have

brought her here now – perhaps it was improper – except
that the child would not have come willingly without her,
much as she adored her Papa. In any case Eileen was
easy-going, at least so long as nothing was pointed out to
her: and it should not be.

A sudden desire for wild remembered things, the garden,
the old house, the primroses by the way, had come to him
lately in England. They had had a few clothes packed –
dressing did not matter greatly here – and had set out, and
during the short voyage he himself had stood at the rail of
the ship, staring down at the green turbulent water of the
Irish Channel. He saw a pattern of his life in it; wild,
undirected anywhere save by the wind and the moon. What
would be the end of him? To die, still alone, at Fenfallow,
after Kate had married and left? He must give Kate a season,
when she was old enough. A duenna would have to be
found, and palms greased, no doubt, to present a bastard.

Meantime, he had seen the little blue hill by Dublin at last
with relief. In this country he could forget himself, forget
both past and future. He was no poorer than half the
aristocracy of Ireland. And he was no longer as poor as he
had been: careful farming and management, and staying at
home at all times of year, watching Kate grow, had half filled
the empty coffers. But he was still in debt to Guy for rescuing
him from bankruptcy, all those years ago; and the knowledge chafed him, because he and Guy never saw one
another, or corresponded. As far as he knew Guy and his
family went on very well.

He saw a cloud of dust on the deserted road; it was
Johnny, come with the carriage. The horses' bridles were
mended with string. Johnny looked no different, and still
wore the same old patched coat.

'How did you know I would come so early?' Felix asked,
after the effusive greeting.

'Ough, none of us knew, but Miss Eileen said to go in and
watch the ships, and now here you are, and welcome.'

'Go on to the inn, and wait for my housekeeper and my daughter. Tell the hired coachman he is no longer required.'

'He will make a terrible to-do over that, my lord. Trade's bad always, with the gentry mostly having their own.'

'Then give him his fare.' Felix handed over the coins; they would be safe with Johnny, except maybe for a bit on the side. He walked on, smiling, while the old carriage jolted off.

He had made his way to the house past the stables and through the garden, and at this season it was a delight; lush growth everywhere, and the roses heavy-headed and dripping with dew despite their scent, and scent also from the masses of creamy honeysuckle. Eileen, in a battered straw hat, was moving among them, dead-heading the roses. Somewhere, someone was playing the pianoforte.

'It is yourself, at last. Where is Kate?' She raised her face for his kiss; like Johnny, she hardly looked older, although in years she must be getting on for seventy. He told her Kate was still asleep, and that Johnny would bring her and her nurse. The music had swelled to a Chopin nocturne; the unseen performer played very well.

'That is Valentine,' said his aunt. 'Go you in and meet her.' She watched him go, staring after his tall figure; she did not try to follow him. He knew that the heads of the dead roses would be shredded, salted, mixed with blue cornflowers for the fragrant pot-pourri she made, drying it out on trays in the fitful Irish sun. He thought of it as he went in through the glass door, which was open; and then his heart stopped.

The woman who was playing was not so very young; she must be thirty or more; he remembered that she was three years younger than himself. A great knot of curling light-brown hair was piled up on her head, untidy ringlets of it escaping against her milk-white skin. Her nose, as memory suddenly rose in him from boyhood, was delightful, in some way both twisted and tip-tilted. She heard him coming and before the end of the piece stopped playing, rose from the music-stool and turned; she was dressed untidily and even then, Felix knew that she never cared what she looked like, any more than she had ever done or ever would. The sense of coming home was so strong in him that he could have walked into her arms.

Instead, he took her hand. 'It is useless to ask who you are,' she told him. 'I would have known you by your nose.'

'And I you by yours, and your hair, which always fell down your back when it was out of pigtails.'

They stood staring at one another, smiling. Miss Eileen came in from the garden. 'Is he not become a tall fine fellow?' she said to Valentine. She set her tray of rose-heads down near the window and their scent soon filled the room. He would always associate Valentine with that luscious scent of Irish roses.

'He is quite glorious,' said Valentine wryly, in a voice as soft as honey. Eileen made as if to slap her, and said: 'Valentine is grown very impudent since her life with the old baroness. She had it all her own way there, and here too.'

'Then I also must have my own way,' said Felix, and meant more than he said. In fact the blow, which the French call *coup de grâce*, had so overcome him he did not know what he was saying. As for Valentine, there was no artifice about her at all; she was the most natural being he had ever met.

'You must be hungry,' said Eileen. 'Could you do with a mutton chop and some tay? I can have it freshly made, the kettle is always boiling.'

'Aunt Eileen makes tea all day,' said Valentine. 'Do men drink it? I have never seen one do so.'

'Then you will see it now,' said Eileen. 'Come, all of you.' The dog – there were always dogs at Marishnageen, as well as donkeys – stood up and wagged his tail. 'Not you, Master,' his owner said. 'He always stands by for scraps; he is greedy, like them all.'

Felix was still looking at Valentine. 'How long are you staying here?' he asked her in a low voice.

'As long as she likes,' answered Eileen for her, 'and you too.'

They went in, and the maid brought two overdone chops for Felix and a pot of tea still steaming at the spout. The pot was of magnificent old embossed late Stuart silver, the china fine but chipped. Felix ate his fill of the blackened mutton and the good fresh soda bread. For some reason Eileen was talking about the Battle of the Boyne.

'And they blamed King James for riding off, and him with a bad nose-bleed that poured down the lintel of the summer-house they stopped at, leaving his poor face white as bone and him not young. It will never be forgotten in Ireland, that fight.' She spoke as if she had been there.

Felix changed the subject. 'You have a good mare in the stable, I saw as I passed by,' he said. 'I am no judge, but I noticed her.'

'That is Una, the only thing my poor father could leave me, but she is worth the rest,' said Valentine Shannon. 'I would not sell her for all the world's gold. I have been out on her this morning already.' Perhaps, he thought, that accounted for the rose-flush still on her cheeks, or perhaps it was the hot tea; or perhaps himself. He felt happy as a schoolboy or a lark. Nothing in his life, until this moment, mattered. Yet one had to say something, to be polite. 'Do you hunt here?' he asked her.

'In the season. Aunt Eileen will maybe have to put up with me this winter as well,' said Valentine.

She will not, thought Felix, because by then you will be married to me. And there is no hunting at Fenfallow, but you can ride her about the fields and lanes.

Kate was running. She ran past the rose beds and the

catmint and the lavender hedge and the climbing shrubs, leaving Papa with the strange woman, the pair of them not seeing anyone else but only each other, shutting her out. She knew it would be like that always; she had said to Papa here one day: 'When can we go home?' and he had smiled and looked at the tall woman by his side and said: 'Soon, my darling, and Valentine is coming with us.' After that it would be different, with no more games on the rug in the library while Papa read or wrote; no more rides on the pony Sixpence with Papa walking by her and holding the reins, though by now she, Kate Sutbury, could ride very well by herself. It would all be different, and she hated the thought of it. And it was different here; she didn't even like Aunt Eileen, who hardly noticed her after the first, when she had made a little fuss of Kate and said: 'What a lovely child, to be sure,' and then had forgotten her and everything but those two, and had even said to Papa when he addressed some remark to her: 'Yes, and you're the fortunate man, because the old Gräfin left her all her money. Why hasn't she married before? You great stupid, I was keeping her for you, and you were long in coming.'

Long in coming. That meant that she, Kate, had kept him at Fenfallow too long. That was always the answer to everything; too much time had gone by. She might have been a leaf blowing about in the wind for all anyone noticed, though Papa still gave her her goodnight kiss, a little absently. He was like a different person. Everyone was different, except Cathy; and it was to Cathy she was running now, seated as she would be with the other servants by the fire in the kitchen. The back door was open, for it was a fine day; and Kate hurtled across the stone floor and flung herself down with her head buried in Cathy's lap.

'Why, my darling, what is it, now, what is it?' And her hands began to stroke Kate's disordered hair. 'You have got yourself all of a tangle, and I brushed it well this morning,' she said now, but not as if she was scolding; Cathy never scolded. The other servants were talking among themselves while one of them stood up to her wrists in dough, making the dark soda bread they ate here and which Kate did not like. Kate heard one of them say a thing that branded the truth on her soul, if it were not there already.

'To think of Miss Valentine marryin' an English lord! And him so handsome and free in his ways.'

Cathy was smiling a little. Kate looked up, her eyes filled with tears, and saw the smile. Even you think it's good news, she thought; and began to sob against Cathy's apron.

'Why, now, here's a to-do, and all about nothing; she'll be a kind stepmother to you, will Miss Valentine. And she's rich, and that will help your father.'

Kate burst out into stammering words. 'She can't be rich. She has darns in the heels of her stockings.'

Everyone laughed. 'Hark at the little miss!' said one, while the breadmaker kneaded on. Suddenly the laughter stopped. 'You take it from me, missy, it's lucky for anyone in this country to have stockings at all, or shoes; many folk go barefoot, even in the cold winters.'

And the talk turned towards the everlasting chip on the shoulder which was and is Ireland, and Cathy went on stroking Kate's hair.

It was some time before Cathy could obtain a word with Lord Fenn alone; his lady was always by him from the morning ride until they all went to their different beds. 'I would like a word with you, my lord, if you can spare the time.'

'What is it, Cathy?' He was a little uneasy about Cathy. There had been nothing, of course, said at Marishnageen about a relationship they knew nothing about; but it had existed, and Felix's conscience troubled him. He would have thought of ways to find Cathy a place elsewhere, but she was good to Kate; he could not in fact imagine Kate without her, the child thought of her as a mother.

Cathy looked him straight in the eye. 'First of all, my lord, I'm glad you are happy. You have found the right lady to be your wife, and that makes all of us glad, except Kate meantime; but she's young and will get over it. Secondly I had a thing to tell you about myself. I am to be married when we return, as soon as can be.'

'Married?' Relief flooded him, but he did not let her see it; who was the man?

'Saul Fingerhut, up at the Knocking.'

'The ranting hellfire man, the lay preacher? Oh, Cathy, that's not the man for you.' He remembered the fellow; thin as a shag, and dark eyes glaring to boot, as if he would cast your sins in the fire and you along with them. 'And his house is a shambles,' Felix added.

'He has been at me to marry him these five years, ever since I came out of mourning for Joe. Men need somebody to look after them.' Cathy managed a little smile, and did not say that she had only just sent a note to Saul with three words on it: *I will come*. It's not that *she* would mind me at Fenfallow, she was thinking; but *he* would, in time; and I couldn't bear that. 'I'll make Saul's house all right and tight for him, you can be sure,' she said. 'I'm used to living rough, you must remember.' What my lord had taken her from, when all was said, wasn't any better than Saul's house; a pack of brats to be washed and fed at the table, with holes scooped in it for soup because there weren't any plates like the gentry had; and her father always drunk, and her mother forever seated by the door in daylight, mending, or on the floor, scrubbing, or in the bed they mostly shared, bearing more children. No, Saul's place wouldn't be any worse than that.

She saw the relief she had known would come, though he tried not to let it show on his face openly. 'Cathy, I'll give you a new thatched roof for a wedding-gift. And of course you must see as much of Kate as you can. You say she's upset? I must see to it.' But in fact there was a matter which troubled him at present more than Kate's whims; he had been outraged to learn, some time after proposing to her, that Valentine was in fact a rich woman. The old German baroness had had no close relatives living; she had left everything she had, except the castle in Thuringia which was the property of the unknown heir, to her young paid companion of eleven years. Valentine had not expected it; she was not used to money and could very well have done without it; but now she was glad for Felix's sake. But he would have none of it, and rounded on her.

'You will spend every penny on yourself, do you hear? I want none of it, nothing to do with it at all. My brother fattened on his wife's inheritance and she led a life of misery. I do not want that for you.'

'I shall not be miserable with you,' said Valentine softly. She did not argue about the money. It was there, if he ever changed his mind and needed it. And they would have children. She must make friends as soon as possible with Kate.

She tried. She bent down over the little girl and said: 'I saw you talking to Rebecca the donkey.' It was a different Rebecca, the last having died horribly of eating yew. 'Have you a donkey at home at Fenfallow?'

'No.'

'Would you like a donkey? I will buy you a little grey one, a baby one, that you can feed with bits of carrot, and sometimes a lump of sugar.'

'I don't want a donkey. I have a pony.'

'Have you, now? And what is the pony's name?'

Kate stared at her own shoes. For some reason she was not going to tell Valentine that the pony's name was Sixpence. She was not going to tell her anything, or pretend to be friends with her. Everything at Fenfallow would be spoilt, and Cathy was going away. But not very far, Cathy had said; only to the top of Knocking Hill, and that was not very high, just a lump of rock in the middle of the flat fields. She, Kate, would be able to ride there often. She turned away and pulled at a piece of grass, sucking the sweet pallid end when it came up. Valentine watched her kindly. It would be difficult at first, maybe; the little thing wasn't used to other children, let alone a stepmother.

There were other difficulties. Father Jonathan Filey – ironically, he shared a Christian name with the gloomy Dean – had prepared Valentine for her confirmation when she was a child, and made no bones about telling her what he thought of her marriage to a Protestant, an Englishman, lord or not.

'Do you think I do not know about England, and the blessed martyrs who shed their blood there for the Faith?' he said bitterly. 'And you will deny all that, giving yourself to a heretic and the son of persecutors, living nowhere near a Catholic church, having to miss Mass, getting used to that and ending with no religion at all, or any hope of a happy death?'

Valentine smiled; she knew the old man well. 'I will not forget the Faith, father, and if there is no Catholic church I will build one.'

'That would be something, certainly; but your children? Will your bridegroom promise that they will be brought up in the Faith?'

'I do not want to hold him to promises.' She faltered slightly; she could not yet visualise their children, and surely no Catholic was permitted a degree at a university, a commission in the armed forces, and so on? Or had all that been overcome? She knew she was ignorant; having lived here in the safety of her faith all her life, and also in Germany, where the Gräfin had had a beautifully painted chapel, a resident priest, and a relic of St Nicholas, Valentine had been sheltered in such ways. Now – but surely her love for Felix, and his for her, would overcome any difficulties that might arise?

She talked the matter over with her betrothed. He had given her the moss-agate from Aunt Eileen and Valentine fingered it where it lay on her breast as they talked. 'I suppose you did not know,' she told him, 'that you are marrying a black Papist, who God willing will never change.'

'I don't care if you are a Moslem or a Hindu.'

'My dear love, that is a little different.'

'Well, let us meet the trouble when it comes. Will the priest refuse to marry us?'

'He will do so, but unwillingly, and only if we promise that our children –' she flushed a little – 'will be brought up in the Catholic Faith.'

Felix frowned; he was too greatly hedged about by promises. It was an indication of the strength and passion of his love for Valentine that only now had he remembered his long-ago oath to Guy.

After she had left him, Felix wrote to his brother. He made no apology because he did not feel apologetic. The oath should never have been made or asked for; as for payment of the debt, had not Guy deprived him of a part of his own land that had repaid tenfold whatever Guy had laid out that time on his behalf? He tried to persuade himself along these lines, and partly succeeded.

Within the week Guy's answer came. *I curse you and all of your blood and descent*, it read. *I understand that the woman you are marrying is rich. I ask God* – Guy seldom invoked God – *that everything you undertake will nevertheless fail, that your wife will be barren, that if there are children they will be deformed in mind and body, unfit to inherit. I wish no good thing to happen to you and yours till the end of your lives. If right can ever come out of wrong, my son will one day wear the title, in spite of you. I regret that I ever set eyes on you or helped you financially, and I spit on your name. Any future communications from you will be returned unopened.*

Felix tried to be amused; Guy, he thought, had unsuspected melodrama in him. But Felix did not show the letter to Valentine. It breathed too much sulphur.

Later, after they were married, Felix stayed with his wife for a few nights in London to let her see the sights. Cathy and Kate had been sent on to Fenfallow. Felix excused himself to Valentine on the second evening and took a cab, alone, to Arlington Street. The servants there knew him and had evidently not been told to refuse him admission. He walked into the drawing-room, where Guy and his wife and son were seated after dinner. They rose to their feet, Lilian's framed skirts rustling.

'This is an outrage,' Guy began. Felix held up his hand for silence.

'I have to tell you, as a result of your letter,' he said, 'that you have no claim whatever to inherit the title of Fenn, or my estate. You are not the son of the late Earl, but of a lawyer whose evidence I have obtained and kept. As regards my so-called debt to you, I swear that it shall be repaid with interest, either during my lifetime or after my death. This, as I believe, makes our erstwhile bargain and your curse worthless, if so biased a document – I put it mildly – were in any sense valid in the first instance. You live on the fruits of our arrangement well enough, I see. The railway has paid good dividends on what should have been my land, and Isabel's money you no doubt enjoy also.'

No one replied; Guy's face was the colour of ashes. Felix made a slight bow to Lilian, cast an eye over the son – Guy's spitting image, but with some humour about the eyes and mouth – turned, and went out. As the door closed behind him he knew that it was the last time he would ever cross that familiar threshold. He cared nothing now. He went back to Valentine, to her warmth and her loving milk-white arms.

*

'You must keep up your piano-playing. I will buy you a piano and have it sent to Fenfallow, to be there when you arrive.'

'Hold, hold, where's the fellow that has no money? Auntie Eileen will send me over the one from Marishnageen; no one ever plays it now but myself.'

'Then I will pay the carriage-costs.'

'They are paid. I did it before we left.'

He was dejected. 'Valentine, it is going to be very difficult to live with a rich woman.'

'Do not trouble your head, I shall not be rich long. I have a notion which will use up all my money and perhaps more.'

'I am glad of it,' he said with truth. 'May I know what it is, this wonderful notion?' She was a creature with moods like the sea; calm, stormy, brooding, welcoming. He loved her deeply, more so than he had formerly known it was possible to love. She was his other self.

'You may not know yet,' said Valentine. 'It may not be possible after all. But I have had the idea in my head ever since we talked with Father Filey. I must do something to atone for having married a black Protestant.'

'Whatever you will, but let us keep friends with the county,' he told her. He wanted nothing more than to be rid of the damned money; as regarded the county families and the rest, he would not have them say he was living off his wife, as Guy had done. Meantime, Valentine was spending freely; she had already been to a coach-builder's and had bought a pretty little carriage, light enough for a woman to handle and yet with room for two or three. It was finished in a very dark shining green, with fine gold tooling. They would buy the horses for it when the sales came on at Newmarket, and the mare Una had come over with them from Ireland and had been handled by Joshua and taken carefully home. As for the piano, it would come in good time.

'Do you know Una will go into season in a few weeks?'

Valentine said to her husband. 'They will advise us at Newmarket on a good stallion to mate her, and we could establish a bloodline. That will mean money for us both, with the stables your own, and Joshua; be thankful for him.'

'I always have been. My love, do not talk of stallions and mares when I only want to talk of the two of us, together.' He kissed her and fondled her hands. 'Very well,' she said, smiling. 'I will say nothing more at all, for silence is best between us.'

He kissed her again, and for a long time there was indeed only silence between them, and much love.

There was the homecoming to Fenfallow, with the assembled servants on the steps to watch Felix carry his bride over the threshold. The elegant little carriage was ready housed, driven up earlier in the week and lovingly polished by Joshua himself. In the drawing-room the grand piano waited, gleaming and tuned. The whole house had been gone over for the homecoming; everything shone with care. Valentine looked about her and smiled at the waiting servants, among whom was Cathy still, for she had not yet married the lay preacher but had stayed to look after Kate until Felix should have returned. Aprons rustled dutifully, stiff with starch, as all the servants from Mrs Canning down were made known to my lady.

Suddenly there was a disturbance. A tall thin bearded figure like a scarecrow erupted into the hall, shouting and waving his fists. The maids gasped and retreated from him; Felix and Valentine stared as he crossed over to where Cathy was and took her by the wrist.

'I'll take my wife out of this accursed dwelling. Shame on you for harbouring a Popish woman, and may the Lord avenge His innocents in His own time. Catherine, woman, come away; you have been here too long, looking after my lord's bastard daughter; now his Romish wife may take her, and lose her soul in her own fashion.'

After the first astonished silence, embarrassment began to creep into the assembly. It was true Papists weren't often seen here; no doubt my lady was one, but what of it? It wouldn't make any difference to having a kind master and a gracious mistress. Valentine herself stood firm, looking at Saul Fingerhut with her clear eyes. 'I am proud to be a Catholic,' she said in her soft, telling voice, 'and Catholics as well as all others who come will find welcome and friendship at Fenfallow.'

Felix strode towards the intruder. 'Get out of here,' he told him sternly. 'Cathy is too good for you; you do not deserve her. Do not come back here; if I see you I will turn you over to the magistrate for a public nuisance.'

Cathy stood forward then, her lips set. 'I said I'd marry you, Saul, and I will,' she told him. 'But if you ever say a word against her ladyship again I'll leave you flat. You hear me? I'll leave you flat.'

They had none of them, in the angry murmurings that followed, taken heed of a small white-clad figure which crept down the stairs. 'Cathy, don't go,' Kate cried. 'Don't go with him. Stay here.' And she began sobbing. 'Kate, get back to bed,' her father told her. 'You should not be awake at this hour.'

'I want Cathy.'

'Cathy will come to you, darling,' said the name's owner. And she turned from Saul and went to the child, took her hand and coaxed her upstairs. Saul started his roaring again; Felix and Joshua, who was present, took him by the upper arms and thrust him out. The maids bobbed, a little uncertainly, again to Valentine. They thought she was a sweet lady, but a Papist? My lord should perhaps have known better.

But on the first Sunday Valentine came into her own. She had asked where was the nearest Catholic church; it turned out to be at the market town, at the far end, only an old hut which had been hired for the purpose out of the scanty means of those who desired a place of worship. Valentine stepped into her little carriage and drove off, and along the road there were many walking who in days to come would be uplifted, and taken with the Countess. But now she found the little place, had a word with the priest, who showed her where to leave the carriage and horses safely, and went in. The church was packed with poor folk; some of them had walked a long distance. There was not a Mass said oftener than every third Sunday, as the priest had to cover more than a hundred miles in his parish. He came in wearing his vestments, Mass was said, and the Countess knelt among the poor folk to receive the Host.

Afterwards she heard more about the little church. 'They tried to destroy it with stones, and even set fire to it, when they heard we were to come there, and at first the men used to take turns in an all-night watch, but things are a little better now,' the folk told her. 'But during the day it must risk it; the men have their work to go to, and can't afford to lose their wage, and so things have been these five year, a bit better now than they were. But it's a poor place for God to house Himself in and we dare not leave the Sacrament there in case it is desecrated.'

'I will build you a better place,' promised Valentine.

She had already thought of a site, and there was a reason. At some time early in their marriage she had asked Felix about the place where Saul's cottage was, Knocking Hill. 'That's a queer name,' Valentine said. 'What does it come from?' But he had refused to tell her, and she had found out from Cathy instead; in Reformation days they had hanged the priest up there, and the knocking was the sound of his feet clattering together as he hung from the destroying rope. Valentine swore that she would put the wrong right. 'We will build a chapel for the perpetual adoration of the Blessed Sacrament on the spot where he was hanged,' she swore.

Felix was doubtful about the project, although he had no personal views on the matter; Valentine might do as she chose. But there would be opposition, he knew; yet already his wife had made herself so beloved among the people that perhaps, as it was the Countess, the matter would be let go. As for Saul Fingerhut, he would have to be moved elsewhere; it was a pity, for already Cathy had made his place more seemly and habitable, and seemed happy enough as a preacher's wife.

But there was still one person, apart from Saul, who had not fallen under the charm of Countess Valentine, and that was Kate; nothing would make the child smile or speak in her stepmother's presence. She cried constantly at the loss of Cathy, was forever riding to Knocking Hill on her pony, and in the end Felix sent to a bureau for governesses, run by a certain Mrs Uttley, for a suitable person to take charge of his daughter in all ways. A small thin sandy-haired personage arrived from London, flustered with the journey and with the very sight of Kate; the child glared like a cat, and would do nothing she was told. Miss Gertrude Oakbury was too gentle to whip her charges, though Felix had given his permission; it seemed the only way to control Kate and prevent her from doing harm to herself and others. He was particularly anxious about Valentine; to his deep pleasure, she had told him lately that she was expecting a child. They laughed when Una the mare went into season at the same time, and was mated to her stallion, bred in Wiltshire. 'I hope we will both do well,' said Valentine. She was in radiant health and very happy. A surveyor had come to look at the site on Knocking Hill and said that it would be ideal for building on; there was even an artesian well for water. Everything seemed hopeful, and the new Countess settled into her new life, and the Earl was content.

About then there was an accident to Tupman the lawyer,

an old man of eighty now. He still travelled by train on Tuesdays to London to see to business there; it had been his fixed habit ever since the railway started. On a dark November day he was found dead on the line, having evidently threw himself out of the carriage door. Enquiries were made, the police called in, but no useful information emerged as to why a sane, settled, businesslike old gentleman should suddenly wish to end his own life. Likewise, it seemed unlikely that anyone in the world would want to end it for him; and as nobody had seen what happened enquiries were difficult. The ticket-collector remembered a stranger who had handed in the return half of a ticket and who might have got into the same carriage as Mr Tupman, he couldn't be sure; nobody was sure of anything. The police traced the holder of the ticket, who protested that he was a salesman for agricultural tools who had been to collect orders from the farmers in the neighbourhood, and was returning with his books only half filled. He did not add that he had had any incentive to come at all by means of a large advance from a certain city bank directed by none other than the Honourable Guy Sutbury.

The old lawyer was buried and soon folk ceased to remember him, or talk any longer about the way he had died.

'I don't want to do writing. I want to ride Sixpence.'

'It is not a question of what little girls want, but of what they should do to become accomplished young ladies. A good clear hand is an essential for any lady.'

Kate had not listened to the latter part of the sentence, and the meaning of the word essential was one about which she was not yet clear; anyway it didn't matter. She thrust her way past silly old Miss Oakbury and the copy-books with *Economy is the Best Policy* and *A Stitch in Time saves Nine* ready in copperplate, and ran downstairs and out of the house, pursued by Miss Oakbury who of course could not move quite so fast with decorum. Kate ran to the loose-box where her beloved Sixpence was generally kept; once she was on his back she could get away from Miss Oakbury and everyone else. But Sixpence was not in his box; Joshua, having told the stable-boy to clean the latter out, had let the pony into the near field.

Kate turned her head quickly. The governess was already crossing the cobbles, her dun-coloured skirts held high to avoid the dust, her feet in their buttoned-up boots picking carefully over the uneven stones like a chicken's claws. Kate saw the mare Una still in her box, and nobody about; Una was bridled, but not saddled, so that Joshua could lead her out presently. Quick as thought Kate slid back the bolts on the lower door – the upper was open – climbed up to the hayrack, and launched herself on to Una's back, seizing a crop from its hook. The mare reared, knowing an unaccustomed rider, and Kate dug her heels into Una's sides as she was wont to do with Sixpence and flogged her. But Una was no tough, docile pony. She charged out of the box and into the courtyard, with Kate, frightened now, clinging to her mane and still flogging; and kicked out at the nearest object, which happened to be Miss Oakbury. That unfortunate lady fell down, clutching her stomach, and screaming aloud for Lady Fenn. In a flash Valentine heard her and was out of the house, running across the yard after Una and her rider. 'Kate! Kate! Don't pull on the bridle, you'll ruin her mouth! Don't beat her! Don't beat her!'

Joshua and the boys came hurrying from the coach-loft, and Felix, disturbed from his occupations, came out also, wondering what the disturbance was. He found his wife in a state of alarm, wrestling with the distracted mare; Kate slipping down from the mare's back, helped not gently by Joshua; and Miss Oakbury shamefacedly picking herself up, but still with a hand to her side. Felix took three strides forward, seized the riding-crop from Kate's hand and gave her one hard blow after the other on her back. Kate screamed; she had never before been touched in anger. Felix flung down the crop.

'That is what you made the mare suffer. Now get out of my sight before I strike you again.'

Kate fled. She left them all in the yard, Felix with an arm about his wife, the frightened mare soothed and led back at last into the box, and Miss Oakbury soothed also and offered brandy and a doctor. Kate shoved open the gate into the field and ran to Sixpence, to escape; he would not come, and she ran past him, past the further hedge, past the gate and ditch and the next field of growing hay; wet with the dew which had not yet gone, her face stained with tears, still sobbing; knowing nothing but that she must find Cathy, who would know what to do.

The mare miscarried next day. Miss Oakbury, amid much fuss, had been led back to the house by someone; Felix was troubled only about Valentine, who had turned pale and subsided, half-fainting, into his arms when everything was quiet. He carried her up to their bed and laid her here, kneeling by her.

'My love, is it all right? Is it all right?' He could not rid himself of the thought that she might have injured herself and the child. She smiled weakly.

'It will be all right, my dear. But I fear poor Una will not have her foal now. Go soon to see her; I love her and want to be with her now, but I will lie down for a little while, I think.'

'I think you should do so,' he agreed with her, and when the physician came for Miss Oakbury, who had after all sustained nothing but a bad bruise, he sent him up to Valentine, who was reported to be out of danger but who, the doctor recommended, should stay in bed for a couple of days and be kept undisturbed as much as possible. The days passed and there was, to Felix's great relief, no accident. But the doctor had given a warning; a shock in mid-pregnancy might affect the child in some way as yet unknown. Felix found it difficult to forgive Kate.

The governess did not as a rule dine with them down-stairs, but as she was recovered from her fright Felix invited her courteously to dine with him, Valentine being still upstairs, and discuss Kate. The latter had been found at Cathy's, eating stew at the far end of the scrubbed table from an unwilling Saul, who had said he had hoed the turnips and why should another eat them? Cathy, standing behind him in her apron in the time-honoured way of wives, said Miss Kate was hungry and there were plenty of turnips, and plenty more rabbits come to that, if Saul cared to shoot them. Kate was enjoying the fragrant stew when the door was kicked open to reveal Joshua, with Sixpence outside and Cathy's elder sister Molly, who had been sent to help in case Kate proved difficult. Molly had few words and a pair of strong red arms which worked well in the dairy. She seized Kate as soon as she had finished her stew and dumped her in the saddle. Kate was crying again. 'Now, miss, none of that, or you'll get a clip on the ear besides what my lord gave you,' Molly told her. Kate fell silent with indignation. A clip on the ear, from someone as rough as Molly! Kate held her nose in the air all through the ride home, and said nothing at all.

'I do not want to seem disobliging, Lord Fenn, especially in view of your kind invitation to dine, but I – I cannot control Kate, as you have seen, and perhaps it would be best if I were to ask you for a reference, if you will give me one, and allow you to find somebody more – more suitable.' Images of bespectacled dragons disturbed Felix's mind and he said: 'No, Miss Oakbury; we are perfectly satisfied with your work – you have at least taught Kate to sign her name clearly.' He smiled, the engaging smile which had never failed to win women's hearts, and Miss Oakbury was forever lost. 'Per-haps –' she began, but Felix already had an idea in mind.

'Molly Maverick is a good strong woman and will sit by you

both during the lessons, and if the little monkey tries any tricks will punish her in the only way I can think of. Kate must learn that there are other people in the world besides herself. I have been remiss in not making it clear to her sooner.'

'Lord Fenn, she is not a stupid child, and she is devoted to you and to – to – Sixpence.' If she had known, Miss Oakbury's hesitant speech had struck a chord in his heart, remembering Isabel. He was angry when he remembered how the governess had been kicked in the side.

Kate had by then been brought home, taken upstairs, washed, made to undress and prepare for bed, so late was it after all that had happened. She stamped her foot and wanted Cathy. 'I'll give you Cathy,' said Molly Maverick, who had been forced to walk all the way to Knocking Hill and back because of this little animal, who was no different from Sammy and Polly and the rest of them at home, and a bastard at that. Molly seized Kate by her hair, turned her over her knee on the wooden nursery commode, pulled up her nightgown and spanked her until the child's yells ceased and she lay quietly sobbing. 'And now you'll go to bed, and I hope you have to lie flat on your face, and that's what comes of being a bad girl,' said Molly.

Kate cried herself to sleep, notwithstanding the pain, the humiliation, and her back which still ached and stung. For Papa to have struck her! Papa! And now this Molly person. It was all Valentine's fault for making everything different. She hated Valentine and always would. She hated Valentine.

It was Valentine who in fact was most worried about Kate; lessons after the daily advent of Molly proceeded quietly, but the child was sullen and unnatural, never smiling or speaking of her own accord; and the adage that children should be seen and not heard was not one under which

Valentine herself had ever been brought up. She would have liked to see Kate happier, enjoying her learning of geography and history and spelling and other things. One evening after dinner, when they had dined alone, the Countess spoke to her husband about the matter. She was wearing a loose dress of brown velvet; her body had begun to thicken, and Felix looked at her with great tenderness. It would not be so long now till the child was born.

'What is the matter, my dearest?' he asked. She let her white fingers rove over the moss-agate, as she always did when she was thinking of some plan, or asking a favour.

'It is Kate,' she said quietly.

'Do not trouble yourself about Kate. She has caused enough harm.' He had still not forgiven Kate for her action that day with the mare, and was thankful that Valentine had not lost her baby as well as the foal. In fact, she had seldom been quite well since, and the knowledge disturbed him.

'She needs the company of children her own age, I think. Would it be possible to get one of the cottage children to share lessons with her? That might spur her on.'

'We will have to see if Miss Oakbury agrees,' he said, not knowing enough about the usual lot of governesses to guess that Miss Oakbury felt herself extremely well off in the conditions of this employment, with a room of her own and Molly to keep order. She would be dining now off a tray which was sent up to her, as was the custom.

'There is Molly and Cathy's brother Ned, who is only a little younger than Kate. He is a good, quiet child and would repay teaching, if his parents will let it happen.'

'Perhaps if she knows she is having lessons with Cathy's brother it will make Kate behave herself,' said Kate's father.

So Ned Maverick began to come to lessons, arriving well scrubbed with soap by his sister Molly each day before she brought him in. He was, if anyone had known, as anxious to learn to read and write, and better himself, as had been his great-great-uncle Hugh Maverick in the Ryden times nobody now remembered. Ned worked diligently and soon Kate was having to concentrate to keep up with him. Halfway through the morning they were given a glass of milk and a newly baked bun, and at twelve Ned went back to the cottage for his dinner. The scheme worked very well meantime. Valentine told herself that her idea had been a good one. She began to think less about Kate and more of herself; she was not at all well, though she could not have told anyone exactly what was wrong; it was a general feeling of unease, no doubt without reason.

The labour was late in starting, and for the past few days Felix had been anxious about his wife. The doctor had been called and had said that there was no cause for alarm; the child was alive within her, babies sometimes delayed a little, or perhaps there had been a mistaken date. In any case he had the midwife ready to be brought at once to Fenfallow.

She came next day, and found Valentine walking up and down in her room, holding her body. 'Let it come, let it come,' said the midwife. 'Lie down, my lady, and rest. There will be enough for you to do at the proper time.'

There was indeed enough, and the labour was prolonged; both mother and child were exhausted when the midwife at last, after eighteen hours, dexterously brought out the child, a boy, cleansed him and saw to the mother. He lay in his cradle, the same one Felix and Guy had in their time occupied. He was a bad colour at first, but that was to be expected; there had been bruising. At last it was time for Felix to come in and see his son; but he went straight to his wife.

'You will get well now,' he told her, holding her hand and kissing it. 'The nurse is ready waiting for him; nothing need trouble you any more.'

'Go and take a look at him,' she said, smiling faintly. 'I have hardly seen him myself.'

He went over to stare into the cradle, but could not take to the little purplish creature which lay there, warmly wrapped. Why did women have to suffer so? He would not have wanted Valentine to suffer, to know anything but love and joy. But she seemed quiet and happy, ready to sleep, and he left. He met the doctor, arrived from another patient, coming up the stairs.

'I hear you are to be congratulated,' the latter said. 'The news is all round Fenfallow that it is a son, and will live.'

He was right in that; Clonmagh Gerard Ryden Shannon Sutbury, third Viscount Harmhill, would live.

They brought Kate to see her new half-brother. By then his hair had dried and the bruising was fading. Kate looked down at the cradle, said nothing, and was taken away.

Some days later, when Valentine was up, the nurse came to her. 'I don't like the look of him, my lady,' she said. 'His head twitches and his eyes are rolled up, and he doesn't kick and cry like most babies.'

Valentine went to look, and her heart stopped for instants. It was true; Clonmagh, as she would always call him, was not like other children. As he grew, they found that he would never talk; that he had convulsions very often as an infant, though he grew out of those later; that his legs would never grow strong enough to support his weight, and that at best he would be an imbecile. Valentine, weeping, went to break the news to Felix as best she could. He was silent, then suddenly spoke.

'Send Kate away to school,' he told her. 'I do not want to see her; it was that day with the mare that caused it. Send her up to Cathy until it is time for her to go. I do not want to set eyes on her again.'

May your children be deformed in mind and body, unfit to inherit. The phrase floated up into his memory later; it had been one of the several ill-wishings of Guy's curse.

It was a fine windy day in spring before Valentine rode out

again on Una. The mare cantered amicably along the flat, but when the ground began to rise towards Knocking Hill slowed a little; Valentine patted her neck and spoke to her in a low voice. The sensitive mouth had not quite recovered from Kate's mishandling of last year. Valentine slipped out of the saddle and they went up the sharp slope of the hill together, with the wind high here and whipping the little veil Valentine wore about her tall hat, and the mare's mane. As they neared the stony top Valentine took her flapping skirts in one hand; then at last stood and looked about her, with Una's rein over one wrist.

There was no sign now, except for a flatness, of the place where the gallows had been. Yet Valentine could feel in the very keening of the wind, the blurred green countryside below, the stones above, the echo of an ancient wrong, the shadow of hatred. She said a prayer for the dead priest's soul and another for those who had hanged him. Even as the peace of prayer reached her, it was broken by a man's harsh voice.

'What is a Popish woman doing up here? This is God's ground.'

God pity him, Valentine thought, he is as full of hate now as any were then. She felt no fear of Saul, and answered him gently enough; but found she could not exactly recall his name. Surely it could not be Fingertip?

'It is indeed God's ground, and God's world,' she said, 'and I will build a church to God here, with His help.'

'I have seen your paid surveyors and folk with their heads down, measuring and consulting with one another, sons of Belial all. They may save themselves the trouble. There will never be stone left on stone of any Papist church raised here. God's people rid the last idolater of his soul long ago, before the Rydens' time.'

'It was indeed long ago and these are old enmities we should have outgrown, Saul.' She did not know why she tried to reason with him; this man was beyond reason, wrapped in his own fanatical hate. It glared from his eyes; his long hair and beard fluttered in the wind like ragged banners. They were all of them blown about, her skirts, her veil, Una's mane, the man's beard and hair, on the rock's height. Valentine felt weakness suddenly; was everything to perish, her hopes, her love, her good intent? She was resolved that should not be. She put up a hand to catch at her veil and faced Saul Fingerhut.

'My lord may have told you that they will start building next month, when the weather is settled. He will find you a better house.'

'I am content with the one I have got.' She had already passed, and hardly noticed, his bit of garden, with cabbage-stalks rank in the wind; and the rickety house, with some of its windows boarded up and the thatch blown bare. 'It must go,' she said firmly. 'You will be able to plant your vegetables in a better plot, dug ready, away from the wind.' The wind indeed carried away half her words. She made ready to go, but Saul was still raving.

'I ask for no favours from your lord. I have lived here snug these fifteen year and here I will stay, and my wife Catherine with me, and maybe our children. I will not move out for any Roman notions of Roman churches. The whore of Babylon herself! I will die before I let it be. God's folk won their freedom long ago, with the help of God's Word in the Bible, and our swords.'

'Is it freedom, Saul, when many shed their blood for the old faith, endured fines and torture and fire and the rope and block, and in the end died gladly? You have maybe heard little of them.'

'They were a superstition and a reproach. I will avenge, saith the Lord. Not you nor any Papist shall build here while I live.'

She left him still talking to the wind. After that he began to gather a little knot of godly folk week after week on the hill, to listen to his fiery preachings. The result was that the blasting for foundations brought an angry crowd, afraid to come too near but shouting and throwing stones and rubbish. The explosions rocked them, but still they stood; and later when the hired builders came daily they would find their previous day's work destroyed in the night. In the end Valentine went to her husband.

'They have set a watch over the building, with lanterns burning all night; the folk from the towns have walked all the way here to help stand guard. But nothing is safe if anyone turns away for an instant; that man leads his followers on, and nothing is safe; the builders are insulted and fists are shaken, and I am afraid lest they are frightened away or discourged, and we will not be able to find others once that is known.'

'I will have the fellow arrested; they'll soon stop, lacking him,' promised Felix, and accordingly had Saul up before the magistrates at the next sitting. He stood erect like the martyrs of old, stubborn in his defence of his own beliefs. 'You may throw me in prison, but others will come after me,' he swore. Cathy, his wife, had not come to the hearing, nor did she know, till Valentine rode up to tell her, of the eventual sentence passed on Fingerhut.

'It is bad news, Cathy, and I am sorry for it. But he brought it on himself.'

'Will they hang him?' Cathy was pale, but in control of herself. Valentine wondered how the clean, energetic woman could endure life here, with any work done soon undone by the wind and weather.

'Not that, but they have sent him to Botany Bay for four years. They call it a light sentence.'

'So,' said Cathy, and closed her eyes for an instant. 'As you say, my lady, he brought it on himself. He always was one for making trouble; it's in his nature.'

'You would not want to go out with him? They would grant you a passage.'

'No, I would not. He can preach away to his convicts

without me by. I never was one for listening to all of that.'

'Well, then, my lord has a new cottage all ready and clean for you; it is the one the old Johnson couple had, and the wife died and the old man's in the almshouse, for they had no family as you know. Shall I send Joshua to help you move your things down in the cart?'

Cathy bowed her head. 'My own brothers will help me, my lady. I would not be beholden to my lord.'

'Well, I myself will be glad to have you near.'

Cathy smiled a little. 'Maybe I'll be glad to be there, my lady, after all. I told Saul often enough he'd be in prison if he didn't mind his tongue, but he never would; he must go his own way, always.'

'He may do well out there. They say the voyage is terrible, but once there he can make money, and there is good land to be bought cheaply, if he wants to stay.'

'I'll stay here for all of that, as long as you and Miss Kate need me, my lady.'

Kate was by now at a convent school near Dublin; Valentine had chosen it because it had a good reputation for turning out well instructed, mannerly pupils, gentle as the nuns were. Kate might respond best to a lack of harshness, and it was too far away for her to try to run home. It was also near enough for Eileen Clonmagh to invite her for some of the shorter holidays, if she would; yet Valentine felt this on her conscience, for Aunt Eileen was growing old. Time would tell; meantime Valentine spoke of Kate to Cathy, as there was nothing more to be done about Saul and she did not feel welcome; she left Saul's wife seeing to her packing, ready to come away from the draughts that blew about the house on the hill.

Gertrude Oakbury was still at Fenfallow. After Kate had been left at her new school – Miss Oakbury had gone with her to see her safely bestowed – the governess had returned to Fenfallow for her belongings, anxious and tearful. She

did not want to go to a new place; they had been so kind
here. Finally she saw Valentine alone.

'Oh, Lady Fenn – my lady, could I not stay at a reduced
wage to help with the little Viscount when he gets beyond
nurses? I – I had a little brother like that once, and he
needed great care all his childhood and died when he was
fourteen, of a chest complaint; you know, it generally –
well, at times it affects them then, when they are a little
older. I would take great care of him, my lady, and see that
he was not neglected or – or bewildered. They have
feelings, as you know, the same as ours, only they cannot
express them.' She fell short of words, and stood staring at
Valentine, her spectacles perched on her birdlike nose.
Behind them the eyes were full of tears which, properly,
did not spill over.

Valentine said as always that she must ask her husband.
But she knew, sadly, that Felix would subscribe to anything
which kept poor Clonmagh out of his sight. To have no joy
in either of his children! Valentine looked at him; the lines
on his face had grown harder, and the lock of hair at his
temple was already white. He was always gentle and loving
with her, but she felt that she had grown away from him;
they no longer shared the same thoughts so exactly that
talk was scarcely necessary between them. Perhaps such
happiness as they had known never lasted. The Earl was, at
any rate, amiable enough about Miss Oakbury and later
saw her himself and said that he was glad to have her help
with poor Harmhill.

He was himself helpful about the new chapel, making
suggestions when he saw they were needed. The architect
who had been employed was a young man, brimful of
aesthetic notions but leaving something to be desired in
practical ones; it was Felix who suggested that, as Cathy
was still in her house, it should be rebuilt to make a priest's
dwelling with Cathy installed as housekeeper.

'Saul will not be best pleased when he returns from

Australia to find his wife housing a Roman priest, as he calls them,' said Valentine.

'Saul will most likely never return. There was a boy sent out once for stealing a hare; I remember the case. Once there he was convicted again and again for petty thefts and the like, and ended up a caged maniac.'

Valentine shivered. 'I hope the like does not happen to Saul.'

'That is forgiving of you. Saul hardly treated you very courteously.'

'Ough, it is only a part of the hate they have against us. I meet it now and again still, but hope it is dying down. Saul's bullies lack a leader now.'

And certainly it seemed as if the chapel project had come into favour. Acquaintances who had hardly spoken to Valentine in their lives sent gifts; embroidered kneelers from Lady Iffley, the Lord Lieutenant's wife; sums of money for embellishment of the inside of the chapel, with gilded ironwork and some carving on the pillars that supported the roof, from others, many of them far away from this part of the country. Best of all, Valentine had a letter from Belgium.

'There is a community of nuns there who are being evicted from their premises. They ask if they might come and live – there is an endowment – and perhaps open a girls' school there. It would be small at first, but they could teach French and fine needlework. It would be a wonderful thing if the scheme began to pay for itself, even a little.' Valentine had not yet spent all her money, but a great deal of it had gone. She did not grudge it; day after day, leaving poor Clonmagh with Miss Oakbury of whom he had grown fond, or at least was content with, she would ride or drive out to see the progress of the building, which now was left in peace and appeared to have been accepted. She began to think of planting trees; silver birches at the top, and lower down, where a flight of steps had been cut in the rock, a double hedge of laurels. When the trees were grown the building would be quite private. It could not be better.

Little Clonmagh Harmhill loved music. When his mother played the pianoforte or the harp he would sit for a long time rapt and attentive, his big lolling head stilled from its twitching, his finlike hands trying to beat time to the tunes. Miss Oakbury would sit by him and get on with knitting or tapestry work, which she did very finely; she had given Valentine two cushions portraying bunches of flowers, which adorned the sofa. The question of lowering her wages had never been considered; she was invaluable with Harmhill, dressing and washing him, changing his fouled and wetted linen, seeing that he slept comfortably in the bed of specially plucked down that was necessary if his flaccid body were not to develop bedsores. There was nothing more to be done with him, and, the doctors said, no hope of improvement. Valentine would play by the hour, her heart breaking, knowing the bright brown curls that were so like her own were close by; they were Harmhill's only normality, his only beauty, except for the long lashes which shaded the poor squinting upturned eyes; and his smile, which could be radiant.

Cathy was living with them at Fenfallow while her fine new house was being built. She wrote at times to her husband in Australia, but Saul did not reply, whether because he was unable to write, or because he was in one of his queer moods, could not be ascertained. Cathy was, as Felix said, well rid of him; the old relationship between himself and her might never have existed, so separate were their ways now as master and servant. Cathy ate in the kitchen with the housekeeper and maids; all of them respected her; the fact that she herself would return to the house on the hill to be housekeeper to a priest had caused some comment at first, but not any more; one became accustomed to everything.

There was one change. Gradually, with a fearful trembling that could not yet be called joy, Valentine became increasingly certain that she was expecting a second child. She did not tell Felix at once; she felt that she could hardly bear it if he were not fully glad, if he feared another malformed birth and hesitated to say so. She herself was not young, was nearing forty now; she prayed that she might give birth to a normal child, and that it should be a son; Felix had always wanted an heir. Poor Harmhill would not live to inherit; it was expected of him, Valentine told herself wryly, that he die conveniently when he was fourteen, or soon after.

In the end she did tell Felix; but his pleasure was in any case spoilt, because that same day a letter came from Dublin.

Dear Lady Fenn, it ran,

We regret that we must ask you to remove Kate from school at the end of term. We have never in all our experience had so difficult and intractable a girl; we have tried every way of gaining her interest, if not her love, and have failed, and for the sake of the other children, who are either frightened of her or else try to copy her in her disobedience, she must go. It is the first time that we have ever had to write such a letter, and we hope that you will forgive and understand the necessity of it.

We will continue to pray for you, for your husband, your son, and for Kate.

It was signed by the Mother Superior.

'You will do no such thing,' said Felix when Valentine suggested that she go across to Ireland to fetch Kate, and perhaps stay for a little while at Marishnageen with her. 'Kate was responsible for what our son is now; we must not hinder this new happy condition in any way. You must do less, not more. I will send Cathy over, and perhaps Miss Clonmagh will have them both for a time at Marishnageen, till after the birth.'

'But what is to become of her later, the poor child? She is at a difficult age.'

'That is not your responsibility; she abused your kindness and my trust. I do not want to see her, as you know. We – I – must find some institution that will accept her, and perhaps train her to some skill.'

'They are harsh places.'

'If she will not respond to love, she must do so to harshness.'

'How hard you are becoming yourself, my dear! You used to love Kate; could not you try again? She would respond to that better than to anything. And there is no need for her to earn her living.'

'It is impossible,' he told her, and turned away, his eyes resting briefly on Miss Oakbury's cushions. 'We cannot expect that poor woman to cope with her again, in addition to looking after Harmhill,' he said absently.

'Then shall we get a second governess? It will be like a hen-coop.'

'I do not know, I tell you,' he answered testily. 'At all events you must not upset yourself.

Cathy was sent to Ireland in June, leaving the walls of her new house rising. It was of rose-red brick, like the chapel and convent building. The trees on the hill were beginning to grow in full leaf: and Valentine began to be heavy. She spent much time in prayer, asking that this might be a healthy son: and almost forgot to wonder how Cathy and Kate and Eileen were faring at Marishnageen.

The sisterhood of Belgian nuns arrived before the carriageway up the west side of the hill was completed, so they stopped at the rock-cut steps. The very old Mère Rose, the Prioress, a French aristocrat whose parents had been guillotined, after which she as a child had been conveyed out of France, set her tiny foot on the first step, followed by a sable drift of women, their veiled heads down; they must not look at the world through which they passed. When they reached the new building everything had been swept ready for them, and some of their belongings, including certain carved Flemish cupboards of old wood, set in place. A cold collation was ready under one of Valentine's fine Irish lace cloths from Marishnageen; sliced chicken, bread baked that day at Fenfallow, and the dairy butter; an urn of steaming tea stood newly made by the Fenfallow servants, who as instructed had removed themselves before the sisters arrived in the convent. Father Maetens, the priest who had accompanied them from Ostend, would say Mass on a portable altar, as the chapel had not yet been consecrated. The sisters heard Mass, said grace and refreshed themselves, then filled the building like ants, each with her separate task. Never again would Knocking Hill be empty, sad and alone with its gruesome memories.

Valentine had left a letter of welcome from her husband and herself, saying that if there was anything they needed they were to send to Fenfallow; but no word came except an elegant little letter, in French, from the Prioress, thanking her and, like the nuns of Dublin, promising her and Felix their prayers. Father Maetens could not stay long; he had to return to his parish, and the local priest could not long contrive the nuns' confessions and Masses as well as his own. A second priest would have to be found, and quickly. The Bishop had already been written to and was said to be doing what he could in this direction. Meantime, Father Maetens departed uneasily; his own substitute in Belgium had other duties which must be urgently fulfilled.

Marishnageen, 5th August

Valentine my darling,

I wanted to write to you about young Kate. She is so happy here, much more so than when she came, and takes pleasure in Rebecca the donkey and all my other odd daft things. As you may know I had made a Will leaving Marishnageen to yourself, but you have your hands full with Fenfallow and the good work of the chapel and convent. I pray God that He may prosper that. Well, as I was saying, I thought I would just write to you that I am a very old woman now and the end cannot be far off in the nature of things, although thank God I feel very well at present.

In fact I have made a new Will leaving you and dear Felix as my Executors, and Marishnageen to Kate. There is enough money to make her a little Trust Fund, as they call it – the lawyers tell me all these things. I know that I shall be happy at the thought of Rosaleen's granddaughter living on in Marishnageen, and perhaps tending the garden. I know also that you will not grudge it to her as you are the most generous soul in the world.

The servant Cathy is a good obedient creature, but not very happy here; she confessed to me that she is anxious to get back to Fenfallow and to the post of priest's housekeeper you have built her a little new house for. Kate will want to be with her meantime and as the Sisters talk of starting a school, you tell me, perhaps Kate would do better there than she did in Dublin, meantime. I have a sympathy for the child as when I was her age I was very naughty and did nothing my dear Mother and Governess told me. Kate is no trouble to me here but as you will agree, she needs more schooling to turn her, as they say, into an accomplished young lady. She tells me she does not mind about that but meantime, you and Felix will decide. She is certainly a Clonmagh; one only has to look at the eyes.

All love to you, my dearest, and to Felix and poor little Clonmagh Harmhill. I pray that the coming child will give you much joy.

Your devoted Aunt and Friend,
Eileen Clonmagh

'She must stay with Cathy,' said Felix. 'I will not have her here again when you are in your present state.'

'Maybe she will prefer that,' retorted Valentine. 'I think that if she could attend the convent school as a day girl, and go home to Cathy at night, it might settle her.' She did not add that she herself thought it best not to have Kate at Fenfallow before the birth of the coming child.

It was arranged, and Cathy and Kate would instal themselves in what was now a comfortable draught-free house with warm fireplaces and thick curtains, and a load of dry wood for burning. Valentine knew that she would not go to visit them after their arrival as she was no longer riding, and only drove in the carriage when it was necessary, such as for Sunday Mass in what was still the only centre for people outside the convent, the rickety hired shed. A letter meantime came from the Bishop to thank Valentine for all she had done, and saying he had found a priest for the nuns. Valentine stared at the letter for so long that Felix asked her if something troubled her. She raised her head, its brown hair by now beginning to be peppered with grey.

'Yes and no,' she said. 'It may be a very wonderful thing; or it may not. The priest they are sending is blind. They had difficulty in finding anyone, as they are so short of ordinands. The place will suit Father Smythe, the Bishop says, because he will be able to find and touch familiar things in so small a space. He is active, and anxious to come.'

'He must be a brave man,' said Felix quietly. He stared at his wife and thought for the thousandth time how much he loved her; like Eileen, he prayed that the birth of the baby would not be difficult; Valentine by now grew quickly tired, and lay often with her head resting on Gertrude Oakbury's cushions. She would rouse herself to play to Clonmagh: but the boy showed such excitement now at the sound of music that the playing had to be short, lest it put him in a convulsion. If only he – But Felix made his mind turn away sharply from the notion that he wished his son were dead.

Cathy and Kate had bidden farewell to a wildly waving Eileen, with wisps of white hair showing beneath her battered old felt hat, her body shapeless beneath cobbled clothes and her feet in stout boots for gardening. 'She will go on that way till she is a hundred,' said Cathy, who was glad to go; her own brisk, punctual habits had been constantly irritated by the slow easy way of life at Marishnageen. They would stay a night in London after crossing, take the train next day – it was the second time now that Cathy had been on a train – and be met by the Fenfallow carriage to drive up to the new house. There had been no word of leaving Kate at Fenfallow.

When they arrived it was dark, and the steaming, snorting monster made its way off into the night, lamps gleaming fitfully. There was a yellow steadier glow from the carriage-lamps where Joshua, the same as ever, waited for them. He was grinning from ear to ear. Cathy began to hand him the bundles of baggage, but he delayed putting them in the carriage-boot.

'There is a piece of very fine news,' he told them. 'My lady has given birth to a son. He is very small, they say, but very well, and so is she, thank God.'

'His lordship will be delighted,' Cathy said.

Kate said nothing, and began to climb into her seat. She has grown, thought Joshua, but does not seem any more pleasant. He had never taken to Kate since her long-ago mishandling of Una.

They were able to drive up to the new house door, for the dirt carriage-way and wide space outside the convent had been tamped down, and there was only slight jolting. Cathy looked at the rearing roof and level chimneys of what used to be Saul's cottage. She had not been very happy with Saul. It was almost time for the end of his sentence and he had never written to tell her whether or not he proposed coming home or staying in Australia; nor had he ever asked her to come out to him. She supposed she would have gone: but meantime, this was better. She walked through the opened door, fresh as it was with green paint, and saw a fire lit in the kitchen, the lamp lit and a kettle on the boil. My lady must have sent someone, or perhaps it was the nuns. A queer religion that would not permit them to wait and greet her arrival! Yet Cathy understood that they must see no one, except by special arrangement behind a grille, or the priest in the confessional. What could a nun have to confess? But she must stop asking herself questions and get on with the unpacking; nobody knew when the blind priest would come.

He came next day. They heard the sounds of a carriage drawing up and then a man's voice. 'No, no, there is no need to come with me, thank you; I will find my way.' Then there was the light quick sound of footsteps on the path, and a thunderous knocking at the door.

Cathy flew to open it, Kate close behind her. A fairly tall broad man with blunt cocky weather-reddened features stood on the threshold, his thistle-down fine silver hair blowing about his head. There was no sign that he was blind, except that one of his eyes had a bloodied look; he carried a stick in his hand and held it forward, not straight like the rest of mankind. Cathy hastened to help him.

'Don't grab me by the elbow, woman,' Father Smythe said irritably. 'Tell me which way to go and I will find it for myself.' She learnt in a very short time that this was the best way of dealing with Father Smythe. Any small thing, like finding a missing wineglass or a key, he preferred to do for himself, even if it meant going down on his knees and searching the floor, and it pleased him greatly when he found what he was looking for. He quickly identified Kate and Cathy. 'How do you know which one of us is which?' Kate asked him one day; she was never afraid of Father Smythe. He smiled, and his perky face lit up as if from within.

'I can tell whether your skirts are short or long by the rustle they make. And I know Mrs Fingerhut because she moves more quietly than you do, with a different way of walking.'

One day he told Kate how he had become blind. He had been sitting outside a cafe in Paris, near the statue of Henri IV, reading a newspaper and drinking coffee; he had just completed his training at the seminary, and was having a short holiday before going to his first charge. 'Suddenly the paper turned white in one place, and I found I could only see with my other eye,' he told her. 'I can still see a very little with it, but after consulting the doctors I knew it would go too in the end.'

'What did you do then?' Kate was sitting at his feet; the fire blazed, and the orderly arrangement of objects in the room was as Father Smythe had placed them. In the kitchen, Cathy was baking; there was a homely smell of risen bread. Kate gazed at the crucifix hanging on the wall.

'What did I do?' said the blind man, and laughed a little. 'I went to see as many great paintings as I could while the sight of one eye remained to me. I saw a Leonardo, certain El Grecos and two Rembrandts, at last the Arnolfini Van Eyck; I can still remember each detail in every one of the little scenes in the bowl mirror, and the dog at the bride's foot.'

'How brave you were!' said Kate, who knew nothing of paintings.

'It is a matter of taking what comes, of looking – if that is the word – ahead; it is not bravery,' said he. 'And there is another thing; they say the blind live in the dark, but I see only light, with a brighter rim round that part of one eye that can still see a very little, close at hand.'

'How do you contrive to say Mass in a new place?' She had already watched and admired his quick, nippy motion about the altar in the chapel: he had made no mistakes, no fumblings. The joy on his face when he said '*Sursum corda*' to the nuns behind the grille she would remember, she knew, all the days of her life. She had never seen such complete happiness and fulfilment on the face of anyone.

He was growing testy. 'In the same way as I manage anything anywhere,' he said curtly. 'By rehearsing my exact movements, knowing how many steps to take, where to lay my hand on objects I have placed there myself. It is like a game of blind man's buff, only the bandage will not come off.' He smiled; this analogy often pleased him. 'It is not so very difficult, once one is accustomed to it.'

'It looks difficult if one knows that you are blind. If one did not know, it looks the same as every other priest would look.' She remembered the ones at the Dublin convent; but they had had their sight.

'You have given me great pleasure by saying that,' he told her suddenly. 'What do you want to do with your own life, Kate? Shall you marry, or take vows?'

'I want to breed racehorses,' she said.

She began to help Father Smythe in small ways, walking with him – but never taking his arm, except in slippery weather when they could pretend it was for her sake as well as his own – to the chapel doorway, hanging his vestments brushed ready where he would find them, on a precisely specified hook. She would even – and this was something for Kate – mend his worn washed hose, for the Dublin convent had at least taught her to be adept with a needle. If she had taken time to think about it, Kate would have marvelled at the difference others saw in her. She was no longer purely selfish, a grabbing little wildcat; her face, her manners, even her walk had grown different. When the lists of pupils for Knocking Hill began to be made up from parents' letters, and Cathy said she was to put down her name, however, Kate rebelled. To be with stuffy nuns again! Then Father Smythe let it be known that he would be taking the girls for religious instruction: at once, Kate agreed to be included. All this was arranged by letter from Fenfallow, for her father never invited or visited her. As for Valentine, she was still under doctor's orders after the birth of her son.

He was named Henry Shannon, after the old Earl and Valentine's father. From the beginning it was clear that he would not be another Clonmagh. His eyes were blue and watchful, his hair straight. He was small – the doctor had told Felix that Valentine had a tired heart, and that babies born to such women were often of small size because the blood flow to them in the womb was less abundant. But small or not, Henry was energetic; he kicked in his binder, seeming impatient of restraint. His mother had him lying by her on her sofa often; he was carried for poor Harmhill to see, but Harmhill knew nothing, or at least showed nothing, neither smiles or tears. Gradually the two boys were kept as though they led separate lives in separate houses; there was plenty of room at Fenfallow. But there was one time they were brought together, and that was on the day of the Bishop's consecration of the chapel on the hill, on the Feast of the Annunciation, 1849.

'I do not think that you should take Harmhill. The crowds and the music will upset him.'

'He of all people needs the Bishop's blessing. And the little organ is being played by a fine musician from Birmingham, they tell me. We will take both the children; it can do them nothing but good.'

Felix acquiesced, because at times his conscience troubled him over the promise he had made when he married Valentine, that any children they should have must be brought up as Catholics. He had done nothing about it, although on the other hand he had not prevented his wife from doing as she would in the matter. Harmhill had been baptised, but confirmation was out of the question. Henry's future was a different matter, and Felix had given it much thought. It would be a hindrance to Henry in most walks of public life, and Fenn was anxious to see his son succeed in the world. At his birth Felix had put him down for Eton, as he had indeed done for Clonmagh, but had withdrawn. As soon as might be Henry should go to preparatory school; a tutor was not enough for him, he needed to be with other boys of his own kind as early as possible.

At the chapel's consecration, the Earl and Countess and their children were given an honorary place at the front, where Lady Iffley's kneelers, and some Valentine had herself sewn, showed their bright colours enhanced by the brightness of the windows. The Lieutenant and his wife had in fact come, an honour which warmed Valentine: and taking this hint, almost all the county families had sent a representative. In their plain straw bonnets the still scanty number of boarders at the new girls' school were shepherded in; and last of all had come, from far and near, the walking poor. They crammed the tiny chapel and its doorways, kneeling as the Bishop's procession entered. A burst of music from the little organ, played by a nun, amazed the pressing faces; and there was the splendour of the Bishop's mitre and robes, the great gilt crucifix carried before him, the candles, and the silver chapel vessels gleaming in their light. The nuns knelt behind the grille and no eyes were turned in their direction; it was already accepted that they had renounced the world. In the privacy they had chosen, from now on, a light would burn constantly all night above the sanctuary, and the Blessed Sacrament would never at any hour of the day or night be alone; a single nun would always take it in turn to come, watch, and pray.

Harmhill had heard the music, in an explosion of sound which reached his imprisoned soul in a torrent of healing. He was filled with a great joy he had never before known. It no longer mattered that Miss Oakbury was not here (her Anglican scruples would not allow her to come in, and she waited in the carriage). Clonmagh was aware of her absence but now accepted it, also that Henry, who he knew did not

love him, was nearby. A world above and beyond what he
had ever known resounded in the clear chords. He tried to
beat time, but found his hand caught and held by his
mother's. The restriction troubled Harmhill and he began
to wag his head, mouthing sounds which had no meaning
for anyone but himself. His mother placed a finger on his
lips, while Henry looked on smugly. Already he was aware
that other people did not have such brothers, and could feel
an embarrassment that this abnormal, in fact revolting
being should play any part in his life.

The homily was short, to allow for time already taken in the
long ceremonial of consecration; but the Bishop reminded
the listening crowds that instead of the hatred and ignorance that had once hanged a priest on this site, they now had
the presence of the Lord Himself, crucified also for love.
Many of the women in the crowd were weeping: nobody
noticed a bearded wild-eyed man until he tried to interrupt.
'Idolatry,' he shouted, 'superstition and idolatry. The dogs
licked the blood of Jezebel in the streets of Jezreel,' but at
this point he was silenced by angry voices, and shoved out of
hearing. He continued to rave more quietly in the distance,
then was heard no more. The Bishop had proceeded to
speak calmly on, as if nothing had happened. Afterwards
Mass was sung, to the pealing of the organ, and the Bishop
took the Sacrament first to the nuns, who came one by one to
the gate of the grille; then to the congregation. When it came
to Harmhill's turn his father lifted him up in his arms to
receive the Bishop's blessing. Harmhill gurgled as the sign
of the cross shaped itself on his forehead; he did not know
what it was, but liked it. Henry was blessed as well; he took it
as he took everything in his life, as his right. Valentine
received the Sacrament; and as she did so Felix became
aware of the kneeling figure of a young girl by one of the
pillars which had been consecrated on this day, receiving the
seal which would forever proclaim to anyone who came here

that this was a sacred place. Felix looked at the girl for some moments, and knew his daughter Kate, her muscles taut as a panther's, her rich hair hidden under a tied kerchief. Cathy was not here; she was busied in helping with preparations for the collation later, then would go back to her house. Father Smythe followed the Bishop in the procession, having rehearsed it yesterday. Only a few of those present knew that he was blind.

It was Father Smythe who, later, stumbled over the body of Cathy across her doorstep, sending him sprawling for the first time since his blindness. He did not understand what had happened, only that something was there which was not there as a rule, upsetting his calculations; and was climbing to his feet rubbing his forehead when Kate came, having left the crowds who still swarmed about the convent grounds, admiring the new building. Kate ran forward, seeing the priest first. 'Father, you've hurt yourself, let me – Oh, Cathy, *Cathy*!'

Cathy had been strangled. Her face was livid, the eyes staring out of her head. Any cries she made must have been drowned by the sonorities of the organ. There was no other sign that Saul had been.

Kate ran. She ran back to where the Fenfallow party was preparing to leave, Harmhill having been lifted first into the carriage beside Gertrude Oakbury, who took charge of him. Kate thrust her way past Valentine and Henry and his nurse; her need was for one figure only, a tall figure in a frock-coat, with a great long nose and greying hair, his hat still in his hand.

'Papa – oh, Papa! Saul has killed Cathy. She is lying dead at the door of the house. You must come, and bring help. Father Smythe didn't see her – he's blind, you know – I was the first, and oh, she looks dreadful.' The tears began to flow and without thinking further, Felix took her in his arms; she stood there sobbing with her head against his coat. He spoke quickly to Joshua, who waited.

'Get the women home and I will see to this. Inform the police; a statement will be needed. Do it quickly; get away now, before the crowd blocks the road.'

He did not wait to see the carriage drive off, but hurried with Kate to where the body lay, by now discovered to the shock and horror of bystanders. Father Smythe was on his feet now, feeling his way about the dead woman.

'This is a terrible thing, terrible,' he was saying, not knowing whether anyone was there to listen. 'It must have happened during the Mass. Poor woman, poor soul.'

Felix knelt by Cathy, making certain she was dead; there was no pulse. 'We should carry her inside, I think,' he said quietly. 'I will remain here until the police come. Kate, sit down and rest, my dear. You have had a great shock. Is there any wine in the house, or brandy? You should take a little.'

Father Smythe knew where the wine was. It was communion wine. He filled a glass and carried it carefully over to where Kate sat, and handed it to her. They all three remained with the still body until the police came, and a doctor.

Later, Saul was taken as he walked slowly along the roads, not troubling to hide himself. 'It was justice to kill her,' he said when they took him. 'She was the priest's whore. To think of a Romish priest in my house, and my wife with him! I have meant to do this thing since ever I heard of it, since ever I heard.'

There would be no transportation for him this time, even allowing for his probable insanity. He was hanged after trial, in early June.

Valentine had sent the carriage back at once on the day of the murder to collect Father Smythe and bring him to them at Fenfallow. She was told that the police might want to question him about the death. 'Let them do so here,' she begged. 'He has nobody to look after him now; there are no lay-sisters yet in the convent. He may stay here as long as he wishes, until someone suitable is found to keep house for him.'

The arrival of Father Smythe roused Kate out of the shocked torpor in which she had remained since finding Cathy's body. She had answered the questions of the police calmly and sensibly, but it was like listening to an automaton. She would talk to nobody except her father, and Felix accordingly did what he might to comfort her. 'You shall stay here, Kate,' he promised her. 'You cannot go back to the priest's house; it would not be proper when there is nobody there except yourself and him.' She had grown, he saw, into a violent kind of beauty; her small breasts pricked against her gown, and her cat's eyes emitted a glowing power. Her manners were better than they had been, for which he had to thank poor Cathy. The death of Cathy had shocked him profoundly; he remembered, for the first time since his marriage, what they had been to one another before the coming of Valentine. Meantime, he talked, when he could, to Father Smythe, who was driven up daily with Kate to the convent and performed his duties of hearing confessions, saying Mass and teaching the girl pupils. Kate remained for the religious teaching and returned with him at midday. She had found out, in the days of Cathy, what he would tolerate and again would not; she was tactful with him, knowing when to say, at Fenfallow, 'There is a bureau on your right, a little way ahead,' and 'The door is on the left of the passage: you are almost there.' In return, he gave her his friendship, so difficult to obtain; they were often to be seen talking to one another, beside silent Clonmagh with whom the priest soon established what was almost a relationship; it was as if one crippled personality relied on the other. When Valentine played her piano, Clonmagh delighted in it and Father Smythe endured it; he confessed afterwards to Kate that he did not greatly care for music. 'I know the blind are supposed to be musical, but there it is, I am not; I don't enjoy it. But it affects him and is perhaps the only thing that gives him pleasure, apart from Miss Oakbury's presence and that of his mother.'

Valentine was disturbed about Gertrude Oakbury. She felt that the governess was wasting her fine mind on the hours spent looking after Clonmagh, tasks a servant could have done. She spoke to her one day.

'Would you be willing to teach for an hour or two at the convent, Gertrude? They need a teacher of English grammar; I told Soeur Placide, the Bursar, not to spend money on advertising until they had asked you.'

'Oh, Lady Fenn – a Roman Catholic school – I do not think –'

'Many of the girls who board there – and the numbers are increasing – are not Catholics. There would be no pressures put on you in such a way; you would be free to continue in your own beliefs as long – and you will understand this – as you do not speak or imply anything against the Catholic religion in the course of your duties. And it would mean some diversion for you, and a little extra money.'

So it was arranged. Whilst Valentine sat with Clonmagh, Miss Oakbury drove up daily with Kate and the priest. Her English lessons were a success. One day the Prioress sent for her.

'Would you be able to include elementary mathematics, geography and household accounts among your subjects?'

Gertrude assented wryly; they had not offered her more money for the extra duties, nor was she permitted to teach history which was done by one of the nuns. However board and lodging was offered during the week, in a small cubicle curtained off from the girls' dormitory. She missed the comfort of Fenfallow; but enjoyed her teaching. Valentine laughed when she heard.

'I myself could teach them German,' she said, 'but they would want me to do it for nothing. Nuns have to be parsimonious, I dare say; every penny counts, for there are so many growing old within the enclosure.'

'The one who sweeps round is ninety-six, hale and hearty, but she speaks in such a broad accent I cannot understand her, and I believe she thinks I am deaf.'

'I am glad to hear that the school is doing well,' said Valentine. She was glad, too, to have the company of the former governess at weekends; Gertrude was always glad to sit with poor Harmhill, Felix nowadays spending much time with his son Henry. He was proud of the boy and it kept showing itself in small things; more pocket-money, a ride on a bigger pony. In the first place Henry had been taught to ride on Kate's beloved Sixpence, old now. The new mount was a colt of Una's, broken in by Joshua. Felix took great pride in riding out beside the small erect figure of his younger son; at first within the bounds of the estate, later the lanes and roads. The pair would be watched passing by the cottage; one could almost predict what the tenants were saying; a pity such a fine lad could not inherit the title, and Fenfallow, the elder being like he was.

Father Smythe bent forward to stir the logs on the fire. It was mid-November, and he had lived at Fenfallow for four and a half years. He reflected on this ironically while he felt for the head of the poker; it was of iron, in the shape of a ram, and had been made by the blacksmith nearby. He knew very well that the nuns had no intention of finding him a housekeeper while the Earl entertained him so generously; at times his conscience troubled him, especially when he heard that they were, in the house where he had briefly lived, taking in occasional paying guests who came to hear the Masses and perhaps make a retreat. But he knew that his presence in the house gave the Countess pleasure, and he was glad to talk with her often. He knew that she was troubled about the lack of religious upbringing of her children; but Fenn himself was curt on the subject, and one could not force one's host.

Father Smythe had done what he could in accustoming the small Henry to the fact and mention of the Faith, that it should not seem strange; that was all he could do, and the small boy had not seemed very receptive; but one never knew. As for the other, all that could be done was to pray.

Young Henry and the Earl had left Fenfallow yesterday, to drive to the preparatory school for the second half of term. Fenn was expected back this evening. The boy seemed happy at school and, again, Father Smythe knew that nothing better could have been done; there was no school of any status that would have accepted a Catholic boy on equal terms. No, he must continue his prayers for the family at Fenfallow; my lady at least was faithful, and so, by now, was Kate. He had received her into the Church with pleasure two years ago, on Easter Sunday.

He replaced the poker in its holder and moved over to where the logs lay drying; he could not see that a small piece of burning wood had rolled on to the rug. But he smelled the odour of burnt wool, tried to trace it, was satisfied that he had done so, took two cut logs, threw them on, and went out. It gave him pleasure to be left to do such things for himself: otherwise the Countess would have bidden the servants to come to replenish the fire.

He walked briskly down the corridor, turned left, reached the side door of the east wing and went out to the garden, where Valentine was working in an old pair of gloves and a hat tied on by means of a scarf under her chin. It was not very cold; they had had mild dry weather 'but the weeds grow just the same, Father, and if I don't do them now, it will be a wilderness next summer.' Again, he knew she could have employed a gardener; but she liked to do things for herself, and had a great love of growing things. He remembered the very old aunt who had come to visit them from Ireland three years ago; tall, frail and silver-voiced, and a good Catholic. She had been kind to Kate; the Countess had told him in confidence that she had left Kate all her goods, but not to mention it yet; so he had not.

'I wonder if Henry is back at school safely,' said Valentine. 'The roads will not have been too bad. My husband will have had time to visit town. Let us go now and sit on the bench, and talk; it is not too cold.' She peeled off her gloves. 'I am an old woman now, and get tired with too much bending,' she said. 'It will be a refreshment to talk with you. I hope you are happy with us.'

'Too happy, and too kindly dealt with. It will be a blow to make do with ordinary fare after the luxury with which I am surrounded here, and the kindness.'

'Why, that is our privilege,' said Valentine, as they sat down on the stone bench. 'In old times we would have put you in the priest's hole. Did you know that Felix found one, or rather the workmen did, when the old fireplace was mended? It opened off it, and whoever was inside must have roasted if the fires were lit.'

They talked on, and some time later Valentine remarked without concern that there was smoke coming from under the roof. 'I had best go and see about it,' she said. 'The servants notice nothing.'

Felix came back in the evening to find his house enveloped in roaring flame.

He had seen a horseman lately thundering along the road, and thought it looked like Harry's colt mounted by Ned Maverick, who helped in the stables. The speed at which he himself drove prevented him from seeing, in the gathering dusk, clearly who it was; but there must be some growing cause for such speed and misgiving was in his mind as he saw the distant sky bronze, as if with a late sunset; but suns do not set in the east. He made his tired horses hasten; and as he approached he saw that the worst of all had happened. The road near the house was thronged with people carrying away belongings from Fenfallow, chairs, pictures, sofas, beds, the harp, but not the piano. Their faces were lit up in the orange glare that came from what was by now a maelstrom of flame, though all the servants not engaged in rescuing valuable stuff were busy handing, passing and throwing bucketfuls of water from the pump, Father Smythe among them. Joshua had got out the old water-extinguisher with its leather bag and metal pipes, and was trying ineffectively to quence a patch of roaring fire; but the cracked and leaking leather made the effort useless. Felix flung the reins to a boy and strode forward. The whisper grew. 'My lord is here! My lord has come!'

'Where is Lady Fenn?' It was his first anxiety, after thanking God Harry was safe at school. Valentine was nowhere to be seen, and a frightened maid told him my lady had gone to try to rescue the Viscount, but nobody could follow for the heat. 'Oh, sir, my lord, I fear they're both gone,' she wept, but he did not stay to hear the end, thrusting his way into the places which were become charred ash, almost beating back the flames to find the way Valentine could have gone. The place was unrecognisable; doorways had fallen, leaving jumbled beams and rubble; the shattered windows spurted broken glass everywhere. He was cut, bleeding and burned before he thankfully found Valentine, prone on her face in the burnt-out ash; she must have been overcome by the fumes.

He carried her out, stumbling over the uneven mess of charred wood and stones: he left her with Gertrude Oakbury, whose face was streaked with smuts; she was helping with the water. 'Lord Fenn, they have sent for the fire-engine,' she told him. But it would be too late: the engine, though quickly manned, could not get here in under an hour, and would only be starting out now after Ned's alarm. It clattered up as Felix made his way back into the fire; he did not yet take time to admonish himself; had he not always wished that his son was dead? Now he was groping to try to find him, bring him out despite everything into safety.

The contradiction rising in his mind he thrust down; there was no time to do anything but pick one's way, duck aside from flaming timber, discount the universal roaring that came from the melted tar below the roof, dripping down in scalding patches. He felt the heat come at him like a wave, and went on. A spar fell across him as he blundered ahead and he smelled the burning of clothes and flesh; his own.

Harmhill was alive. He had fallen out of his chair and was soaked in urine, his hands thrust forward. Felix picked up the helpless burden and carried him, unresisting, out of the smoke and enveloping flame; at one time he went through a wall of it and felt his hair on fire. A jet of water from the fire-engine reached him; it saved him, but blinded him meantime. The reek of burnt wood and hiss of steam came to his ears; he was almost free; at last he saw the outside world again, and was about to carry Harmhill towards it; but a warning shout: 'My lord! My lord!' came too late; a lintel crashed forward, and Felix had only time to thrust the bundle that was Harmhill forward, propelled somehow, knowing his own imminent danger but unable to escape it; as he felt the boy's weight leave his arms, the lintel crashed down. He felt a sickening pain in the small of his back, fell on his face, and lay concussed and helpless, knowing no more. Outside, the firemen hosed on, reducing the whole area first to smouldering ash, then wet dark ruin; afterwards they were to find that only the west wing had been saved. Two hundred and sixty gallons of steam a minute from an engine already kept boiling by hot water circulating in pipes at the main station performed their task ably. The horses, trained marvellously to stand still while their harness was dropped ready on to them, not to panic when they saw fire, no matter how vast and terrible, continued to stand quietly by the engine until all was over. It was a fireman with a blackened face who rescued the inert body of my lord Fenn. Beyond, propped against others, the portrait of Judith Ryden stared out into the flame-scattered night, her painted hand caressing a long spiralled lock of painted hair.

He came to himself at last in a strange bed, with Valentine by him, her hands in bandages. She had turned her head so that she could watch him when he awoke; his eyelids raised themselves painfully, he was all pain to his waist, and below that felt nothing. His tongue was in his head, however; he asked, with a dry mouth, 'Is Harmhill safe?'

'Yes, my love, and you saved him.' Valentine was weeping. 'You saved him, Felix, and you might have been killed yourself in the doing of it.'

'I feel odd. What has happened to me?'

She shut her eyes for a moment. 'The doctors say – we are at Lord Iffley's house – they say that at present, you will not be able to move. Later it may get better.' That last was not true, but she could not face him, all at once, with the whole truth; which was that he would never walk again, would be a helpless hulk requiring nursing, as Harmhill did; incontinent, as Harmhill was. And all for such bravery!

They were able to return to Fenfallow within the week; the west wing had been made habitable. Felix was put to bed in what had been the blue room; its ceiling and walls still showed signs of water staining them. He used to stare at them by the hour, unless Valentine came to read to him, or Father Smythe to talk to him. The priest was overcome with guilt.

'It was I, my lord, in my foolish vanity, my determination that I could do everything alone,' he said. 'I should have sent for a servant to make sure the burning fragment was extinguished. You have given me hospitality, and I have repaid it by destroying your house. If I had sight I could not look into your eyes for the shame that torments me.'

'I am glad to know how it happened,' said Felix. 'At first I thought that perhaps some malice, arising from the ceremony about the chapel – there is ill-feeling in some places as you know – was responsible. But you have been honest. You need have said nothing and we would never have known.' He smiled, a smile still not brought about without pain; the hair had begun to grow again on his scorched scalp, the skin to repair itself on the roasted hands. 'Perhaps it was a corrective to my own vanity, father. I was riding back home proud of Harry, of his school and the fact that he is doing well there and that the other boys like his company; and I was thinking that in time he will be Viscount. Then I had to rush in to rescue the one who will prevent that, while he lives.'

'It was God's love made you do it. Had I known they had not brought him out I would have gone myself, as it would have been the least I could do to repay what I had already done. I would have seen and known nothing, and my life would have repaid my fault.'

'Well, well, it is all over. Fenfallow will be a smaller place, I hear. It will do us no harm to keep less state. The Iffleys have been kindness itself.'

'Here is my lord now,' said Father Smythe, who had heard a carriage stop and knew the tread. The Lieutenant appeared in a grey morning-coat, his handsome face creased with sympathy.

'Better today? A little easier, perhaps?' He had nodded to the priest, whom he did not like. 'Hair's growing,' he said to Felix.

'It certainly met a thorough barber.'

'How do you feel, Fenn?'

'Nothing at all, which troubles me.'

Lord Iffley, who knew the outcome, did not allow his distress to show. A splendid fellow like Fenn turned into a cripple for life! It made one wonder if there was a God. Yet God was the support of the man's wife, for she never stopped praying, and as soon as she was able to drive had gone up to her chapel, taking the blind priest with her. They said he'd taken his turn at the buckets, as well he might. They said the whole thing was his fault. It was a mercy no lives had been lost: but poor Fenn, poor Fenn!

Kate was unharmed. It was she who had met the blind man blundering down the corridors, shouting of something burning, of smoke he could smell, of his own faulty behaviour with the log. 'Come,' she had said, and taking him by the hand led him at a run down and out of the house to the yard, where the men were already fetching buckets at sight of the smoke pouring from the upper part of the house. 'You stand there, father,' said Kate, 'and hand the buckets on as they come,' and so he had done, untiringly, with tears running down his face, while Joshua filled his ancient fire-extinguisher and found it to be useless; while flames burst from the roof, so that the wind caught them and flung them towards the main part of the building. There had been no rain for weeks and the timbers were dry; they caught like matchsticks, and before anyone could think of those left inside, the fire blazed merrily. Joshua turned to Ned Maverick, who was pumping at the well and filling the buckets as they came and came again.

'Get on Master Harry's colt and ride like hell to the fire-station. We shall need every man before this is done, and women too.' And he shouted to those in the stables and cottages who had not yet come running, so that by the end the yard was filled with women carrying jugs, children staring and helping to throw the water on the fire, old folk peering uselessly.

So Ned had gone, and Kate was aware of loss; her hand had touched his in exchanging buckets, and she had felt a sensation far removed from the urgency of the fire; a sweet liking. In the back of her mind was the remembrance that Ned had shared lessons with her once, and was younger than she was; what of that?

Then someone shouted for my lady. Valentine had run

straight into the house to where the nurse and Harmhill should be, to find the boy alone; the nurse had run off, and Valentine pulled Clonmagh from his chair and tried to carry him, but he was too heavy for her; she had dragged him a little way, then run out of the room for aid and collapsed with the intense heat and the thickness of the smoke. She remembered awakening at last to the awareness of pain from her burnt hands; then she had seen Felix, lying nearby on a stretcher made by the men with blankets from the cottages. Harmhill was safe, seated on the ground, the nurse again by him, biting her lip. The fire was under control, and would soon sputter out.

Young Henry Sutbury had heard the news at school and was made to write politely to his father and mother, expressing his condolences and hoping that Mama's hands and Papa's back would soon be well again. To do him justice, he did feel the appropriate anxiety for them; he was a correct child. But when he came home for the holidays it was different. He saw the appalling difference at once, with the shell of the front entrance rearing naked and blackened, its flat Corinthian pillars scarred with fire and nothing, nothing at all behind them. The west wing, where everyone lived now, looked abandoned and ridiculous, with some scorched ivy still clinging to its walls; it was the oldest part of the house, and, as he was to find, the least comfortable. One couldn't ask other fellows to come to visit a place like this. Henry was embarrassed; he had already known some hospitality from parents who lived near school, had been taken out to tea, even asked to stay at a weekend, and he owed hospitality. There was nothing to be done, and Henry's discomfort grew even while he averted his eyes from his mother's scarred hands in sympathy. Within him an anger was growing, not only against that damned priest who had started the whole thing; it was the anger of being deprived of his rights. One had had a home, and now there was none, to speak of.

Henry vowed within himself that somehow, in whatever way, he would find the money to rebuild Fenfallow and make it as it had been. It didn't matter that Aunt Eileen in Ireland had written and offered them all hospitality; that wasn't the same. Fenfallow must rise again as it used to be, and he would be the builder.

He did not know that he himself carried a deadlier foe than fire. In a few days he began, in his cramped quarters in what had formerly been the servants' attic, to feel distinctly unwell. His mother came to him and stroked his hair and felt his forehead. Her hands were no longer bandaged and he could see the red scars.

'Why, you are flushed, Harry,' she was saying. 'I think you should keep your bed for today, till we see how you are. Papa sends his love; you know he cannot come upstairs.' Felix had been housed in the library, its leather-bound books mercifully free of the effects of water and fire.

Next day Henry had spots, and the doctor confirmed measles. In the cramped space Harmhill soon caught them from his brother. Henry recovered in due course and was able, though still languid, to walk about and even go into the cold garden if he wished; Harmhill lay in a fever, then one day grew pale, his breathing harsh and reversed. Valentine stayed by his bed, having dismissed the nurse; Molly Maverick, married now and with a young family at the cottages, helped her when she could. The doctor came, and shook his head, saying gently: 'Is it not for the best, my lady? It is pneumonia.' It was like Fanny's death over again.

When it was all over Valentine went, her eyes full of tears, to Felix where he lay. 'He is dead, poor Clonmagh,' she said. 'I still have you, thank God.'

He laid his hand over hers; he could still move his arms. Then: 'So Henry will inherit,' was all he said.

A train screamed and passed in the night, then silence fell again on Fenfallow.

THREE

On the day after Henry, fourth Viscount Harmhill, came of age his father the Earl sent for him to tell him about the family curse. The rejoicings of yesterday were over and the great bonfire, at which they had roasted four sheep and dispensed ale to the tenants, was out, leaving a blackened patch on the grass of the near field.

The Earl lay in his room near the window, his couch comfortably arranged with pillows. His hair was white but still thick, and his face, with the years of annoyance from bedsores despite all nursing, was lined with pain. He watched his son come in with pleasure; a handsome boy, Harry, handsome and like others! It was wise of him to have chosen the military profession; he looked well in Guards uniform. He had had good reports from his senior officers during the late brief war against the Zulu in South Africa, in which the young Prince Imperial had been killed. With this as a background, the Earl permitted himself a slight smile; Guy's curse, however it had been perpetrated, made poor sounding now.

Henry Harmhill listened quietly. It was his habit to judge everything impartially as it was dictated by the notions he held of his own class. One would not dismiss a saying of one's uncle in the same manner as one would dispose of the drunken ravings of some farmworker on the estate. Nevertheless there were resemblances. He smiled, the gesture lending lightness to his long-jawed face, which as was the fashion among young officers wore a neat moustache. He had not inherited his father's notable nose, but that of his mother, the Countess, who was not present today as she had gone to visit Father Smythe, now an invalid whose remorse over the long-ago fire at Fenfallow had at last turned his brain; he no longer ministered to the nuns, but resided at a private nursing home financed by Valentine Fenn.

'You smile,' said the Earl, 'but at the time it was not pleasant. I have another thing to say to you; by accident, at the time he was dying, I was informed that the lawyer Tupman was in fact the father of Guy Sutbury, as he still calls himself. I understand his health is not good. His son Gerard, when last I heard of him, was on an expedition to North Africa; that was many years ago.'

'Our ways have not crossed, but I have heard of him in the City,' murmured Harmhill, who maintained a discreet interest in the stock-market. 'They say Gerard Sutbury returned from Africa safely, though no doubt his experience there was almost as warlike as my own.'

'I do not wish to hear about him. The question is whether or not you consider that the relations between the two branches of the family are to be left, or mended. I myself would have preferred to mend them, but Guy was adamant.'

'I do not see any reason to disagree with your findings. If he wishes to be reconciled to us it is for my uncle – which you say he is not – to make the first overture, not ourselves.'

'Your mother would say that is not Christian charity,' ventured the Earl. He had still not followed his wife into the Catholic Church, chiefly for Harmhill's sake; he did not want to hinder the boy's progress in any way; perhaps, when oneself was actually dying, it might be thought of.

He turned his upper body restlessly. How much he would have liked to be out on this fine day, riding round the farms! He had supervised a certain amount of rebuilding of Fenfallow from his bed; the architect had brought him the plans and he had studied them carefully, but it was still not what it had been, although they had enough room now for privacy and for a few guests. He knew Henry had an interest in restoring the place as it had been; he thanked God he had such a son, not a spendthrift as he himself had proved in youth, but a worthy and virtuous young man, suitably instructed in the ways of the world though not led astray by them. He should do well when in time – Felix now prayed that it would be short – he should inherit the title. The question of Harmhill's marriage had been much in Fenn's mind of late; he would like to see grandchildren before he died. But of all the marriageable daughters of county families Harmhill had surveyed, none seemed to suit his fancy; and after all there was plenty of time, the boy was not yet twenty-five. If only Kate had been as tractable! Felix made his mind turn away from the remembered scandal of ten years back, when Kate had eloped with the groom, Ned Maverick, a man younger than herself and out of her class. Fortunately Eileen Clonmagh had died that year in Ireland and Kate came into her inheritance, and was now doing well with her husband there in the business of horse-breeding; but they had no children.

He returned his mind to Harmhill.

That young man had meantime ridden to the former offices of the lawyer Tupman, long since dead. It was now served by a firm of solicitors who had purchased the business somewhere in the sixties. There was no longer the old family rapport, but familiar names still showed on the shelves in their white paint on black deed-boxes; Iffley, Ryden, Sutbury, Fenn.

The partner was young, perhaps forty. He was a handsome dark-haired man with bland grey eyes, said to be somewhat too fond of the women; but able enough as regarded his profession. Harmhill sat in the proffered chair and set his blue gaze firmly on Matthew Radice, Bachelor of Law and Notary Public. 'I should like, as I wrote to you,' he said quietly, 'to see the original deed of entail as fashioned by the first Gerard Ryden, particularly as regards that part of the estate formerly known as the water-meadows, on which a canal was built.'

'And dug over a generation or more ago, in process of preparing the land for rail travel,' replied Radice, who knew a determined client when he saw one; the Viscount was only just of age, but evidently knew his business. He produced a yellowed scroll, and spread it out before Harmhill's eyes on his desk. 'As you see, I have everything ready for you,' said the lawyer softly.

'As I would expect, having given you warning. My father is no longer able to conduct such business for himself. I trust that you can safely regard me as acting in his interests.'

'If it came to formal business, his lordship's power of attorney should be obtained.'

'That will be readily available. I have already consulted my fahter.'

The hard blue eyes stared down at the spread scroll, stained and marked by age and time. The map portrayed Fenfallow as it had once been, with a dotted line ceasing beyond the water-meadows. 'I understand the canal was built by Hugh Maverick, who married Margriet Ryden by a shameful trick,' said Harmhill. 'Has there ever been any question of compensation by the railway company for disuse of the canal?'

'The canal had not been in use for many years.'

'But was a means of communication, which was duly cut off. You might enquire as to this; but mainly, I want to establish the exact borders of the entailed estate with regard to a bargain made between my father in his youth and his brother, Guy Sutbury, who is still alive as you know, and in business in London.'

'We have no record of the bargain here. I can consult Mr Sutbury's solicitors.'

'I do not think you will find much to help you there. It was, as they say, a gentleman's agreement, heavily baited against my father.'

The lawyer studied his fingers. 'I suggest that it would be in order for you, with your father's consent, to approach your uncle directly,' he said. 'It might be the best way of resolving the dispute.' He looked discreetly at the young man before him; determination there, not as much charm as his father; an air as dogged as a mastiff, but predictably without that beast's size; small, determined, reliable, possibly lacking in humour. Harmhill's eligibility as a bridegroom should not be overlooked; it was a card he could well play, here and there. Guy Sutbury had, was it, a niece? Had she not been presented lately at Court? One's memory failed. The lawyer placed his fingers together as though they had been roof-timbers. Such a marriage might solve everything, without litigation.

It was a chilly November day with the kind of fog that can only exist in London. Guy Sutbury sat in the smoking-room of his club, enjoying the good fire. There was nobody else in the room and he rang the bell to summon the porter on duty. 'Bring me whisky,' he ordered.

Waiting for it, he stared into the red coals. He had aged more in the shape of his body, which was a trifle hunched these days, than in his face. He walked stiffly nowadays and his hair was white, balding a little over the forehead. His wife Lilian had tried to get him to use an elixir for this, but it had made no difference.

He was not thinking of Lilian, although she fulfilled her duties as a wife and hostess admirably. The upbringing of her son she had left to nurses, tutors and schoolmasters, as was correct. There was no explaining the sudden wild streak that had burst out so unexpectedly in Gerry shortly after he had come down from Cambridge; an urge to

explore foreign countries, evidently the less civilised the
better. That expedition into the interior of Ethiopia had
nearly cost the boy his life; and moreover ...

The whisky had come. The porter placed it on the small
table beside Guy's armchair, and departed, reflecting on
how singular it was that some gentlemen were liked and
others not at all, although it was impossible to put a finger on
why. The Honourable Guy Sutbury was generally alone.
There was something sly about him; more than that was not
a fellow's business.

He soon forgot the matter. A smooth long automobile had
drawn silently up to the door, emerging as if from the fog's
embrace. It was still an unusual enough sight to cause the
porter, moving decorously to the door, to feel inward
excitement. What a beauty, with her gleaming metal parts
and dark-blue chassis you could see your face in even on a
day like this! The bloke who owned it must be very rich.

He watched the chauffeur spring out, open the door and
click his heels in precise fashion. Foreigners, that was it. The
emerging inmate looked foreign, even before he spoke and
in stiff English, asked for none other than the Honourable
Guy Sutbury. He had, the porter saw, one of these
new-fangled monocles in one eye, and his face bore a
crosswise scar.

He proffered his card and the porter took it. He would
see, he said, according to the ancient formula, if Mr Sutbury
was in the club. Meantime he took the foreign gentleman's
hat and his coat, which had an astrakhan collar. The visitor
spread out long thin hands to the hall fire, to warm himself.

Guy, on being informed, nodded; the card had read
Baron von Schweiz zu Gedern. He was not acquainted with
the Baron, had no idea why the latter should want to see
him, and was accordingly intrigued.

When the man faced him at last he seemed very tall,
overtopping Guy by half a head. He clicked his heels as the
chauffeur had done. 'You are the Honourable Mr Sutbury?'

he said in his slightly too formal English. Guy admitted his identity and allowed himself a narrow smile.

'Do you drink whisky, Baron?' he asked. He found that he had no idea of the habits of Germans; one pictured them in beer-gardens, but not this man.

'A small one, if you please. Permit me to offer you a cigar.' They sat comfortably in the leather-upholstered chairs; Guy had accepted the expensive brand and both men lit them. They fell into general polite talk until the porter brought more whisky; then for a few moments drank in silence, agreeably savouring the fifteen-year-old malt. Guy awaited whatever it was the Baron had to say without eagerness; already he felt that that sentiment must not be apparent. He was aware of the scrutiny of the other's eyes, which reminded one of dead fish, with the one behind the monocle unnervingly enlarged to outward view. The Baron's hair possessed no colour, being smoothed back from a middle parting which in some way reaffirmed the fact that he was not an Englishman.

'You are wondering why I have come,' said the Baron. 'Confess it.' His smile was hard, jerking the taut skin into folds as though a mask cracked.

'It is a pleasure to have your company,' said Guy smoothly. 'In what way can I be of service to you?' One might as well get down to brass tacks, as Lilian often put it.

'In a way that your position makes possible,' said the Baron slowly. 'As an English aristocrat, you have connections with persons of high rank as well as acquaintance with many City of London bankers.'

Guy forbore to let his smile widen and the Baron spread out his hands. 'For instance,' he said, 'you go to your weekend house parties, *ja?*'

'I am known to be something of a shot, but I prefer reading to society nowadays.' It was true; he spent much of his time these days alone in his library, studying the markets, reading the gazettes. It gave him a certain prescience which, for instance, assisted him with this particular visitor. 'Of that I am aware,' said Baron von Schweiz. 'I know a great deal about you, Mr Sutbury. I know, for instance, that you have recently been approached by the board of directors of a certain merchant bank, hoping that you will join them as you have joined others. You are a man who has made his way in a manner seldom seen among the English aristocracy.'

Guy flushed. This fellow knew too much, and his constant reference to one's social standing was irksome. It had in fact been manna to Guy to be asked to join the elite board, but his name was not yet on the writing-paper among the others. He began to take the Baron more seriously. 'What has all that to do with it?' he asked directly. If only – one hoped that that state of affairs was still confidential – it did not come out that the Baron also knew about the suit at law that that young pup Harmhill had brought, evidently with Felix's consent, over the matter of ownership of the railway cut near Fenfallow.

'We have our own ways of knowing what we wish to know, and keeping silent about the rest,' said the Baron, as if he read Guy's thoughts. 'Let me say only that the fact of your election to that particular board will confirm us in the opinion we had already formed of your abilities.'

'Who are "we"? I would be glad if you were more open with me.' He glanced about the empty room, where wisps of fog had drifted through despite the closed windows and the thick curtains. 'We are not overheard,' said Guy quietly.

'Nevertheless I must make sure that it is safe,' said the Baron. He rose, stalked to the windows, inspected the alcoves behind the curtains, stirring the fog as he went, and returned to his place. 'I will not, in this talk or elsewhere, say the name of my employers aloud, and I beg that you will not do so either, here or elsewhere. Walls, as you say here, have ears, even though our countries are close by reason of the *freundschaft* of our Kaiser and your venerable Queen, also the Crown Prince's fruitful marriage to your Princess Royal.'

He showed Guy a name engraved on paper and the other kept his face carefully blank. One must not appear too greatly impressed. Guy fixed his glance thoughtfully on the Baron's scar; he remembered reading somewhere that young Prussians of a certain rank sought to acquire these as a reference, in a way, that their swordsmanship was admirable. This scar had long whitened; the duel must have been a long time ago. Guy wondered if it had been about a woman. The Baron did not look passionate, but perhaps he nourished hidden fires. It was amusing, or would be later, to speculate.

'Frankly, my friend, what we want is an Army contract,' said von Schweiz. 'Certain conservative interests in England make this difficult, despite our two countries' friendship. It is perhaps not wholly a secret, among those who know about such things, that in the late Franco-Prussian war we, as a subsidiary firm whose name I have not yet told you, supplied arms to both sides.' The smile wrinkled again. 'This is of course not publicly spoken of; you will keep it – how do you say it? – in confidence.'

'I had heard rumours, I admit. But how does all this concern me?' Guy drew on his cigar, enjoying the flavour. He had the certainty that power, no doubt money also, was within his grasp. But on the surface he must be the helpful, mildly puzzled aristocrat, as von Schweiz persisted in calling him. The thing was to keep a grip on oneself, not sell oneself at too low a price.

'As I have said, you are familiar with dukes, earls, generals. You may well be on speaking terms with the highest-ranking officer of all.'

'I am.' He thought of the irascible personage named, and grinned to himself. It should be possible to get behind Cambridge's defences; his bombast was bluff, he was privately as uncertain as the next man.

The Baron leaned forward. 'Recommend our work. I will arrange that the finest possible rifle is sent to you without delay, and its precision, in your hands, will no doubt be remarked upon. You will say where you obtained it and that the price was reasonable. What they will not know is that you will be in charge here, operating by means of your railway, with raw materials coming by way of Scandinavia.'

'Where are the headquarters? One does not discuss the price of one's rifle.' The cigar was finished and Guy stubbed it out in the huge glass dish on the table. For some reason he would always remember the crushed, lonely stub. The Baron's was still alight. He offered another and Guy shook his head. Von Schweiz smiled again.

'Ah, you English! You can make the price known subtly. You yourself, I am happy to find, have that subtlety many of your countrymen lack. They are naïve and you are not. That will suit us very well.'

'I have not yet said that I agree. There is a certain risk for me in the matter; my social position –' He thought of the outrage the truth would rouse at Belvoir, Chatsworth, Woburn, not to mention Sandringham. But with care –

'You have already accepted in your mind,' said the Baron softly.

He named a sum. Its amount would normally have made even Guy blink, but he was careful to make no change in his expression. Isabel's fortune was not yet spent; he had doubled and trebled it already. Compared with this, however –

'The address?' he said. The Baron's thin lips made a light grimace. 'It is open enough,' he said. 'Gillinghall and Sons of Bishopsgate have been in business since the days of your George the Fourth. It is not generally known that the business has lately been sold to a new owner.'

Guy knew the name of Gillinghall; old-established, craftsmanlike makers of small guns. He set down his glass.

'I cannot commit myself without some guarantee,' he told

the other. 'I have experience in the matters of merchant banking and of the purchase and sale of rail stock, but not ... your subject.'

'We already know of your railways. They will be a great convenience. The manufacture itself will take place in your Midlands; arrangements have been made and only wait to be finalised by you. You will have no trouble, I think.' He took out his wallet with a confidence that would have been offensive half an hour ago. 'As regards guarantees, I have here a cheque. It is to be cashed at a certain bank; do not operate through your ordinary account.'

'I am hardly a child, unable to guard my business.' Guy was by now a trifle sullen. Once let these fellows get the upper hand and one would become a mere cog in their monstrous wheel. He did not want that; what he still wanted was the power to make his own decisions. But the cheque itself was almost fabulous. Guy felt his fingers itch to seize it, but accepted it at last only with a show of reluctance.

The Baron rose and clicked his heels. 'I shall not come here again,' he said. 'We must not be seen often to meet. The risk is great.'

'How did you know I was in?' He did not come every day to the club. 'The door of your house was watched daily and your direction noted when you came out,' the Baron said. 'We are efficient, *nicht wahr?*'

And ruthless, no doubt, thought Guy. Despite everything little shivers went up and down his spine. By accepting the cheque he had put himself in their power in spite of all his protestations. He knew it, but could not bring himself to return such money. Once a tool became useless it would be thrown on the scrap-heap, no doubt. He must make himself useful, that was all. A skeleton within him grinned, showing all its teeth.

He escorted the Baron back to his car and they talked generalities as they went down the curved stairs, such as that the fog was lifting a little. 'I will say farewell,' remarked the

German in the hall. He extended his dry hand and Guy took it, and they went out together to the car. Afterwards Guy returned to the smoking-room, into which a few members had by now ambled, and remembered the headed writing-paper the German had shown him. It bore the name of Krupps of Essen, the giant armaments firm inspired at its beginnings by Bismarck.

He thought for some time, exchanged brief pleasantries with the members, then went to consult the Almanach de Gotha where it stood on the club's shelves. The Baron's quarterings proved impeccable. One might have foreseen it.

The Earl of Fenn was gravely ill. The doctor had called repeatedly and had left lately, his bearded face solemn. It was a recurrence – and might be the last – of the trouble in the chest that commonly visits people in Felix's case since the night of the fire. For the past few years he had been, in this way, doubly an invalid, tormented by the necessity of having to be helped to lean over and cough. His wife seldom left him and Harmhill, on this recent leave, spent much time with his father, hearing the weak voice talk when it might; he himself had replied as best he could, but he was not demonstrative and could not make clear the grief he felt. At last, now that drugs had been given to relieve the pain, he saw that the drowsy, moss-agate eyes contained a kind of irony, an almost comic sympathy and understanding.

'Father – what is it you want to say to me? I am – I am listening to every word.' Stiff, formal he knew he was, conventional and shy; it was not the thing to show one's feelings. Now he was beset with them and could not give them expression. The Earl turned restlessly on his pillows and Harmhill shifted them until the wasted body lay more comfortably.

'Thank you, my dear boy,' whispered Felix with difficulty; his breathing, after the tossing and movement, was laboured. He raised a weak hand to touch his son's face.

'Glad you ... have done well ... enjoy life a little ... not all duty and burden. Try ... to laugh.'

He fell back on the pillows as Valentine entered the room. She hurried to the bed.

'My darling, how do you feel now? Father Corcoran is here.'

Harmhill was aware of a sense of outrage. Ever since his father had become a total invalid she had been at him with hints, prayers and bringing priests to Fenfallow. She had even asked the local Anglican vicar not to call. The Romans had no business here. When there was a funeral – and God knew he would grieve for his own father as much as was proper – it would be Church of England, with the parson, and no nonsense. His mother could make her own arrangements privately; but private they should be. Harmhill turned a cold face to the little Catholic priest who now served the community, as he came along the passageway carrying the Viaticum under its cloth. Harmhill had no idea how far things must have gone for that to be possible; he had not been able to be at Fenfallow all the time, there were duties with the regiment. He turned and stared out of the window at his mother's garden. It was late summer and the flowers were sparse; there was little colour at this time of year, only green.

He waited for a little, but did not want to see the priest or Valentine immediately. He went downstairs to the library, took a book from the shelves at random and opened it. The page made him frown. *He that comes as near uprightness as infirmities admit, is an upright man, though he have some obliquities.*

Donne Harmhill had never cared for that personage. He dared say there was insecurity behind the smugness. When Donne's wife had had a miscarriage the man had written: 'I have lost half a child.' Later he lost his wife herself, at the birth of their twelfth; she was still young. When he, Harmhill, came to marry he would treat his wife very differently. There was no haste about that in any case; he would prefer to get this dispute with his uncle Guy settled before committing himself in any such way. To date, the lawyers were still working on it; how damnably slow they were!

He became aware that his mother had entered the room and was standing by him, her eyes full of tears. Harmhill laid a hand on her arm; he was fond of her, after all.

'It is only a matter of hours now,' she was saying. 'They tell me he will not last the night.'

The priest's footsteps sounded outside and Valentine turned away, leaving the library and closing the door gently. Harmhill went upstairs again to sit by his father, seeing briefly his mother walk outside to bid farewell to the priest. Felix's breathing was easier; it was possible that he slept. The long-nosed face was at peace.

He died that night, shortly after midnight, with Valentine's hand in his. Harmhill closed the hooded eyes and later sat, writing notices to the gazettes, until morning. He could not yet grow used to the fact that he was Earl of Fenn.

Sir Guy Sutbury – he had, to his own and his wife's great satisfaction, received the knighthood as a reward for his labours in industry and gifts towards charity – sent a stiff black-edged letter of condolence to his sister-in-law and nephew. As he closed the envelope he pondered on the fact that it was many years now since he had held any communication with the elder branch of the family.

Glancing at himself in the looking-glass before he drove to his office, Guy gave a small smirk of self-congratulation. He had worn better than Felix, which was to be expected, for he had not wasted his energies in youth nor misapplied his gifts and intelligence. He had made a great deal of money, not only by means of the continuing arrangement with the Baron but, on a smaller scale, in a field concerning which he would never have admitted himself openly to be interested; to wit, wholesale grocery. The less often he thought about that aspect of things the better; he had financed, successfully, an enterprising individual who put wood chips, gelatine and colouring in what had been sold on the shelves as raspberry jam until complaint made it prudent to concentrate on some new product instead. In any case as Guy had from the beginning made it a condition that his name would in no way be connected with such matters, he was safe from scandal. The dividends were satisfactory.

As regarded the other, and admittedly more dangerous, concern he had done rather better than he had expected in the matter of personal commissions, to the extent of interesting even one bluff and hard-headed member of the Royal Family in a certain gun whilst shooting in Norfolk. Not only his business existence but his social life had been enhanced as a result. Lilian of course was pleased. As to Gerry ... well, nothing now would make any difference.

Guy thought of his son, which by now he seldom allowed himself to do, with a sense of doom and defeat. Only one other happening had ever made him feel so; the time when Felix had informed him, to his face and his family's, that he was not the son of Fenn at all, but that of a lawyer. Although Guy had continued to deny this to himself and would certainly have done so to others, the stigma remained, hidden in his mind; perhaps it had spurred him on to further effort. To hope, in certain directions, was after all to lumber down a blind alley; but one could always rely on oneself and ... certain means. It was a pity Lilian had borne no more children; he himself seemed unfortunate in that respect.

But nothing could touch his innate self-satisfaction. He had shown care, cunning and had met with success. By the time he left the house he was wearing his smile again, though not too broadly as the polite world knew by now that his brother was dead.

Valentine bore up bravely for Felix's funeral, with never a tear shed behind her veil; but afterwards she went into a state of total collapse which lasted for many weeks. It was almost Christmas when she felt able to venture out, in the carriage, to visit Father Smythe; only to find the blind, deranged man as usual, with his head turned downwards and sideways, as if gazing at the floor, in silence. The effort of trying to make him talk was too much for Valentine; she left early, and on the drive back, in the deep cold, caught a chill despite the fur rugs in the carriage, and was put to bed again. Countess Valentine was no longer the woman she had been when the long nursing of Felix began. The rich hair was grey now, the eyes large and wistful in her worn face. There was little except conventional affection between her and the new Earl, though Henry showed kindness enough, as and when he could; but there were few occasions for it, and the gulf between them widened.

As soon as she could, Valentine drove out again to the convent hill, causing Joshua to stop at the flight of steps; she picked up her black skirts and ascended them slowly, trying to encourage her returning bodily strength, feeling her knees betray her at the end. She saw, for it was spring by now, the delicate buds on the growing birch trees, almost scenting the lacelike forms of the branches borne in the cool air. The laurels had grown and were green. Valentine went to the chapel door, turned the iron handle and went inside. It was cool and dark. The window she had already donated to Felix's memory shed coloured light on the floor; behind their gilded iron grille the nuns were praying, and the altar itself was draped in an embroidered cloth the nuns had brought with them from Belgium, the tabernacle clothed in some of the same work, gathered so as to make it seem almost like the shoulders of a man. Valentine knelt in the oak pew and remained there for a long time. A great sense of peace and comfort came to her as she prayed; she felt certain that Felix's soul was not given to the darkness, that she herself, left lonely, could help him by prayer. By the end her knees had grown stiff, her hands and face cold; she did not know how long she had knelt there. She rose slowly and, without looking towards the grille, made her way out, round to the great front door, and rang for the portress. A small grille opened presently and a voice asked her name.

'I am Lady Fenn. I should like to speak with the Prioress if it is convenient.'

She was led along the tiled passage into a parlour where a great crucifix hung on a wall and a further grille would open presently in the wall opposite. Presently the Prioress came, a nun in attendance. Valentine looked and saw an ageing woman whose face was serene; Mère Rose had died some time ago and one of the sisterhood had been chosen to replace her. They spoke in French. Valentine put back her veil.

'Madame, I want to ask you if I may be received among you. I have thought of it for very long, ever since my husband died; in fact, while he lay dying. I have no life in the world any more. I would like to end my days with you in peace. I received great comfort just now in the chapel.'

The wise eyes assessed her and the voice answered slowly. 'We could not admit you, madame, because of your age. We need young women. Your help to us has been great and we will continue to pray for you, also for the soul of your husband.'

Valentine was desolate. 'Is there no possible way?'

'We have no Oblates as yet. They are the dedicated ones who live in the world.'

'I would not have the strength to continue as an Oblate. I want the sisterhood about me, to encourage me in the habit. I am not a strong-willed person; I would do as I am told.' She smiled a little, and the Prioress continued to regard her gravely.

'We could take you as a lay-sister, but that involves rough work.'

'I would not mind that. I have helped at home with the farmwork in the dairy, with the lambs, everything of that kind.' She recalled, at this moment, how she and Felix had been delighted in their first year when the lambs came, and had taken it in turn with the farmhands to sit up at nights to scare away the dawn crows, who a little later would be waiting to peck out the new lambs' eyes. And she had worked hard at making comforts for the soldiers in the Crimea.

'Think of it,' said the Prioress. 'Take time to think, and pray. I will pray for you, my child, that your decision may be the right one for you.'

The grille closed and Valentine was left alone.

Henry, Earl of Fenn, was going through his late father's papers. Felix had not been a meticulous correspondent; there were many accounts rendered and even respectable demands, at last, for an early reply at his lordship's convenience. However a full statement on the financial position would be available from the accountant and the Bank. Fenn put all such bills on one side, and concentrated then on the rest, prudently tearing in two that which was to be burned.

He had almost finished, and was clearing the last papers out of the small mock-hidden door which one opened with a separate key. It sat between two carved panels of the rosewood of which the desk was made, and escaped notice easily. A single paper lay there, and Fenn's glance roamed over it and then returned. He was shocked. Its language was so violent that at first he thought it must be an anonymous letter; no doubt there had been incidents in his father's past which might have accounted for one. Why, in that case, had it not been taken to the police? But flicking it over he was astonished to see, on the other side, the signature of his uncle, Guy Sutbury. He recalled some curiosity of his own as a boy as to why this uncle, whom he knew to exist, never came to Fenfallow. 'There was a quarrel,' Valentine had said quietly. 'Do not mention the matter to your father.'

Now he read the letter. Its terms were abusive. He studied the signature of his unknown uncle for moments; one often deduced a man's character by the way he signed his name. Then, his small mouth in its long jaw tightening, he rose from where he sat and, tearing the letter in fragments, threw these on the fire. A curse on his father's descendants! What tasteless melodrama! Guy Sutbury must be unbalanced, despite all one had heard in other ways of his wealth and his position, which he had evidently made for himself, culminating in the knighthood recently. He was married to somebody of whom one had never heard; and he had a son whom one never met. But there might be many explanations for that; one need not give way to prejudice.

But Valentine's wish to enter Knocking Hill convent as a lay-sister was another matter. 'I cannot permit it, mother. My father would have been furious. The Countess of Fenn a scrubbing-woman! Have a little regard for my position; what is everyone going to say?'

Valentine smiled sadly at her son. Fenn, as she must now call him, could seldom see beyond obstacles of his own making. 'If it is so very objectionable to you,' she began, but he cut in.

'For God's sake spend a little while at their guest-house, if you must be near them; that way the carriage will not be seen going up there and back every other day.'

'The guest-house is expensive.'

'I will meet the expenses. Only oblige me by not making a laughing-stock of yourself and me. I have never heard of such a thing. Thank God you mentioned it.'

'You have mentioned God twice in five minutes, Henry,' she said wryly. 'Do you want me to serve Him by appearing week after week in your pew in the parish church, when I do not believe in that, when I believe nothing but that the true faith is guarded up there, at Knocking?'

'God knows –' Fenn bit back the third mention. 'It was evident in my father's lifetime that you would not accompany him there, but went to that tin shack instead. Everyone talked of it. It has been a great drawback to us, to me in particular; the other chaps in the regiment knew of it, and had to be tactful. It is asking too much to demand more of me.'

'My poor boy, nothing more will be demanded,' said Valentine sadly.

She spent a little while in the convent guest-house, and came back to Fenfallow to find it empty of anyone except the servants; Fenn had gone off to his turn of guard-duty with the regiment. Valentine did a little gardening, for the beds were full of thrusting green spears of the bulbs she and Felix had planted years ago now; they had doubled and trebled. She began to plan her life like this, part at the guest-house, part at Fenfallow. The nuns had made a little parlour for her, with a sofa on which she often lay; after Valentine died it was always to be called the sofa of Madame la Comtesse. As for the Earl himself, he would not admit that his mother had died in a Papist place, with the comfort of a Roman priest, and in the notices, and on her tomb in the Fenn vault, it was to be stated that Countess Valentine had died at Fenfallow.

But that was not quite yet.

Fenn had been more deeply disturbed by his mother's attitude than he showed; when he had leisure to think of it it tormented him so much that he did a thing which he seldom allowed himself; instead of going to his military club for a drink, he turned into a public house. He ordered whisky and water and sat drinking it, dispassionately eyeing the new crimson plush upholstery and gilt-lettered glass. He was in the middle of his third drink, thanking God there was nobody here that he knew among the blue tobacco-smoke and jostling press of humans, when a voice hailed him.

'Fenn, my dear old boy. May I join you? Looks as if life had got on top of you. Got on top of me, too. Not worth worryin'; be like us all and get blotto good and proper, as they say in the halls.'

It was a fellow-Guardsman, Major Geoffrey Ellison; both he and Fenn were out of uniform. Ellison sat down and set up his own kind of conversation, which was amusing if one wanted to pass the time; he was a mimic, and took off so many of their acquaintances so well that Fenn found himself laughing and drinking, drinking more and more. Presently he was so drunk that a clear-sighted vision came to him; nothing was worth troubling about, as Ellison had said, and another. *Enjoy your life, my dear fellow* ... were those the words? Remembering was not a good thing, but in the circumstances ...

'Lookin' a bit under the weather, old boy,' remarked Geoffrey Ellison again. 'Tell you what, when this place closes let's take a cab and go and see old Chummy.'

'Who is Chummy?' Even now his pronunciation was careful, so was part of his mind. Geoffrey Ellison laughed, his splendid teeth and bright brushed moustache setting off his surprisingly clear blue eyes; he had been a pretty child and somehow had taken the innocent quality with him into manhood. He was unmarried, and very popular with women.

'Lord bless you, we all call him that. There's no harm in him, but he likes his drink.'

Fenn found himself shortly in a hackney cab, with Ellison's shapely legs in their peg-top trousers stretched out beside him on the straw-littered floor. He was still not

certain where they were going or to whom, and almost
nodded off to sleep as the cab turned into Arlington Street.

Fenn had a brief recollection of astonishment when the
butler, after admitting them to a handsomely furnished
hall, led them upstairs to a room whose door was locked,
and turned the key for them to go in. The man inside
seemed to know Geoffrey Ellison, who no doubt came here
frequently; but now was not the moment to ask him the
reason for the locked door. They found themselves in a
room where a man sat by himself at a fire, drinking brandy.
A tray with more bottles sat by his elbow. The furnishing of
the room was sparse and contained only, in the old manner,
a curtained bed and some chairs. Evidently the inmate slept
in this room. He had turned his head idly as the pair of them
came in and Fenn received a shock; the man was an alco-
holic far gone in his disease, and his jaw trembled in a
ruined yellowed face. He rose unsteadily, came forward
with hand outstretched, the brandy in the other, and said:
'Ellison, my dear fellow! Come to the fire and join me. Trust
y'well.'

Ellison had mumbled introductions but these were lost on
the hearer. He refilled his own glass, then two more, turned
and said urgently: 'C'mon drink, drink till it's all gone. Then
they'll send more. M'father, damn him, says I am to have as
much as I need. If that were so they'd stack the room with
bottles, eh? You know me. Your health,' and he raised his
glass to the incomers. But Fenn was not looking at him. He
was looking at the portrait of a girl, hung on the wall. She
was the only pure thing in that appalling room. She had
great dark eyes in a heart-shaped face, and her dark hair
was a cloud of curls. She wore pale blue, with a locket at her
throat. The hands were not shown.

'That's m'daughter,' mumbled Gerard Sutbury. 'Spanish
blood, as they say. Don't see Sabrina now, m'father has
taken her away, keeps her in Hertfordshire now she's
finished school. Says I'm an unfit parent. No doubt he's

right. Pretty thing, Sabrina; taking ways. Her mother died, y'know. Her mother –'

He had begun to weep. Ellison took his arm and said: 'Come on back to the fire, Chummy, old chap. Here's health to all of us.'

The night grew blurred with drinking, and then the dawn. When Fenn awoke next day it was to find himself, with a violent headache, in his own bed at the club – he had no recollection of getting there – and the memory of two things about the evening before. One was the girl's face; he would remember it all his life. The other was the recollection, as they left, of a door in the house shutting quietly, some way off; as though somebody had watched them come, and watched them go. He did not yet know the name of his shaky host, apart from the fact that he was called Chummy, and he did not greatly want to meet him again.

> *Fenfallow, 28th April, 1884*
>
> *My dear Ellison,*
>
> *I fear that I have behaved in a somewhat remiss fashion by allowing you to take me to a house the owner of which I do not know by name. I would be obliged if you would send me, by return if you will, this person's direction, as I am not fond of lending myself to enterprises of such a nature and would not in the ordinary way have allowed myself such a liberty as to drink in the house of someone whose name I do not know.*
>
> *If you will oblige me with this information I shall be grateful. I turst that you remain in good health.*
>
> *Yours obediently,*
Fenn

> *10 Half Moon Street, 2nd May, 1884*
>
> *Fenn, dear old boy,*
>
> *I seem to have made a most frightful boob; admit that we were both under the weather. Our host the other night was poor old Chummy's father, Sir Guy Sutbury, who I understand is a relation of your own. He keeps Chummy locked up these days but allows one to visit him. I*

wasn't in a state to think of it at the time and I do apologise to you and, if necessary, to the old man; but I go there a good deal, as Chummy has very good brandy and used not to be a bad sort when he was himself. There is a story told about him, that he ran off with a Spanish heiress, who died when the daughter, whom I have not met as she is not yet out, was born, and Chummy took to the bottle thereafter. Anyway all that is water, so to speak, under the bridge. Do forgive me for my gaffe.

Affectionately,

Geoffrey M. Ellison
Fenfallow, 8th May, 1884

To Sir Guy Sutbury, C.B.E.. at
   18 Arlington Street, W.1.
Sir,
   It is with regret that I have been made aware that I entered your house the other evening without knowing whose it was. Being aware of the nature of certain correspondence of yours with my late father, and of the terms pertaining between you, I would in no circum-stances have permitted myself to enter your house, and I trust you will accept my apologies for having done so.

Your obedient servant,

Fenn
11th May, 1884

To the Earl of Fenn,
   at Fenfallow
My dear Nephew and Lord,
   I received your letter and pray accept my assurance that no one regrets more than I the necessity of its having had to be written. Nothing is of greater importance to me than to repair the relations your late father and I broke off some years before you were born. It is my earnest wish that this breach should be repaired, and if you will forgive an old man's somewhat precipitate haste — after all we cannot tell, as it is said, how soon our soul will be required of us, and one ought not to let the sun go down on one's wrath — not that I am the least of sinners in that respect, or rather was not formerly — it would give me great pleasure in any case to meet my brother's son.

Would you find yourself able to take luncheon with me at my house in Hertfordshire on a date soon to be named by yourself? I can suit your convenience, as I live a retired life nowadays. My young grand-daughter lives at Harmings since her return from her school in Paris, and it would be a pleasure for her to meet you although she is not yet launched formally into society and is somewhat shy. I myself have heard much about you and would greatly like to make your acquaintance.

Your devoted (and repentant!) uncle,
Guy Sutbury

'What are your wishes in the matter, mother? I feel that you should be consulted.'

They sat together in the little parlour in the convent guesthouse. Valentine lay on her sofa, as she often did nowadays; the state of her heart had left traces on her cheeks, and her nose bore a small throbbing vein. She raised a hand, discoloured and spotted with the brown stains of age, and fingered the Clonmagh brooch in the way he remembered her doing from the time when he was a child.

'I do not think that we were the only ones wronged,' she said slowly. 'Before we were married, your dear father confided to me that Kate, whom you remember –'

'I remember indeed. She was like a wild cat. There was a scandal when she ran off with the groom.'

'Well, they seem happy enough although your father would not allow me to keep up with her at Marishnageen over the years; I wonder how she is? At any rate, she was your father's child by his brother Guy's first wife, Isabel.'

Fenn was frowning a little; what unsavoury secrets there were in the family! 'That is a story I should not like to get about,' he said, and Valentine smiled a little; how much older than his age dear Henry – that is, Fenn – seemed! One would think, to hear him, that he was fifty.

'Have no fear, I do not talk about it, and nobody else remembers,' she said. 'But at least I think that, now that Guy is in a frame of mind to repair matters with us, we should not rebuff him. They say he has grown extremely rich, not that that is a reason for – for forgiveness, but perhaps he will forgive us too, and that is pleasant, is it not? I think you should go to Hertfordshire, and meet Sabrina. What a beautiful name! It is, I think, from a poem of Milton's when he was not as heavy as he became later. It was a masque, I recall. My dear boy, I shall be so glad when things are mended; it will be a great relief, and perhaps – well, one never knows – at any rate, go to the luncheon.'

'I do not suppose that that will be any great matter,' he said, and rose shortly to take his leave. He never liked visiting the convent guest-house, and preferred it when his mother was available at Fenfallow; but he had been in some haste to have her decision and to be able to reply punctually, and courteously, one way or the other, to his uncle's invitation.

Fenn caught the train into Hertfordshire and alighted at the station. A chauffeur in a leather cap was waiting; there were few others getting off the train, and the man saluted him as though he knew who he was.

'The car is here, your lordship.' A Daimler was waiting, its gleaming parts and basketwork spotless, its spoked tyres as though they had never known dust; the man must have spent the time in giving everything a final polish while he was waiting for the train. Fenn got in at the door the chauffeur held open and declined the offer of a knee-rug; he was wearing tweeds and the weather was warm for May. The chauffeur wound the starter and jumped into his place; for the first time Fenn tasted the delights of an automobile. One of the men up at Oxford had owned a bumpy Austin which seemed more trouble than it was worth but was the delight of its owner's heart; Fenn had never been invited into it, but in any case this car was superbly different. After starting it purred on, like a great contented cat. If one were rich! But his dream of rebuilding Fenfallow must come first; meantime, he settled back for the journey, which was about five miles, along pleasant leafy roads dusty with summer.

The car slowed at last and turned in at a tree-shaded entrance, on either side of which sat two tall pillars bearing crouching greyhounds, their features a trifle worn. This must be an old house that his uncle had acquired; perhaps he, Fenn, was acquainted with the former owners. It would make a talking-point; otherwise he felt that he knew very little of what to say.

The grounds were not extensive, and soon they passed a patch of azaleas in full, bright bloom. On the lawn beside them a girl played with a leaping spaniel puppy. He recognised her, across the clear flame of the blossoms, as the subject of the portrait in Chummy's room. She was dressed today, again, in something light; a small straw hat was balanced on her dark curls. She looked up when the car passed and he saw one slim hand touch the dog, who sat still. As he had seen, her face was heart-shaped and her eyes enormous and dark; the painter had not flattered her, had somehow included not the grace of her movements, which seemed instinctive as a sea in the wind; it was as though she could never do anything against nature.

Fenn came to himself, alighted at the door – the house was not so old, perhaps rebuilt earlier this century – and was received by a bland old gentleman with a jowled beard, wearing a shooting-jacket, and whose blue eyes Henry felt summed him up shrewdly. 'Come and take a glass of sherry, then we will go out on to the lawn,' said Guy Sutbury. He showed no emotion at the meeting and Fenn felt none, not even animosity. This old gentleman seemed harmless; but there was the memory of the letter. He tried to crush it down; all that had been a long time ago, and his father was dead.

They went out on to the shaven green lawn, a manservant behind them carrying the drinks on a tray. The girl and the dog had gone. Guy took evident pleasure in showing his nephew the flower beds, the shrubbery, and the glass-houses, where early begonias were being brought on in a smell of good damp earth.

'My granddaughter could tell you as much about plants as I can,' said Guy. 'I have had her carefully educated. She will be our hostess at luncheon, as my wife is abroad. You must forgive Sabrina if she is not quite up to it yet; it is the first occasion since she returned from school in Paris.'

Fenn muttered some disarming comment. He was not unaware of the fact that Guy might have invited him here on purpose to meet Sabrina, and he did not intend to be taken in in any way. He commented on the shrubs and begonias and said that his mother no longer kept up the garden at Fenfallow. 'I do my best, but have not her knowledge, and it is of no use telling the fellows to dig if you don't know why,' he said, with an attempt at lightness. Guy laughed, showing expensive false teeth.

'I make sure they dig as I tell 'em. It is a pity Sabrina is too young for you; she might have done a lot of good to your garden. My wife will present her when Lilian comes home in the autumn. We expect a good marriage for Sabrina; she will have an excellent dowry, a factor which many English parents do not acknowledge. If it were my wish, I could leave her penniless; but I am fond of her. Let us go in.'

He led the way through the hall to a light, bright dining-room, with the mahogany table set for three persons and the shutters flying wide. The quality of the sunlight made Fenn think of a French painting. A slight figure appeared, and he was made known to Sabrina Sutbury, his host's granddaughter.

'Sabrina, my dear, this is your cousin Henry Fenn. It is too long since both branches of our family met. He has come here to repair the omission.'

He sounded like a tom-cat purring. Henry took his young hostess's hand and was aware of the huge dark eyes, strangely defenceless, and of the sweetness of her low voice as she said clearly: 'How do you do?' pronouncing each word as if it had separate value. He was early aware of this sensitivity in her, and of the way she spoke; not, like most women, incorrectly at the back of the throat, but using her lips and her tongue. Her hand in his clasp was soft and dry.

They sat down, and the servant brought in chilled soup. During its consumption they all talked of everyday things; but Fenn was continuous in his assessment of the girl. He did not know exactly how old she was, but she could not be more than eighteen; too young for him? The remark had nettled him somewhat; perhaps that was why it had been made. He was to admit afterwards that he had not at any time been ignorant of the intention to trap him; but it was not Sabrina's fault, except inasmuch as she had been taught to use pretty manners to any eligible man.

When the time came to leave he regretted it. He had found out a thing about her which she strove to conceal with every art and gesture no doubt taught at the Paris finishing school; her teeth were soft, well filled with gold. It gave the feeling of conspiracy with her that he should know her only fault. Her little ears beneath the dark silky curls were like shells; how often had one heard of a shell-like ear without noticing it? Her complexion was smooth and of an olive colour, neither raddled nor flushed. She was the most perfect thing he had ever seen, except for that one defect of the teeth; and her sweet red mouth made its vowels, performed its duty, prettily despite them, aided by the fluttering movements of her hands. Fenn would not after-wards have said that at that moment he made up his mind to marry her; he liked to think of himself as one who would conscientiously plan, examine a situation for possible faults, before committing himself. Yet he should have known he was lost before seeing Sabrina, slight and graceful with the puppy on the lawn.

'My mother will write and invite you both to Fenfallow,' he

heard himself saying. 'It will do her good to see company; she is too much alone.'

'It would give us pleasure to see you here again,' ventured Guy. 'You have not heard Sabrina play yet.'

'Grandpapa, please – I am not ready –'

'The child plays when she thinks she will,' said Sutbury. 'I like to hear her. Do you enjoy music, sir?'

Fenn heard himself replying. 'I know less about it than I should, as my mother is a fine pianist. I should greatly like to hear Miss Sabrina play.'

'Another time, then,' smiled Guy. Fenn took his leave with a feeling of unreality; he must see her soon again. It was only when he was returning to London on the train that he recollected that there had been no mention of the parents, either father or mother. Perhaps one could not, at this stage, have expected it, given Chummy's condition and the fact that the mother had died at Sabrina's birth. He already had the impression that in everyday things of life Sabrina could be hurt. He would protect her.

Valentine was at Fenfallow, but not well, when Lilian Sutbury's invitation came a few weeks later. There was a familiar pain, sharp enough to be called anguish, down her left arm, and even the drops the doctor customarily gave her only helped a little; she lived in dread of further attacks, knowing one might be the last. One always had to be prepared for death; she remembered Felix, and the long years he had lain in this very bed an invalid, and was thankful that at least she herself had remained able to travel and to get about, though she no longer played her piano; effort was dangerous and her hands rheumatic. She opened the letter with its unfamiliar handwriting when Henry was in the room, and looked up smiling.

'It is for Sabrina's coming-out ball.' Lady Sutbury had the pleasure, etc., for both of them. A vision flitted across Fenn's mind of Sabrina in an enchanting ball-gown, floating in someone's arms, but not his; the thought perturbed him. 'We cannot accept, mother,' he said firmly. 'You are not well enough for me to leave at present. Can you write, or shall I do so on your behalf and explain that you are ill?'

'My dear boy, I feel guilty at the very thought. I will try to write for myself, but presently. It is a pity that you cannot go, as you say.' Her eyes lingered on him thoughtfully; he looked older than his years, and his hair was beginning to thin a trifle over the forehead. She knew, or rather guessed, for he had said nothing, of his attraction for Sabrina, whom he had described to her briefly in his unassuming way. The result of this coming-out ball might well mean other proposals of marriage for Sabrina; would it not be wise for Henry to ensure his own, if he wished as much? She tried to put the matter to him and was pleasantly surprised when he did not rebuff her. 'I was thinking along the same lines myself,' he admitted.

He left her presently, and went down to the library; in that familiar atmosphere of old leather bindings, sunlight and dust he took a piece of paper and a pen, then hesitated, searching for words. The correct thing – this necessity always troubled Fenn – would have been to write to the girl's father, but Chummy, as far as he could judge, would probably be in no state to make a responsible reply. In the end he wrote to Guy, enclosing a letter for the girl's father if he thought fit to deliver it. Fenn had to write twice over before he could make his confused intentions clear even to himself. Precipitateness embarrassed him; it was far too early in their acquaintance for a proposal to Sabrina to seem anything but hasty, and yet he did not want to be laggard for the very reason Valentine had expressed, and which had occurred to him also. There would be no shortage of suitors for a beautiful, charming and no doubt well endowed wife whose connections at least were blameless. In the end he found the right words for the two letters, sealed both in one and laid it ready for the post. For the next few days he was

aware of an inward excitement, aided by the fact that
Valentine had recovered from her attack of angina. She
was still in bed, and the doctor advised no unnecessary
exercise; but in due course she insisted on visiting her
convent again. It was becoming increasingly rare for her to
stay long at Fenfallow. 'But I will be there when Sabrina
comes,' she told Fenn. It was understood between them
that there should be a return invitation in proper course,
especially as Lady Sutbury had evidently returned from
abroad and could chaperone Sabrina.

An answer from Guy came within three days. It was
pleasant; he was delighted on his own account to
encourage Fenn's suit for Sabrina, although the girl's own
inclinations of course had to be taken into account, and
although she had liked Henry very much she would
doubtfully have any thought of a deeper bond yet, as she
was so young. *As for the girl's father*, the letter went on, *I will
deliver your letter, but it is unlikely that my son will find it in
himself to make a decision. His state has worsened since you saw
him and he is now more than ever an embarrassment, as my wife
wants to be able to give Sabrina an excellent season and there will
be guests and social occasions at Arlington Street. I may consider
putting Gerard under care for the time, reluctant as I am to take
such a step; but you have seen him and will understand. My wife
regrets that you and Lady Fenn will be unable to attend the ball,
and sends her good wishes.*

And that was all; but it was enough. Fenn enclosed the
letter for his mother to read with one in his own hand for
her. *I do not think there will be opposition to my proposal from her
family at any rate; I am glad I took your advice.* In fact the
notion had been his own as well as his mother's; fond of
one another as they were it was rarely that their thoughts
flowed in the same channel. He began to consider what
form the return invitation to Sabrina should take; a
luncheon, no doubt, with her grandmother present, with
or without Sir Guy.

*

'My husband was greatly disappointed that he could not join us owing to a business engagement. How pleasantly the sunlight shines in at these large windows!' said Lilian Sutbury, having settled herself in a comfortably upholstered chair in the drawing-room at Fenfallow. Such remarks were meat and drink to Lilian; she supported them with an outward appearance which was remarkable for her age, notwithstanding the fact that she had in spite of everything grown a trifle stout; she wore a false front of grey curls, a summer gown of braid-trimmed faille, and a long string of genuine pearls, supported by drop earrings; her parasol matched her dress.

'Yes, we were able to choose for ourselves when Henry began the rebuilding,' said Valentine. 'Of course he has not been able to do nearly everything yet, have you, my dear?'

Fenn, addressed, replied in an undertone. He was completely obsessed by the sight of Sabrina, seated here in his house at last in a severely cut suit of cream-coloured linen with a matching wide-brimmed hat from which fell two long dark-brown ribbons down her back. The earrings in her tiny ears were of gold. She had hardly spoken, except to answer politely, since the carriage had brought them from the station; and he was more than ever enchanted with her. She turned her great dark eyes on him now and said sympathetically in her soft voice. 'It must have been so dreadful, the destruction of so much by fire,' and her mouth lingered on the words, pouted a little in a way that was both delightful and sincere. He replied that it had happened in his boyhood and that he had always had the determination to rebuild Fenfallow, but that the building was not yet by any means completed. 'The garden, however, is worth looking at just now,' he told her. 'Will you and Lady Sutbury accompany me to see it?' It was after lunch; they had refreshed themselves and would not depart for the train until tea was over.

'I will stay here with Lady Fenn,' said Lilian tactfully. She

smiled as she saw Fenn give his arm to Sabrina and the pair
go out together into the summer sunlight, the narrow frilled
peplum on Sabrina's waisted bodice flaring, loosely, above
the slender line of her hips. She moved gracefully, her skirts
held up in her free hand to reveal tiny brown high-heeled
shoes with ribbon bows that matched the hat. Guy had given
Lilian free choice as to Sabrina's wardrobe for the season,
and she had indulged herself; and it would be worth it if, as
seemed probable, the child ended up a Countess.

Lilian turned to Valentine, who sat opposite her in a
matching chair. The room was tastefully furnished with the
few things that had been rescued at the time of the fire, and
those acquired since; the latter included a walnut console on
which stood a vase of roses freshly gathered from the
garden that morning by Valentine herself.

'How beautiful the roses are!' said Lilian. 'How fortunate
you are in having such a garden! It is the one thing I miss
from Vevey in Switzerland, the roses; London cannot match
them at all.'

Fenn was transported with pleasure at being able to feel the
touch of Sabrina's light hand on his arm. He led her down
the shaved grass paths Valentine had made, the turned beds
vivid with summer flowers and rosemary, which was being
trained to become a hedge; through the pergola which had
survived since his father's day, and up which twined not only
yellow roses but early-flowering clematis brought by Valentine from Marishnageen long ago. Sabrina showed great
delight and much knowledge of the flowers; he was pleased,
and advanced, a very little, the decision he had already made
to propose to her when the time should be ripe. What better
time than now?

'I should like,' he said carefully, 'to look after you all my
life. Would you permit it?' He dared not say her name. He
was in a morass of feeling which threatened to overcome his
habitual outward calm; within himself he was on fire. She

was silent for so long that he thought he had frightened her, and pressed the hand that lay on his arm. 'I would not hasten you into a decision,' he told her. 'You are young; enjoy your season, but perhaps you will think of me a little?'

She turned to him impulsively. 'I do not care for the season, although the flowers at the ball were delightful,' she said. 'I should very much like you to look after me. I am afraid of so many things, and you are strong and kind and would not hurt me.'

'I can promise that,' he told her, and raised her free hand and kissed it. The dowagers in the drawing-room were able to observe this happening, and were accordingly forewarned of what he would say when the pair came in, smiling and hand in hand, out of the summer sunshine.

'Will you not play to us, Sabrina?' said Lilian afterwards. 'You should let the man you are going to marry –' she smiled, briefly revealing upper dentures, at Fenn – 'hear your prowess on the piano. She is really quite a performer,' she told the company, who had been joined by a caller, Lord Iffley's cousin Jack Inchhope; he was not particularly welcome, but it would not do to let him feel it; so he sat stolidly by them while Valentine poured tea, and afterwards as Sabrina moved to the piano. She played, as Fenn could see, effortlessly; her touch was so light that it seemed the music would make away with itself on a breath of air. Her profile, which he watched with enchantment, was rapt in her task and without any of the appearance most young women had of coyness, self-advertisement or affectation. He knew little of music despite having often sat by his mother as she played by the hour; but he could listen to this creature for hours and days, or rather watch her, so soon to be his own; she was, he thought, a darling; he would soon release her from what must have been the slight beneficent thraldom of Guy and Lilian.

Sabrina had played Schumann. Now she changed to

chords of a strange inchoate music that even he could sense
was not what one was accustomed to hear in drawing-rooms.
Jack Inchhope stared with his prominent light-blue eyes; it
disturbed Fenn and he looked for a moment at his mother,
to perceive her speckled eyes thoughtful as they rested on
Sabrina's back. 'It was strange,' she said as Sabrina finished,
flushed, rose from the piano, smiled at Fenn and returned
to her place. 'It came to me in a dream,' said Sabrina.
'Sometimes I hear music, but I can never write it down. I do
not know where that came from.' She put a hand to her
throat, suddenly troubled. 'I – perhaps I should not have
played it here.'

'You shall play whatever you choose here,' said Fenn. In
the silence that followed, Valentine got up.

'I have not played for many years, but I think my son's
betrothal is an occasion when I should perhaps do so,' she
said. She sat down, moving stiffly, her grey head bent over
the keys; thought for a moment, then faultily at first, but
with increasing confidence as her memory returned, played
very beautifully the Schubert Sonata in G major, with its
wistful melodies and drumming rhythms, finishing at last
on a triumphal note; the scarred, stained hands lay for a
moment on the keys, then left them and dropped again to
Valentine's sides. The company applauded, except for
Sabrina. Fenn noticed that her eyes were full of tears. 'What
is it, my darling?' he asked tenderly. She turned towards
him. 'It is nothing,' she said, 'nothing; only the things I feel. I
am so glad your mother played to us.'

He drove to see them off at last on the train, standing to
wave at their disappearing carriage until nothing could be
seen but enveloping twilight. He was so filled with happiness
that he could not remember ever having known a similar
sensation in all his life. He made haste to write to Guy, who
would put the news of the engagement in the gazettes; and
that, thought Fenn, will put paid to anyone else who had
hoped to achieve Sabrina. He still could not believe his own

good fortune; a creature such as that, to give him charge of her!

As for Inchhope, he had gone home thoughtful. Pretty girl and all that, and Fenn seemed much taken; for himself, he'd prefer something a bit more down-to-earth. And all that music! But they had always lived their lives in their own way at Fenfallow.

There was, at least meantime, no reply from Sabrina's father to Fenn's letter, and he ceased to think of the matter in the midst of preparations for an early wedding.

The wedding itself was splendid but exclusive, very few guests having been invited and of the bride's relations, there were none from the mother's side; evidently, it was whispered, the proud Castilian family with whose daughter Chummy had long ago eloped had forgiven nothing. As for poor old Chummy himself, of course, everybody knew about him and nobody expected that he would be able to be present at the ceremony, let alone give his daughter away. This function was performed admirably by Sabrina's grandfather, looking, as the groomsman Geoffrey Ellison put it, as pleased as a plum as he escorted the lovely, slender bride, her bouquet of Madonna lilies and stephanotis, her dress a plain white satin, her head adorned with a wide circlet of orange blossom over the veil. The vows were said and the register signed; Sabrina came back on her bridegroom's arm smiling, and Fenn himself so pleased that his habitual reserve forsook him and he talked with nearly everyone at the reception. Perhaps he was pleased also with a letter he had received on the morning of his wedding. It had been from Sir Guy Sutbury, and stated that the latter was happy, as a wedding gift to Fenn and his granddaughter, to hand over his full share of the railway stock and the rights to the land so recently in dispute. The dividends would pay handsomely, and Sir Guy must be very pleased indeed to have parted with the object of dispute so readily.

The couple were seen off at last with the bride attired in a pepper-and-salt tweed suit with a flare in the long skirt which was seen to be much more becoming than the bustle, and would undoubtedly influence fashion for the coming autumn. Fenn looked as usual, correct and very proud. The Dowager Countess had been unable to attend because of illness, but everyone knew that as a strict Catholic it would not have done for her to be seen at St George's, Hanover Square. The reception continued accordingly, after the newly wedded couple had gone off, and champagne was drunk well into the night to the health and, under one's breath, the fertility of the new Countess of Fenn.

All that had been delicious; but on the wedding night Fenn found Sabrina nervous, and she sobbed when he touched her, explaining that she knew she was foolish, but she could not help it. He proceeded, therefore, with his intentions very gently, and the matter was accomplished, Henry assuming that his bride would grow accustomed, like any other properly reared young girl, to the state of marriage within a few days. But Sabrina never lost her distaste for the realities, and Henry learned that he could never, in this way, become fully one with his wife. But there were other delights; the very sight of Sabrina, always exquisite, slender and well groomed, for they had taken her maid Quint with them. 'Such a strange name,' mused Sabrina. 'Perhaps she is a descendant of Charles Quint?' and she gave her little delicate giggle. He found her responsive to his least mood; she appeared to have no desire, during the days, other than to make him happy with a word or a look, and no doubt this was as much as an ordinary man might expect; women after all were different. He was glad when they returned to Fenfallow, to find Valentine recovered and once again installed at the guest-house. She kissed Sabrina warmly and welcomed her

home, then left in the carriage after they had all eaten
dinner and drunk healths.

'Don't you think we could make a little water-garden here? It
would look pretty by the gate. We could have water-lilies and
taller plants at the edge. There is that little stream, which
could be diverted to make a small pond. I think perhaps it
would be too small for fish.'

He agreed, happy to encourage her enthusiasm for
everything at Fenfallow; the builders were already at work
on the last wing, which had been partly financed by Guy's
wedding gift. Fenn was pleased with life; he had his bride, he
had some money, the feud was forgotten and the lawyers
paid. He looked forward to seeing his children grow up in
the new, spacious Fenfallow, surrounded as it would be by
gracious gardens in the manner of a stately home. Sabrina
had suggested that they do a thing which was becoming
common among country landowners; they might have an
annual garden party, beginning next summer, the proceeds
of it to go to charity. Fenn, who had resigned his commission
in the Guards on his marriage, began accordingly to interest
himself in the state of the lawns, while Sabrina ordered the
gardeners as she wished during the winter and spring. He
left all such matters to her, knowing that her taste was good;
only he would not permit her to do any practical work,
digging or weeding. She must remain as she was, exquisite
and apart, and merely give orders; and, when she was not
otherwise occupied, play to him on his mother's pianoforte.
He was thankful that it had been saved from the fire.
Christmas passed, their first; then the garden in spring was
thick with daffodils, and he could sense their cloud of gold
as Sabrina played.

The day of the garden party, at last, was fine. The great
marquee had been erected on the main lawn; inside were
trestle tables covered with carefully ironed white damask

cloths. Plates and cake-trays in heaped tiers bore every
manner of iced cake, sandwich and biscuit baked not only in
Fenfallow kitchen but in the cottages, for every cottager by
now adored the young Countess, who took great and
personal interest in them, visiting them often. They stood
ready to usher and to serve, stout red-faced Mavericks most
of them, with a scattering of Harts and Ridleys; the latter,
for Molly herself had married a Ridley, were most of them
already married young or else still children themselves, but
they helped all the same. Molly herself, by now a grey-haired
matriarch in a jet bugle bonnet, renowned for her knowledge of how to bring other people's babies into the world
after ten of her own, supervised the making and pouring,
when everyone should be ready for it, of tea. Meantime
everyone talked to everyone else, high and low dressed up in
Sunday finery, for this was a day when everyone would be
seen and their appearance commented upon afterwards.
The county arrived a little late in its carriages, and the
cottagers knew every one by name and said so, conspirato-
rially and with heavy breathing; there were my Lord and my
Lady Iffley, getting on now, and their daughter the
Honourable Mrs Price-White and her children, little ladies
all, their fair hair combed long and straight. The few from
church who were to be met with every week wore the same
clothes as they always did; old Lady Fazakerley, who had the
third pew on the left as you went in, chattered to old Lady
Brunt, who had another, so that ordinary folk had to crowd
in at the back. It was said the pair had not a penny between
them to put into the collection, but they took respect as their
due, and received no less. Those who had arrived from
further away, having been delivered by train, sauntered
about the garden and admired the shrubs and flowers,
which were at their best, having been tended by her ladyship
and young Joe Ridley, a grandson of Molly's who could work
hard and had green fingers. Certain folk who went out and
in for natural necessity were stamped firmly on the back of

the hand by Nick Ridley, with a purple stamp; that way you didn't have to pay twice, but you couldn't get in without paying once, the entry being by the water-garden.

Later on there was a sensation; my lady's grandfather, Sir Guy Sutbury, and his wife had been driven up from Hertfordshire by motor car. Gasps were exchanged at sight of this new vehicle, which was the first Daimler many here had ever seen. The older among the crowd recollected that this was also the first time *he'd* seen Fenfallow since he was a young man, having left it then in dudgeon. It was a fine enough place now, no doubt, to make him wish that with all his money he could buy it, but that wouldn't happen. It was fair to say that Sir Guy looked pleasant with that smug face of his, and his lady was a fine-looking woman still, if a trifle stout and too well dressed; the removal of her motoring veil revealed a startling hat made of crimson velvet flowers, too loud for summer.

Everyone watched, covertly, the meeting between that couple and the young Countess and the Earl. It looked friendly enough, with kisses given and taken on both sides; then the couple gazed at Fenfallow and evidently answered tentative questions about what had happened to the old motor, which some remembered and preferred. Everything seemed serene: yet Fenn, looking across the trestled table at last over tea, surprised a look in his uncle's eyes that shocked him out of his late well-being; it held not only deep hatred and envy, but a kind of ironic patience. It vanished as soon as their eyes met; Fenn was to persuade himself afterwards that he had been mistaken. He looked instead at Sabrina, exquisite today in an apricot hat and gown, fulfilling her duties as hostess as if she were a much older and more experienced woman. He was proud of her. She already had a wide acquaintance among the county families, many of whom were here today for her sake; there had been invitations back and forth to luncheon or dinner with everyone since their return. Fenfallow in fact was full of

Sabrina's friends; he could not have been better pleased. If only –

He was roused from inattention by a touch on his arm. It was Iffley himself, left behind while his wife made towards Sabrina after tea; they walked together over the smooth green lawns, their skirts trailing. 'Grass well spiked with ladies' heels, eh?' remarked Iffley, his kindly, worldly-wise gaze resting on Henry's face. The young man had done well; this was a slap-up do; couldn't have done better themselves, and that was saying something, for Susan was a past mistress at this kind of thing. He made these sentiments known to Henry, then bent in closer confidence. 'Truth to tell, I've been wantin' a word for some time,' he confided. 'Matter of the Lieutenancy; I'm gettin' old, thinkin' of givin' it up. New generation and all that. You're a sound man, Fenn; would you think about takin' it on? Thought I'd ask; you will want to consult your mother and your lovely wife. Damned fine girl, Sabrina! Hope she and you don't mind Christian names; my wife took a great fancy to her when you were both over; must come to us again soon.'

Fenn was flattered at the idea of the Lieutenancy, which he had half expected; to himself he had already admitted that he would be a suitable candidate and would fulfil the duties ably. He made up his mind to accept later, formally, by letter. It was best to do all those things in correct fashion, though Iffley's sincerity was undoubted, and flattered him: this whole day was a triumph. It must have been a trick of the light about the expression in the other old gentleman's eyes, that time over tea. Nothing must disturb this day of Sabrina's; she had worked so hard to organise it, and had impressed Fenn with her ability for such things, which he had not more than half suspected and which pleased him greatly.

Old Joshua, like Valentine, had been too ill to attend the

fête. For some months now the old man had been bedrid-
den, after, of late years, sitting on fine days outside his
cottage, where he lived alone and had, until lately, kept
everything as spick and span as he had used to keep the
stables. Now a woman came daily to clean and cook. He had
always kept up with racing news, especially Miss Kate's
winners; it was a far cry from the day she'd spoilt Una the
mare's mouth. Instead of Miss Kate, nowadays, it was
Joshua's greatest delight of all when the young Countess
visited him, and would sit perched on the edge of his bed,
slender creature that she was, and listen to his stories. 'Tell
me the one about the turnpike-tolls again,' she would say,
and Joshua would live again through that long-ago drive
with Earl Felix and his four-in-hand, when they'd flung a
couple of guineas to the driver of an insolent motorcar, to
pay his toll-tax. 'The roads are so full of motor cars these
days that it would cost you a great deal of money now to
overtake them,' said Sabrina.

'They'll ruin the country. It was bad enough when they
had a red flag waved in front of 'em. Now nobody knows
when they're comin' or where they're goin'.'

She laughed; she must tell Henry that one. He had in fact
spoken about buying a motor. The thought made her
nervous. 'World'll be a mucky place soon,' said Joshua.
'There's nothing to beat a good shire-horse at the plough;
but they'll oust 'em at this rate, with their machines an' all,
and the fields go barren.' He turned on his side. 'You'll see it,
my lady, you'll see it; but I'll not be there, and maybe that's a
good thing.' Then he began to tell her again of his childhood
among the horse-copers when he was fed with gin to keep
him small, and her wide dark eyes would swim with pity; and
he would smile and say that after all it had made him Earl
Felix's tiger, and he might have been worse off. 'Do anything
for Earl Felix, I would,' he would say. 'He was a lad in his
day; but after he married he settled down, and there was less
larking.'

'Did you miss the larking, Joshua?'

'Nary a bit. I've been happy here at Fenfallow, doing this and that.'

'I must go,' she said, and laid her hand on his. 'I will come again tomorrow.'

But by tomorrow he was dead. He had gone in his sleep, painlessly. All of Fenfallow mourned him, even the cottage children who had been used to run in and out, and chat with him. It would be a well attended funeral.

It was held in church, and Fenn had decided to bury Joshua's body near that of his father, beside the vault. 'The old fellow would have liked that,' he said, and Sabrina nodded. 'He is still there, the tiger,' she murmured. When it was time for the funeral, however, he would not permit her to attend. 'I myself will go, but it is not for you, my dear.' He had a notion she would be upset; she was very emotional. He attended the funeral, saw the small coffin lowered into its grave, and one Sunday later on, when they had been to church, walked with Sabrina in the churchyard to discuss with her what kind of stone should be put up. 'A simple slab, saying he was a good and faithful servant,' she suggested, and Fenn agreed with her; when the stone was ready they saw it put in place. Fenn returned home still saddened. 'All the old links go,' he said. 'Soon there will be only ourselves.'

'There will be another,' she said softly.

He turned to her quickly. 'You mean –'

'Yes, my darling, there is to be a child. It was Quint who told me before I knew for myself. Now I am sure. I know you are pleased.'

He kissed her. 'We must hope for a boy,' he said, and glancing at her narrow hips thought already of the ordeal it would be to her to give birth. He must not allow any single thing to upset or alarm her; he must treat her almost as an invalid, although she herself laughed this away. 'I am well,' she said more than once. 'There is no need to worry about me as you always do.'

'I love you, and I want the world to be a safe place for you, as far as I can make it.'

'I love you too, but I think the world has got beyond both of us. Your mother is delighted; I wrote to her, as you know.' He did not like Sabrina going up to the guest-house among the Romans; when the two women met, it was at Fenfallow. Henry knew his mother would be pleased at the news; he himself was filled with delight and hope. It would be the greatest day of his life, he thought, when he held his son in his arms.

They say death comes in threes. A few weeks after the joyful tidings of Sabrina's expected child came the news that her father was dead. They saw it first in the gazettes and Fenn wrote at once to Guy and Lilian, enclosing a letter from Sabrina. She had wept a little.

'Poor Papa,' she said. 'He was always kind to me when I was a child. Afterwards I was never allowed to see him.' There was no resentment in her tone; she had been accustomed to being ordered, all her life.

Again, Fenn decided he would attend the funeral alone; it was not in any case proper for Sabrina, in her state, to go. He travelled by train on a dreary, wet day. Despite the rain there were more present than he had expected; many remembered Chummy in the old days, even though he had not been seen by anyone for a long time, except his warders. After the burial an unpretentious person came up to Fenn, who was standing a little way off from the body of mourners. The tall black hats and umbrellas shone bleakly in the light rain that still fell, bringing a smell of turned wet earth from Chummy's grave. 'This is for you, my lord,' said the man. Fenn raised his eyebrows.

'I do not know you; who are you?'

'Who I am's not important. He – Mr Gerard Sutbury –

said I was to give it to you when I could, and to no one else. It's private, my lord.'

He was gone, disappearing into the crowd. The package was indeed marked Private and Confidential. Henry put it in his waistcoat pocket with his watch, to read on the returning train; he would not stay for the collation.

Valentine had been reading, and was surprised to hear the new Austin motor Fenn had lately bought skid hurriedly on the gravel that now surrounded the convent and guest house on the hill. She rose to her feet, laid aside her pince-nez, and was in time to greet a white-faced Fenn at the door. 'What is it, my dear?' she asked in alarm. 'What has happened?' She thought it might be something to do with the funeral, perhaps with Guy: surely not Sabrina.

'Come inside where we can be private,' he said, and went with her back to the sitting-room. 'Nobody must know of this but yourself. Read it, and then give it back to me. Sabrina must never see it, never know of it. I am in two minds whether to destroy it, but it is the memorial of a dead man.'

She had taken the papers from him, and sat down, smoothing the sheets. Without her glasses the copperplate writing was blurred before her eyes, and she took a moment to put the spectacles on again. Then she began to read. Fenn was seated in a chair, his head in his hands.

This is the testament of me, Gerard Ryden Sutbury, being despite all that is said in my right mind at the moment of writing; my memory is clear. I shall give this to the friend who has seen to it that I had the materials and the privacy to write it, in my own time and in this place where my father has put me so that, as he thinks, I can do no further harm. I do not want to do harm; I want to make known the truth. The story has been put about that the mother of my daughter Sabrina was Spanish and that I had eloped with her against the wishes of her family. I may state that I have never been in Spain. But I have been in other places; and this chiefly concerns an expedition I made into

the northern Afar district south of the Yemen, when I was
twenty-two.

There are always odd characters to be met on any such expedition
and I soon fell in with one. He was a doctor, who was employed
further south in the pay of a mining company. I think that in his day
he had been rather better than that, but some indiscretion at home
had caused him to be taken off the list. As a result, he drank copiously
and could take a great deal more than I could, in those days. Possibly
he started my own habit of drinking heavily. He was a very tall
forceful man, red-headed with a great moustache that shone in the
sun like bronze. His name was Alexander. The tribes knew him as Al
Tabib Tawil, Him of the Bronze Moustache.

Al Tabib said to me that he was on leave, and wanted to explore the
same places as I did, and knew a little, including the dialect. We
arranged to travel together with my bearers, neither of us taking
much to carry; I was not on one of the pompous organised shoots for
big game, which I think are very cruel, although my opinions are not
popular in England. In any case the places where we were going had
little in such ways other than hyenas and oryx, and the occasional
desert lion.

The landscape grew very strange as we went further inland; not
only were there mountain ranges whose very shapes were fantastic,
but the earth itself had undergone volcanic changes; there were
great rocks in shapes which might have been made by a mad sculptor,
thrusting upwards to an unbelievable height in the sand, and there
were inland lakes of salt. Al Tabib Him told me what I already knew,
that the tribes of the region are very savage and independent and will
kill and castrate strangers. It occurred to me to wonder why Al
Tabib, knowing this, chose to come. He would always smile and
shake his head mysteriously when I questioned him, and not till one
day when he was struck down with malaria did he give me any
inkling as to his errand. The fever was so bad he thought he might
die, and indeed he did not live long after I left him, which he insisted
I do; but he gave me a package to deliver. I would be safe, he
promised, if I told whoever accosted me that I was the Bearer of the
Beads from Ashanti, and made a certain sign. In the intervals of his

delirium Al Tabib told me more, and as you may imagine I questioned him as much as I could in his state. To sum it up, the King of Ashanti was in possession of certain beads which were said to have been a part of the robe worn by Balkis, the Queen of Sheba, when she visited Solomon. These beads are so rare that legends have grown up round them. It is impossible to put a value on them; in appearance they are not striking, being small cylinders mostly of a yellowish green; occasionally a round gold one is found among them, and only a great chief can be in possession of these. There are other laws; they must be given, not lent, and to a son, never a daughter. The King of Ashanti had many sons but none he felt worthy of the beads, and the best of them had made a marriage that displeased him. It seemed to him necessary that he send the beads to his blood brother, Al Akh Fi Addam, of the Danakil tribe in the north, to give him in exchange for his daughter as a bride, and this errand was regarded as sacred. But the first messenger who had been sent was killed by an arrow, the second savaged by a leopard; Al Tabib had treated him with all the knowledge at his disposal, which was considerable, but the young man died. Before doing so he handed the beads to Al Tabib, requiring an oath from him that he would see the beads delivered into the hands of Al Akh Fi Addam. Now again, as if some curse rested on the bearer of the beads, Al Tabib was himself dying. I was young then, and it seemed to me to be a challenge to beat the fate that pursued the bead-bearers. I promised that I in my turn would take them to the chieftain of the Afar, as the Danakil tribes call themselves; they make other claims, saying that in their veins runs the blood of the ancient Pharaohs.

Despite my determination – it must be remembered I was young – ill fortune did strike us soon, and two of my bearers died, one after the other. I did not trouble to bury them because ants, hyenas and vultures would pick the bones clean. A few days later the third man came to me with rolling eyes to say that he too must go back; it was bad country, he said, with bad magic; they took a man's honour away. I told him to go to the devil and went on alone; nowadays I would realise how insane a course this was. I had only a few words of dialect, and no horse; much of my baggage I shed for its weight, and continued with no more than a native would take, except that the Beads of Balkis were safe in my cummerbund, where I felt the package daily. The nights were frozen and the days hot, and the sweat used to roll down into my eyes making me unable to see where I was going: I had dry rations with me, but it became difficult to find fresh water. I began to go mad with thirst, and do not remember where I wandered or how long it took; I could not direct anyone on that way again. Once I found a small group of missionaries, who gave me water and shelter. They said I was mad to go into the country of the Danakil, as they called them; one of their nuns had been taken long ago and never returned, and they had killed and castrated a priest whose body had been found in the sand. But I was stubborn, and would go. I set out refreshed, with directions and my own confidence, and struggled on for two days and nights until I saw an old dark-skinned man seated in the shelter of a rock. I made the sign Dr Alexander had given me, which is to cover the last two fingers with the thumb and project the rest. He answered by getting up and beckoning me to follow him. I called out that I was the Bearer of the Beads and to take me to his chieftain. This he did, and by the end I was confronted with this personage, who wore the robes of the ordinary desert nomad, but with a headband of hammered gold.

He opened the beads with great ceremony, showed his delight, and issued certain instructions to a second man who may have been a servant, but they are all proud. I was led to where an old woman was; she was so dried up and shrivelled that I could hardly believe it when she spoke to me in rusty English; she was the nun they had kidnapped, and had been forced to become a member of the chieftain's harem, though she had never borne any children. She told me that it had been stated that as I had brought the Beads I was to enjoy the second princess, Hadasseh, for seven days and nights and that the elder was to go with an escort to Ashanti as the King's bride, partly by water. Her name was Ambusah.

I have little time to write but will describe, as best I can, my princess. The Song of Songs says that the bride is black but comely and this is perhaps the best way to describe Hadasseh. Her features were not flat, but noble and delicate. She was slender and moved with an incomparable grace, her hair when she was unveiled fell to her waist, and her dark eyes had clear whites and held a gentle fire. I could have sworn she loved me; I did not count the days and nights, or that on the seventh night Hadasseh gave me a drink of the local wine which is very fierce, and made of mares' milk; there must also have been a drug in it. I remember her lips fiercely laid on mine in farewell and that is all. I awoke to solitude, with nobody and nothing near, only the sand; and I knew that a certain outrage had been performed on me. They had stitched the wounds carefully with what I later learned to be sheep's gut. I wandered, fevered, for how long I cannot remember, and was fortunate to have been rescued by the missionaries, who told me that my life had been spared me as an honour, but my manhood had been taken in exchange for the seed I had left in my bride. Altogether I was considered fortunate to be alive, and I was ill for many weeks, when they nursed me carefully. I did not know what was to become of me and it turned out that for the best part of a year I stayed with them, having informed my family at home that I was safe. I told them at the mission about having found the nun, and they said that they would continue to pray for her. Her name in the harem was Rohani. I mention it because I am certain she had a hand in what happened thereafter.

One very early morning a baby girl was found at the entrance to the mission hut. She was carefully wrapped and on her tiny arm was a paper, fastened with sheep's gut, depicting the cylinders of the beads. Her skin was almost white and I knew, from the shape of her ears and hands as well as from the message, that she was my daughter. I resolved to bring her home with me and to devote my life to her welfare.

You will understand that it was not easy to tell my father what had happened to me, and why I could never marry. At first he seemed inconsolable, but soon he began to take an interest in the little Sabrina. By degrees he took her away from me totally, for a purpose which I knew from the first, even in my then state, was evil, for I knew my father. I remembered his feud with his brother Felix, Earl of Fenn, and of how he nourished a desire for revenge on the latter's heirs. By the time I heard of Sabrina's betrothal I was under restraint and could send word to nobody. It is only now, when I know that I shall not live long, that my good friend here, the male nurse, has promised to take this memorandum to my son-in-law for me. I can only think that it is best for him to know the truth and to understand certain things that may happen, or perhaps they may not. In any case one must always tell the truth.

Valentine put down the paper. 'Oh, my dear,' she said, 'my dear son. Poor Sabrina.'

'Sabrina must never be told,' said Fenn. 'She must never know any of this. If the child is born –'

'If anything is wrong, send it here to me. I will undertake to find a home for it where no one will know who it is ... ah, Henry, your child!'

'It may be a daughter, but even so there must be no more. The risk is too great. That devil meant me to endure this. He meant it from the beginning.'

'Poor Sabrina,' said Valentine again. Shortly Fenn left, and she listened to the wheels of the new car turning on the gravel. She had not the heart to wave him farewell.

The third death was Lilian's. For some years now, when in town, she had been in the habit of patronising a well-known but exclusive tea-room where an orchestra on a raised central dais played light music, surrounded on a lower level by the tables of the élite. Lilian had a brand of China tea she especially liked and always ordered. Sometimes acquaintances were to be met with there to whom one might talk agreeably, but of late years, with many of one's friends wintering in the South of France, they had seemed fewer. This particular day there was nobody she knew and the black-gowned waitresses in their dainty broderie anglaise caps and aprons moved about tactfully, carrying trays with pots of tea, coffee or, sometimes, as the new fancy had grown, Russian tea in a tall glass with a holder and lemon slices. The stout, fashionably dressed old lady they all knew by sight always ordered China tea, and insisted that the silver pot be left for at least five minutes before pouring, to allow the beverage to infuse. She had sat for so long on this occasion that a new young waitress, anxious to shine, paused to ask if madam would like a fresh pot of tea. When there was no answer the girl leaned forward to ascertain whether or not the customer might be deaf; and meeting the glazed eyes under the fashionable hat, screamed and dropped her tray. The music was made to stop; the manageress hurried from her place, soothed the other customers, repaired the damage to the carpet, reproved the erring waitress quietly, and, still more quietly, caused a linen tablecloth to be placed discreetly over the corpse until everyone had left, when the police came, and a doctor. Lady Sutbury was known by name to some of the staff who had been there for many years, and there was no delay in informing her husband, who was at his club. Thereafter things proceeded in the proper way, and the incident was soon forgotten; by the next afternoon customers having heard of the incident and dismissed it, were back again, and the band was playing selections from *The Bohemian Girl* and the elder Strauss.

'Will you add a little note to my letter to poor Grandpapa? I have left a space.'

Fenn replied in his curt way that he would send a card with formal condolences. Sabrina was still young enough to attempt to improve the situation.

'Just a word or two,' she pleaded. 'It will seem so heartless only to send a card; you are after all his nephew and his grandson-in-law.'

'No!' The word came out like a pistol-shot; Sabrina jumped in her chair and the pen flew out of her hand, blotting the letter. 'Dearest, I am sorry if –' she began, but Fenn was already in control of himself and again correct, even affectionate, in manner. As Sabrina obediently signed the letter she thought how kind Henry was to her now that she was expecting a baby; he had even moved to a separate room at nights in order not to disturb her sleep. And if he had been a little sharp just now, that must be because he was very busy with the new Lord Lieutenancy, whose gorgeous uniform and scarlet braided hat lay in the livery-cupboard upstairs. It was possible that one of his duties would soon include the official welcome to the Prince and Princess of Wales and their family, who were coming to the district on a short visit. Altogether it had been stupid and tactless of her to insist about the note; she resolved to do better in future for so kind a husband. As for the baby, she was pleased, of course; at times it seemed to her that Henry was too apprehensive for her sake; it was true, women did die in childbirth and it was best not to think of such things, and be glad that that side of marriage, which she had never liked, was over for the time. Sabrina did not know that it was over for ever and that henceforth Fenn and she would live as brother and sister. It might not have disturbed her if in fact she had known. There were so many other things that were delightful, and plenty of friends; Sabrina liked to think that she had made it easier, a little, for Fenn to enjoy the society of other people, different people from the closed circle he had always been accustomed to meeting. He was such a formal person that it had been difficult for him to form wider acquaintances of his own.

at Fenfallow,
28th December 1886

Kate dear,

I have been remiss in writing in time for Christmas, but it has been so cold. The convent is quiet because the school pupils have all gone home for the holidays, and I miss their coming and going and their shouts at hockey, down in the field. They look so neat and pretty in their straw boaters with blue ribbons, white blouses and black skirts.

However there is something I particularly want to write to you and I do ask that it may be told to nobody else meantime, not even

Ned. *I may be looking for a home for a poor little baby soon who has none, and nobody must know where it has gone for reasons which I can tell you when I see you, if you will promise to reveal them to no one. It is perhaps a greater tragedy even than my poor Clonmagh whom you will remember. I greatly hope that you would take this little creature and its nurse at Marishnageen for a few weeks or months till it is weaned, after which I shall have been able to make further arrangements for its upbringing and education.*

If this is agreeable to you, I could arrive with old Molly Maverick, whom you remember, and the poor child and its nurse, some time after the middle of January, or perhaps earlier.

I hope that you and Neddy and the horses are well.

With every kind thought.

Your loving stepmother (what a hard word that sounds! but I hope I was never cruel to you).

Valentine Fenn

Marishnageen, 4th January

Dear Valentine,

Forgive the delay in replying to your letter but we have been having some trouble with the foals, the damp I think has got into their bones too early, and it never stops raining.

I was surprised by the news in your letter. Has Henry gone off the rails? I did not think it of him, he sounded so devoted to Sabrina.

The plain fact is that I will not have Molly Maverick in my house. She was cruel to me when I was a child and I have never forgotten it, and I will not see her. You yourself can certainly come and stay as you know Marishnageen well enough.

I will expect you, as they say, when I see you. Give my regards to Henry if he is to be allowed the knowledge that you have been in correspondence with me. If this is a bastard of his, I should have a fellow-feeling.

Your devoted stepdaughter, is it?

Kate Maverick

*

The cold had persisted, and on the day Sabrina went into labour thin flakes of snow had begun to fall at last, thicker by nightfall, till the land was covered in the dark.

Valentine had come down to Fenfallow from the convent. Nobody knew, not even Fenn, the trouble she had taken to ensure that if this child was not welcome, it must disappear. 'Say that it is dead,' Fenn had himself stated. 'Tell Sabrina at once, after the birth.' So there had had to be tentative arrangements made to hand the child quickly from Molly, as midwife, to her granddaughter who had been named after her, and seemed practical and must be let into the secret; make no noise, show no surprise at anything, cleanse the child and take it quietly out of the room. After that it must go, wrapped warmly, to the old Countess's motor, which would be waiting; and yet a third Maverick was to be in the secret, for Peg, another granddaughter, had had a baby lately, and enough milk to nurse two. Peg and her baby and my lady would go off, and after that it was for my lady to tell Peg what to do; they would take shawls and spare gear for the journey.

So everyone waited; and in the firelit room Sabrina bit her lips with pain. The doctor had come and gone, saying he would return later. She did not want to cry out meantime and make trouble for everyone; Henry would be anxious, listening for any sound there might be; her mother-in-law was near, and this comforted Sabrina more than anything; she had loved Valentine from the beginning, not only for their shared devotion to music. Sabrina tried to think of her baby and how proud she would be to show it to Henry and to Valentine, then everyone. She hoped it would not be a daughter; she knew Fenn was anxious for a son.

The labour progressed. In the end Sabrina had to cry out; not once but again and again, as the birth-rhythms tore at her. The doctor had not come back, but Molly Maverick was there, with her broad red arms scrubbed to the elbow, her sleeves rolled back to be out of the way, and a kettle steaming on the fire. It seemed strange to have a kettle in a bedroom; Sabrina, who knew nothing that was not conventional, had no notion either of how a birth took place; all she knew was pain, and something fighting its way out of her. In the end Molly helped, in a strange way; she pressed down against the child's head, as though wanting it to come out more slowly; why was that?

'Lie still, my lady; lie still; let it come.' And the head came, and after that Molly interposed her broad backside between child and mother, so that Sabrina saw nothing; and brought out the child and twisted it away.

'You see to my lady, Moll.' The child was taken from her; she had not had leisure to see it, did not know if it were a girl or a boy. She began to cry, plaintively; they were doing things to her body which were an indignity, but no doubt necessary; she put up with it uncomplainingly, but cried for her child. Suddenly, after she had been made clean and the sheets changed, Henry was with her, taking her hand. His manner and voice were very gentle, though his own hand trembled; how concerned he must have been for her!

'You must be very brave, my darling,' he told her. 'It was a boy, and is dead. There must never be another.'

Sabrina found leisure to wonder through her tears; after all that suffering, a dead boy! He had felt so lively while he was inside her. And she was certain she had heard him cry. But she was glad, so glad, if there need never be another; she could not endure the thought of more pain.

Fenn himself had had a word with the doctor, who was asked not to return now the Countess was out of danger; the sight of him might alarm her, and she was in good hands with Molly. Later, Fenn and Valentine looked down at the baby, cleansed and wrapped warmly by the two Maverick women, its dusky starfish of a hand waving weakly, its eyes not yet open. When they opened, they would be shining treacle-dark, with clear whites as they are seen in portraits of the

Pharaohs. The wizened little creature looked in fact like an Egyptian mummy of a child; it skin, still wrinkled from the birth, was a dull, leaden black.

Fenn informed interested parties, and also put the information in the newspapers, that the child had been a son, but still-born.

After the birth Sabrina's convalescence was to be slow; she would have fits of weeping and melancholy, later walking much alone about the house and grounds. Fenn was troubled about her; he began to spend as much time with her as he could, but the duties of the Lieutenancy were particularly demanding owing to the coming visit of the Prince and Princess of Wales to Uffield. He tried to rouse Sabrina for the visit; she must make a special effort to appear as lovely as Princess Alexandra 'because you are so.' But nothing would cheer her for long; he tried desperately to think of ways to take her mind off the birth and death, as she believed, of her baby.

Meantime, Molly Maverick was worried about the whole thing. The old Countess had said to her that she was to go with her and Peg and the baby, then had said she needn't come, but not the reason why. Molly knew Peg well enough; Peg wasn't married, had had the baby as a result of high jinks with the men after the spring ploughing, and had no sense worth speaking of; if my lady had one of her heart attacks, Peg wouldn't know what to do. Still, you couldn't tell great folk whom they ought and ought not to take, and she'd stayed where she was, and said to them all as arranged that my lady had found a good situation for Peg, some way off; which would have been a fortunate thing, as not every mistress would take on a new maid with a baby. The little thing was lively and lusty too, the way bastards generally somehow were; as for the other, and the poor young lady upstairs, well – she must do as the old Countess had told her and say nothing of that, and keep silent she would, although if that bitch Miss Kate had anything to do with it all, which Molly suspected, the secret might not remain one long.

As it happened, the secret was already known, in its way: old George William Maverick, coming home drunk as was his custom, had crossed the yard at Fenfallow as the Countess and Peg were getting into the motor, which was being driven by that silent Alf from the convent who did for them up there, cutting the grass and the like. Peg Maverick had been there, and in her arms was one white baby and one black, and whether anyone believed him or not, it was true and he'd seen it with his own eyes.

'George William, if you say a word more,' Molly told him, 'I'll tell my lord about them apples you made off with, last year at harvest, and sold them in the market and spent the money on drink, and that wasn't the first time. And it's drink that's making you talk the way you're doing this night, and one day they'll put you away for a drunken old fool, that chatters nonsense like a babby.'

But whether George William took her advice or not, the thing got out somehow; and with the whispering and the secrecy changed its nature, to end up as a myth that Saul Fingerhut long ago had killed his wife because she gave birth to a black baby, and her ghost still haunted the convent, where the house had been.

'He's a lively one, my lady. He's pulling away already, sooner than my own did; *he* slept for almost a day.'

'Wrap him up warmly. It is still very cold.'

The car had taken them to the port, and rather than endure the cold while waiting to cross Valentine had booked places at the packet inn, where they sat by the fire and ate hot supper sent up to their room. The two babies slept quietly. Valentine did not look at her grandson; she must not let herself have affection for him: very soon she would know no more of him than that he was being well cared for.

On their way she had caused the car to stop beside a tall grey house; the snow had stopped, but her footsteps made marks in the thin white carpet as she had walked to the door with the baby in her arms, inside her fur coat for warmth. The door was opened by the servant she knew.

'Lady Fenn! What a night it is! What brings you and –' He could only see the wrapped bundle, its head hidden.

'I should like to see Father Smythe; I hope he has not gone to bed yet.'

The man did not know, but would enquire. Presently she was shown up. The blind man was still dressed in his black velvet jacket and black trousers and slippers, staring sideways at the floor; but he knew her name.

'Lady Fenn. I remember you very well. May God bless you.' She had the notion that he said this to everyone, being filled with a vague benevolence that was perhaps all that was left to him in the way of feeling. But he was still a priest.

'Father, will you baptise this baby? He is going on a journey, and I want it done before we set out; nobody knows what will happen.' Peg's baby had already been christened at home.

'Have you godparents?' he asked, with one of his flashes of remembrance. He had stood up from his chair, and now felt about for the vestments which had used to hang by the door. Valentine thought quickly. Kate would do, and herself for the other. She named both, one unavoidably absent. She promised that the child would be brought up as a Christian. 'I think,' she said, 'that he will have as good a chance as any.' The tears were pouring down her face as the blind priest made ready to baptise the black child she might never see again. 'It is near enough the feast day of St Raymond,' she said. 'That will do for the name.'

Father Smythe made the sign of the cross on the baby's head with a little of the water which he always kept by him in a jug. 'Raymond, I baptise thee in the name of the Father, and the Son, and the Holy Ghost.' The sightless eyes dwelt

184 The Sutburys

on the black head, its hair dried out to ebony fluff.
Afterwards they went out again into the night, leaving the
blind man alone.

That was what Valentine had to remember, seated now by
the inn fire. She was beginning to feel tired and very old; but
the thing was almost done.

They caught the packet next morning; Alf, who was
usefully taciturn, had gone back on the previous night with
the car. The sky today still held snow, and the flakes began to
fall and mingle with the green water of the Irish Channel.
They watched from the window of the cabin at last till land
came in sight through the snow; there were few aboard in
this weather. Once landed, Valentine hired a closed carriage
to drive them on to Kate's; the wet trickled in at the joints in
the tarpaulin roof, and Peg cried out with it as she
comforted the babies. Her own had begun to burble sounds
which meant nothing, but Raymond lay quiet; he was a good
baby. Valentine wondered how they all fared at home, and
how Sabrina had taken the news that her child was dead.
She, Valentine, would have liked to be at Fenfallow to be
with her for a little while, but had had to leave word that she
was summoned urgently to help a sick friend. In its way it
was true.

Kate had scarcely changed except to grow fuller in the
bosom. She sat in the drawing-room in a shabby old
riding-habit, a glass of whiskey by her, her hair, without a
shred of grey, piled on top of her head.

'So it is yourself, Valentine. I would hardly have known
you. What is it you have there?'

'May I sit down?' said Valentine formally. The tears had
almost come again at sight of old Marishnageen, badly kept
with the yard full of muck, and grazing horses were the
garden had been; and Ned, who had seen to the carriage
himself, with his fair hair still thick, had had bloodshot eyes
and a high colour, as though he were drinking too much. So

was Kate, evidently; her voice sounded faintly insolent, and for the first time Valentine admitted that she herself was disliked, and always had been. It made it doubly difficult to ask a favour of this woman; but it must be done, till the child was weaned. She sat down and revealed Raymond, while Kate let out a low whistle.

'Is it Henry's, by God? Has he been consorting with a female blackamoor?' Suddenly Kate began to laugh, loud heartless laughter; she rose and filled a glass for Valentine, who took a sip because of the cold; it was good to taste Irish whiskey again, though she had grown used to the other, when she had it at all. She answered Kate with a clear look and voice.

'Henry has done nothing he should not. There is no cause to laugh in such a way. It is a tragic happening which must be kept absolutely secret. I trusted you, Kate; maybe I was wrong, but if you will not take him in until he can go to the monks at Inshmara, who will educate him, I do not know where to go.'

'Inshmara is a solitary place. Poor little devil. I will take him for the time, but I cannot be seen about with him or everyone will say he is mine. You have no idea the things they say of me here.'

I can well believe it, thought Valentine. She replied quietly: 'If you will give Peg, his nurse, and her baby an attic room where they may be private with him, and will send up food, there will be no call to do more until Raymond is ready to go. But I agree that as few should see him as possible. It is sad. I have done what I could. I will pay for his keep and expenses.' She began to take out her purse. Kate's eyes narrowed.

'Give me the Clonmagh brooch you wear which should never have left Marishnageen, and I will do the rest.'

Valentine put up a hand to the brooch, its familiar speckled surface comforting her fingers. It should have gone to Sabrina; she had never thought of it. Perhaps –

She unpinned the brooch. The baby caught a gleam of light from the scrolled silver edge and reached out his hand, his newly open dark eyes shining. Kate came over and took the brooch, and pinned it on her untidy bosom.

'I'll not give it to the pawnbroker,' she said. 'Let me get you another drink. It's time Neddy was in.'

But Valentine declined; already she felt warmth return to her cold hands and feet; she knew she could fight on, hopefully, till she was back at Fenfallow. The longing for it which assailed her had not been with her, she was certain, since Felix's death.

'It is time for Peg to feed the two,' she said. 'Will you show them their room?'

Sabrina was having a nightmare. She knew that it was not one of the ordinary dreams that came, in which she would hear music and be able to play it on the following day. There was certainly music here, but it was bad and terrible, something she had never experienced. There was the sound of galloping hooves, strange cries, and the noise of gongs. She did not want to remember it and knew she would never forget it. She did not know either that she had cried out in the darkness, so that soon there was a light, and Henry came to comfort her. By then Sabrina was weeping, the dream unforgotten. She felt Fenn's arms about her, and heard his familiar voice, calling her name.

'Such terrible things – such things – I cannot tell anyone –'

'Forget it, my darling. It was a bad dream. We all have them. Would you like me to send Molly with hot milk? Would that make you sleep? It is quite early, two in the morning; sleep now, and have breakfast in bed tomorrow.' He stroked her hair, as though she had been a child; his child.

'I will try to sleep,' she said. 'Stay with me for a little while. Hold my hand.'

So he stayed with her, while the night passed and the

dawn came, and did not touch her except to hold her thin hand as she had asked. With his presence she seemed to sleep more calmly. He felt an infinite sadness as he gazed down at her, seeing her face more clearly as dawn broke. There were shadows under her eyes and she had lost weight after the birth; the fines bones of her face showed under her skin. He must not lose Sabrina; would not, could not! There would be nothing left in life for him without her. When she was awake and fully well, he must try to get her to interest herself in the things they could still do together; visiting and entertaining friends; the annual garden party, the garden itself; sometimes going abroad for a holiday; the affairs of church, where Sabrina liked to go with him; such things. He must always treat her as if she were as delicate as porcelain. He would give her the happiest life possible for them now. His lips set; he had an appointment, in a few days' time, to meet her grandfather, to whom he would have certain things to say.

'I trust you received my condolences on the loss of your son, and that they were perhaps less formal than those you sent for the earlier loss of mine, and also that of my wife.'

Fenn had not sat down; he stood squarely before the hunched white-haired figure that was now Guy. 'I have to say that I wish to have no further communication with you of any kind,' he said evenly. 'I have come to say so in person because I do not want anything left in writing which might injure Sabrina. Your constant enmity to my father and his heirs has involved you in acts of consummate cruelty even to your own descendants. Now that I have said this I will go, without further discussion, except that I have arranged to return to you the stock you made over to me as a wedding gift for a marriage which should never have taken place without informing me of the truth.'

The faded blue eyes mocked him. 'Has Sabrina wearied you so soon?' Guy said. Fenn felt the blood mount to his own face. 'None of it is Sabrina's fault,' he replied. 'It was a deliberate plot by you yourself to ensure that my heir would be – would be impossible to keep with me, impossible to show to the world.'

'I am not aware of your source of information.'

'The source, as you put it, was your own son, and I was at least forewarned of what might happen at the birth of mine.'

'So it was not a stillbirth,' reflected Guy aloud. He began to laugh, in something the same way Kate had done, far off and in another country. Suddenly, in full control of himself, he stopped laughing and spoke clearly, the gleam of enjoyment still in his eyes.

'What colour was the fifth Viscount Harmhill? Coffee colour, eh? Or black?'

Fenn strode forward. His anger had risen to so murderous a pitch that he could have laid hands on the old man, with what consequences he dared not think, later. Incredulously he watched Guy's laughter turn to a grimace, the frail body topple, till it lay on its side on the floor, Guy gasping like a pallid fish on a grass bank.

It had been a seizure; the apposite nature of the moment ceased to concern Fenn. He knelt by the prone figure, whose left hand was twitching: a sound like that of a boiling kettle came from the contorted mouth. Fenn loosened his collar and tie and laid his head more comfortably. Then he rose to his feet, turned, went out of the room and called to a footman.

'Your master has taken an apoplexy, I believe,' he said coldly. 'It would be best to call a doctor. If I am required I shall be at my club.'

He took his hat and cane and went out. The streets were sunny. Fenn no longer felt anything but the remembered echo of anger. He told them at the club that he would be in for luncheon. He knew that he must not leave town until his testimony had been given about his uncle's stroke. He sat down meantime and wrote to Sabrina, breaking the news to her about her grandfather. It would be hard on her, poor girl; but she must be prevented from visiting Guy, who was more than capable of telling the truth on his deathbed, if speech returned to him.

The Prince and Princess of Wales came in due course, and lunched at Fenfallow. Sabrina had exhausted herself to make the occasion a success; it was the garden party over again, with the grounds impeccable, the notables at the table, the humble folk staring round about the door. The Prince exuded good humour, lavender water and cigar smoke; his guttural voice enlivened the talk so that soon there was laughter except from the Princess, who could not hear anything. But she was so lovely it was a pleasure to look at her, with her close-fitting lavender dress embroidered on the bodice with beads, her hands exquisite, and her face smooth of lines despite her age. Sabrina had seemed almost her old self, but suddenly the Princess said, in her very slightly accented English:

'I was so sorry to hear about your poor little baby. I too lost a son, called Alexander. I have never ceased to mourn him. I hope and trust that you will have other children soon.'

I cannot, thought Sabrina; I am as little use to Fenn as anyone could be; and my child had not even a name. Her talk became forced after luncheon was over, and when the royal couple had been seen off at last on the train she returned home to Fenfallow, flung herself down on a sofa and wept. Presently Fenn came to her, took her in his arms and kissed her.

'You did very well,' he said. 'It could not have gone better. A.E. was pleased.'

'But now – but now – there is nothing I can do – I am of no use to anyone – you, you should marry again, I would be better dead.'

He made himself smile. 'Supposing I were to teach you to drive the Austin.'

She stopped crying and her mouth formed the shape of an O. 'I could never do so! Never, never, never!'

'Why not? Women are already learning.'

He had his own way, as usual; and began to teach her. She proved, in spite of her denials, apt; and by degrees came to enjoy the lessons. After two months it was possible for her, without danger, to drive past the cottages onto the open roads, or even up to Knocking Hill, though Fenn still did not encourage this.

In fact the young Countess, over the years and despite her childlessness, continued to enjoy the success she had first known when she walked, a new bride, on the Earl's arm into the parish church. The invitations with which she had been besieged then did not lessen over the years. In addition, when it became possible, Sabrina undertook much public work which was of great help to her husband. During the Boer War she was president of the newly founded local branch of the Red Cross; the Victoria League, lately spread to the shire, had her support and she was on its committee from the first; there was a country-dancing class at which Sabrina and her friends among the women – no gentlemen were invited – displayed unexpected *élan*; there was the cottage hospital and almshouse, both of which she visited regularly; and there was the circulating library, which Sabrina had helped to found and for which she discovered an efficient librarian. She steadfastly refused, although her talent was known, to play the piano in public; music no one ever heard except Henry still came to her in dreams. But she knew of soloists and small orchestras to invite and the hall of Fenfallow was used, until a public hall was built, for subscription concerts. Between times Sabrina gardened, drove, and read whenever she had the leisure. She preferred French memoirs; St-Simon, Madame Campan, Ida St-Elme. Reading and other matters were always discussed fully with her husband; Fenn was always interested in what she was doing. He himself had had to make a discreet arrangement with a good woman who was the widow of a baker in the village; she had imbibed enough of her late husband's craft always to have fresh hot buttered scones and tea for him when he called, as well as the other necessities. Fenn saw to it that no talk of the situation ever reached Sabrina. There was in fact no one with whom she was on sufficiently intimate terms to discuss such things, except himself. It was a need arising from the conditions of his marriage.

Sir Guy Sutbury continued many years an invalid hulk, looked after by nurses. He outlived Countess Valentine, who died quietly at last in the convent guest-house, on her sofa. There was nobody with her but a lay sister, who had come in with a tray bearing tea, toast and a lightly boiled egg; the Countess had not been eating well lately. But when she saw the state of the grey-faced visitor Sister Josephine set down the tray, crossed herself, rang for the resident priest and stayed nearby while the Last Rites were administered. The Earl was sent for then, but was elsewhere.

Instead, the young Countess came, driving her own car. She was shown quietly into the room and heard the stertorous breathing of the dying woman. Quite suddenly it stopped and Valentine said, in a clear voice.

'Sabrina. Raymond. Inshmara.'

Then she died. It was known that her memory had been failing for some time.

'Who is Raymond, and where is Inshmara?'

Fenn turned away for a moment, took the brass-handled poker from among the tidily arranged andirons, and stirred the logs in the fire. Then he replaced the poker and turned towards the room, walking across to his desk. He answered slowly, as if it were unimportant.

'My mother's mind was affected for a long time. There is no need to attach importance to anything she said.'

'But the words were clear. And she was dying. I think that she meant me to know.'

'Well, perhaps the answer will come in a dream,' said Fenn tactlessly. Sabrina's eyes widened and she was silent with shock; he did not often mock her. What was he hiding from her? Who was Raymond? Inshmara sounded as if it might be in Ireland. She could write and ask Kate. They had corresponded over the years as a family, as a rule at Christmas. Sabrina herself had never visited Marishnageen. She spoke aloud, as her thoughts came.

'I think that I should like to pay a visit to Kate,' she said. Fenn turned on her, his eyes cold.

'You will pay no visits meantime. We are in mourning for my mother.'

'Of course, my dear.' She went to him and kissed him gently on the cheek. She must not hurt and annoy Henry. He was always kind to her, and the icy remark just now meant that she must have upset him. She would be more careful in future.

But a chance meeting, after the old Countess's private funeral and burial in the family vault, encouraged Sabrina in her search, or rather shocked her into it. Among the persons present at the funeral, though not by invitation, was the lay schoolmistress from the convent at Knocking Hill, employed there since Miss Oakbury died. She – her name was Helen Adderley and she had an impressive degree from one of the new colleges for women – would often enough exchange the time of day with Valentine as the latter used to come and go from the chapel, especially on Thursdays when there was Benediction, and the girl pupils were present. Once or twice she had even been invited to take tea with the old Countess in her room. It was therefore suitable for her to be here in her quiet clothes, though perhaps regrettable that she had arrived on a bicycle as she had no car. Afterwards Sabrina spoke of her to Henry.

'It was thoughtful of her to come. Your mother liked her; she spoke to me of her once and said how clever and amusing she was. She teaches the girls any number of things, botany and chemistry and English grammar. I wondered if we might ask her to tea.'

'You could certainly invite her, as long as it is not made into a great occasion; these persons can become too familiar.' One would not, for instance, have agreed to the schoolteacher's coming to luncheon. He smiled at Sabrina, glad that her spirits were lifting again after his mother's death. Certainly they themselves were still in mourning, but a quiet tea-party was not objectionable, especially as this woman seemed to cheer Sabrina. He would, he thought, be glad of any distraction his wife might find to remove the terrible memory of the words she had heard from Valentine when the latter was dying. They must be put, somehow, right out of Sabrina's mind.

So Helen Adderley came to tea. She was perhaps in her early forties, a thin, tweedy and genteel person, but could speak up for herslf with bright chatter if required; she was a little overcome on the first occasion; tea with young Lady Fenn, and a real Earl! Fenn listened in calm silence to the chatter; afterwards, Sabrina confessed herself enchanted. 'So amusing, and so clever! You heard her say that the nuns asked her to teach drawing and botany and games as well as English, for which they first employed her. They were doubtful at first as she is not a Catholic, any more than poor Gertrude Oakbury was.'

'I question if they will have raised her salary,' said Fenn drily.

Sabrina began, mostly in Fenn's absence, to see a good deal of Helen Adderley. Often after school was over, or at a weekend, the two women would drive off together, in the Countess's car, for Sabrina had fallen heir to the great brass-lamped Bentley Valentine had latterly owned and which had been driven for her by the silent chauffeur Alf; but now Alf was retired and Sabrina in any case preferred nowadays to drive for herself. It was a sign, perhaps, of the increasing right she felt to become an individual on her own account; though she would never openly oppose Henry. He knew about the drives; they were seldom long, and at the end of them Sabrina and the schoolmistress would get out and explore whichever part of the country they had reached; Helen to look for wild flowers for the pupils, Sabrina to search for historical landmarks. She had been reading a book of archaeology lately and was afire to find barrows, burial urns, perhaps even Saxon coins or jewellery. She acquired a little hammer to bring back samples of stone, and was delighted one day to find a flint arrow-head, chipped with all the care of a Stone Age craftsman. 'How beautifully it is pointed! Look at the symmetry!' This, also, went to be shown to the girls and to be kept on a shelf that was gradually becoming a showcase for improving objects, though the convent frowned on too much accumulated dust or on bones.

They would often come back to Fenfallow for tea, and although Fenn generally made it his business not to be present – he felt self-conscious in too much feminine company – he was present on the occasion when the talk suddenly ran to ghosts. Miss Adderley chattered on. 'The girls tell me – they talk to me a great deal, and would you believe that they are not allowed to read the newspapers, but are permitted cards on Sundays? – they tell me one of them fancies she saw the ghost, and that it was carrying a little black baby. I told her it was imagination and not to be stupid, and she admitted that she had made it up to frighten the rest. But why black? They are not in fact sure whether the baby was there, or at Fenfallow. But the story is the same in both places; a young mother, looking for it. I wonder what can have given rise to such a tale? There was a man named Fingerhut, a kind of preacher, who lived –'

She fell silent; even to her somewhat blunted perceptions it had become clear that both Earl and Countess were pale and silent, and evidently did not welcome the subject. After she had gone Sabrina looked at her husband with sincere eyes, and said nothing. He turned and went towards the library in silence, but when he had reached the door he turned.

'Do not invite that woman here again. I dislike her.'

Sabrina's eyes had closed and tears pressed heavily behind the lids; she sat among the remains of the tea-things, and did not answer. But as soon as Fenn had gone she went out of the house and across to old Molly Maverick.

The old woman was scrubbing her dresser, an affair of deal with small drawers which were every single one her delight; her son Hugh had bought it at a sale for half a crown, and it held many things which would otherwise have cluttered the cottage needlessly. When she saw the Countess at the door Molly stopped, hid her pail behind the dresser's corner, wiped her hand on her apron and hurried forward. My lady looked pale, she was thinking; what had happened? Since the old Countess had gone life had been very quiet at Fenfallow. Everyone had gone to the funeral service in the parish church, but she –

'Molly, you delivered my baby when he was born. What was wrong with him? Why did he die?'

Sabrina spoke in a jerking, almost breathless voice. Molly pulled forward a wooden chair.

'There, sit down, my lady. I'll put on the kettle for a drop of tea.'

'I have had tea. Do not try to talk of something else; everyone does that. Why did he die, when I heard him cry so clearly? What was wrong with him?'

Molly was flushed with distress; what ought she to say? It was no good denying any knowledge at all. She mumbled something about the baby's head, it must have been hurt at the birth. Or perhaps – she remembered poor Clonmagh

Harmhill – there had been an injury during the pregnancy; one never knew.

'But I want to know. If you will not tell me I must ask Moll.' Moll had married and was living at Uffield. That mustn't happen, Molly thought; the young woman would blurt it all out at once. She thanked God Peg had never come back from Ireland, but had settled down there with Miss Kate and wrote sometimes at Christmas. She never said a word about how the little black baby fared; a schoolboy, by now, he must be.

'Moll knew nothing about it, my lady; she was tending the water boiling on the fire. I wouldn't trouble yourself any more; what's done is done.'

'But *is he dead?*'

Old Molly began to weep silently, the tears coursing down her cheeks. 'How would I know, my lady? I've heard nothing since –'

'Since they took him away. Was it to Ireland?'

Now what in the world made her guess that? What was one to say? Best keep clear of my lord; whatever came of this, he'd blame her, Molly Maverick, perhaps put her out; and the cottage was comfortable and the roof sound, and there was the dresser.

'I do not know anything more, my lady,' she said stubbornly; and no matter how much Sabrina pleaded with her, that was all Molly would ever say. 'I do not know anything more.'

The news of Sir Guy Sutbury's death at last came to disturb them at that juncture; he had died of a final seizure, having been unable to speak or move for many years. His will had been made before he was taken ill the first time; it left everything to his granddaughter Sabrina, and that meant the return of the rail stock Fenn had so resolutely given back. In fact the railway was disturbing Fenn a good deal at that time; he had lately received a request for his approval of a level crossing to be placed between Fenfallow and the main line. He was unwilling to approve: it would mean more disturbance; but with the Liberal element rife in the country it was made more difficult nowadays to show strength of purpose in any matter, and rather than descend to undignified wrangling he had assented, and the work was already undertaken. After all it would only mean waiting, when one went out, till the gates were opened; and a man would stand at the signal-box to press a lever when there was a train expected. Fenn talked of all this to Sabrina, who did not seem to be giving him her full attention; she was pale and distraught, he decided, since his mother's death. He considered taking her on a holiday; perhaps Nice, for the Battle of Flowers? But she shook her head, and suddenly said, to his extreme discomfiture,

'I want to go to Kate in Ireland. And I want to go alone.'

He humoured her; there might be nothing more in it, and the letter he had received lately from the Abbot of Inshmara, thanking him for continued financial support after the death of the late Countess, might be safely destroyed. A phrase from it stayed in Fenn's mind, rather as if it had been burnt there. *He is a most lovable and promising boy. We should consult you soon about his future. It has always been assumed that he would stay on here with us, but we do not force vocations.*

The boy, the dark boy, loose in the world ... but not yet, and he would never know his name until after one's death, that had been one of the provisions made at the beginning. Sabrina in Ireland ...

Fenn spoke briskly. 'As you will, my darling, but I insist on knowing the arrangements for your journey. And you must take a maid with you.' Quint had retired long ago. 'Perhaps old Molly Ridley would make the trip.'

'I do not need her.'

'You must have someone to look after you. You had better write to Kate to say that you are coming to stay. It is perhaps time one of us visited Marishnageen.' Thus he comforted himself; it need be no more than a social visit. Sabrina would take his advice as she always did, although she had grown more stubborn lately, perhaps with the gained confidence of driving. He looked at her, noticing for the first time that there was grey in her hair; her jawline and throat were no longer smooth. It did not matter; he was growing older himself.

'Oh, Ned left me years ago, and a good riddance. He went off to Australia to look for gold there and didn't find it; I don't know what he is doing now. I sold off the stud after he left; it was all of it getting too much for me.' The grass was blowing wild now about Marishnageen, none of it grazed except by the lonely donkey. The house itself had a neglected air; there was dust on everything, and the servants drank tea and gossiped in the kitchen.

Kate talked on, beyond noticing that Sabrina's gaze was fixed on the brooch she wore. Molly had already gone across to the flat above the stables, to visit her niece Peg. Peg's Roddy drove Kate about nowadays, when she wanted to travel, which was not often. Kate no longer cared whether Molly came here or not. The speckled eyes stared at Sabrina; by God, she'd aged; Henry must be difficult to live with, apart from everything else.

The Clonmagh brooch showed its colours below the Clonmagh eyes as Kate breathed. She eventually stopped talking about herself long enough to become aware of Sabrina's glance, and bridled.

'It belongs here by right, so you needn't look like that,' she said. 'Valentine gave it back to me when she was here, the time she came over with the – oh, the dear Lord, I've said it now, and I promised I wouldn't.'

Sabrina remembered the brooch, and the last time she had seen it. Valentine had been wearing it when she leaned over the bed anxiously, when Sabrina was in labour. It had been with her then, and never seen afterwards. There must have been a reason for giving it to Kate. I do not care for myself, she thought; Kate can have it. But the puzzle was beginning to fit; and nobody had told her, nobody.

'You had better tell me everything,' she said to Kate now. 'If you do not, I shall find out for myself.'

'How?' said Kate mockingly. But her face changed at the answer.

'I will go to Inshmara. I am going tomorrow in any case.'

So she had been told everything. She still insisted on going to the monastery alone; Kate had offered to come with her, for the ride, she said. Talking too much now, she'd said how she had driven that road often over the years, taking the boy sweets and the like at Christmas. 'Sometimes I'd drive along the coast road with him a little, as long as I wasn't seen with him.' Then she clapped a hand to her mouth. 'Now what have I said? But they would have thought, you see, that he was mine.'

Sabrina had not brought Kate. The land here had grown wild and flat, with low thatched cottages white against a slate-grey sky, and piled peat dark against them. There was a man working at the bog, who looked up as they passed. He was the only human being they came across, except for the tinkers with their donkeys, laden high. The land was fantastic and broken, with deep holes in the roads.

The monastery could be seen from a mile or two off, for its bulk reared above the sea. The coastline was wild and broken up with tall rocks, against which the tide hurled when it was in. There was nothing to look out on now but the Atlantic, no land until one came to America. Sabrina begged Roddy to hurry; it might rain.

'We can stay in one of the fishermen's cottages if the storm breaks. Miss Kate does that often.'

So Kate had known, always, about her son. Sabrina set it aside and felt her heart thudding in anticipation of seeing him for herself. Why should it always have had to be for others to visit him? Why should he have needed visiting at all? Shut away here, on the edge of the world ... What would she say to him now, his mother?

The entrance to the monastery was along a flat pebbled path, out of the sea-wind, with short green turf on either side. The sea itself sighed distantly, far below; the tide was out. She saw the beginning of rock-cut slopes down to the beach, which turned so that they were out of sight from the door. A metal bell hung by a rope, which Sabrina pulled, sending the bell clanging; shortly the door was opened by a monk in a white habit, a knotted girdle and rosary hanging from his waist. He was not young, but his face was smooth and unlined. She heard herself speak to him.

'I should like to see Raymond. I am his mother.'

The porter bowed, and without further words led her along flagged passages to a room which held a crucifix, chairs and a sofa. In the middle of the room stood a glass case containing very old books, left open at gilded capitals with extraordinarily intricate painted ornament raised and twined in a great square. She stared at these and marvelled at the culture which had not, here in the west, been destroyed by Saxon invaders; this was the last outpost of the Celtic civilisation which had once covered Europe as far as the Baltic. She was still looking down at the books when the monk came back.

'The Father Abbot would like to see you.'

She followed him to the Abbot's office, to be welcomed by a very tall grey-haired man with long ascetic features and humorous eyes behind thick spectacles. He motioned her to a chair.

'You are Lady Fenn?' he said, and she wondered for an instant how he could know her name; but of course, Henry had been in touch with them here. She felt more than ever like someone groping in the dark.

'Yes. I am Raymond's mother. I have only just learned of his whereabouts. He was taken away from me when he was born. I was told he was dead.' She felt herself blurting out matters she would as a rule have kept to herself. The eyes watched her, summing her up, she felt; a hysterical woman, he would think, this calm monk. She clasped her hands together and tightened her fingers; one must be sensible, calm.

'He is not used to the terms father and mother, except for the Mother of God. He does not even know his own surname. The Earl asked that it should not be told to him, and as he has provided for Raymond's education here we felt it best to meet his wishes. We have called the boy Raymond Thomas after our patron, St Thomas Aquinas. He would not know himself as anyone else. Later we hope that he will go out into the world, but it is a world that will be harsh to him, and he must always feel that he can return here when he will.'

'I am glad – so glad – but he will not be in need. I have left him some money.' Her mind harked back to that brief, hurried visit to Grandpapa's lawyers, last time she and Henry had been in town; Henry thought she was going to the dressmaker's. *Half for my husband, half for my son.* The old notary who had known her from a child had been troubled, and Sabrina had smiled at him, a smile like a banner. 'I'm in my right mind, Matthews,' she had said, and that was all; she had the will witnessed and had left it with them; married women could do so now; everything was in order.

'Let me see him,' she said to the Abbot. 'I will not tell him who I am.'

'That will be hard for you, but better for him. He is used sometimes to pilgrims and to visitors. Mrs Maverick comes very rarely. Raymond will show you round if you ask, and that might be the best way to persuade him to talk to you naturally. He is a silent boy.'

'I will be careful,' she promised. The Abbot bowed his head.

'He will be sent to you in the room where you waited. I will pray for you.'

The bespectacled eyes followed her to the door, then lowered themselves before she closed it. Sabrina found herself back in the room with the glass-topped case and the illuminated books, their gilding shining differently with the altered position of the sun. She sat down and waited. Presently the door opened and a dark-skinned boy with fine features came in.

He was not tall. He had the slender body and limbs of his age, an oval face and clear eyes. He was dressed in a grey flannel knickerbocker suit. She felt that she had seen him before; the Book of the Dead, the figures in it, figures of bird-headed gods and animals and dark people. She smiled, and rose, stretching out her hands; he made a little bow, but did not take them.

'You are Raymond,' she said.

'I am Raymond Thomas.' He spoke well, in what might have been public-school English. He had been carefully educated. He felt sorry for this dainty little lady with the great dark eyes; she seemed sad, and nobody should be sad at Inshmara. 'Do you want me to show you round the monastery?' he said politely. He did not in fact know what else to say to her; it was strange that she should be here; who was she?

'I should like to see it,' Sabrina told him. They went together first to the refectory, empty at this hour; its long tables were of very old oak, well polished. There was a reading-stand with the head of an eagle. 'That is for St John,' said Raymond. His facts were accurately conveyed and he remained impersonal; she might have been any visitor; this was the best way.

The chapel was very beautiful, austere, and plain, with groined arches whitewashed and a stone-flagged floor which struck upwards coldly. There were fresh garden flowers on the altar. 'Who arranges them?' she asked in a whisper.

'Brother Michael. Sometimes I help him to choose them from the garden. The soil is very good here; most things grow well.'

'I should like to see the garden, if I may go there.' She closed her eyes for an instant; she had been on the point of telling him about the water-garden at Fenfallow, and the lilies and rushes called water-soldiers.

He showed her the garden, sheltered from the winds on the cliff. Then they went into the pharmacy, where a brother was mixing ointment in a pestle with mortar; he did not look up, but went on with what he was doing. There were blue pottery jars on the shelves with labels in Latin.

There was an apiary beyond the main garden. Raymond talked with knowledge about bees, for he was allowed to help in culling queen cells and occasionally in housing swarms. 'We lose a great deal of honey if a swarm gets away,' he said solemnly.

'But are you not afraid of being stung?' Sabrina herself knew nothing about bees except that at Fenfallow, and earlier at her grandfather's, honeycomb for tea had been delicious and very sticky. She saw Raymond's eyes slew round so that the whites showed, and he smiled.

'No,' they said. 'They are drunk with honey when they swarm, and will hurt nobody. If you shake them down into a box and cover it and put it by the new hive, they will walk up a white cloth in the evening, to their new house. I like to watch that, but it doesn't happen often because Brother Paul is too careful not to keep too many queens.'

He was standing with the clear light from the door shining on him, a young Osiris. Sabrina's heart ached. 'Do you never go out of the monastery?' she asked. 'Do you not swim from the beaches?' A boy should like to swim; but perhaps the tides were dangerous.

'I am not permitted to, because of the fast tides,' he acknowledged. 'There is a little cove with pebbles and shells, below the steps. One can only reach it between tides.'

'The tide is out now,' she said, looking down past the cliff. 'Will you show me the bay?'

'If we go quickly. The steps are very steep; be careful.'

'Let us go,' she said. She followed him nimbly down the steeply cut rocks. The little beach to which they came was small, covered with tiny coloured pebbles and shells. The grey rock rose sheer behind and above them. The sea murmured curiously, as though impatient to get back.

'Would you like perhaps one day to cross the sea, Raymond? There is a world on the other side.'

'Yes. The other side is America. I would like to go there, but I would like still more to go to visit the north of Africa, where Father Abbot says my people came from.'

'So that perhaps you will go?'

'Perhaps,' he said, and stood silently; the excursion was over and there was nothing more to say to the lady. She held out a hand again and then let it drop to her side.

'Will you choose me a shell, Raymond?' she asked him. 'I will take it with me where I am going.'

She watched him bend and turn over the pebbles and shells. The air smelt salt; Sabrina raised her head and let the wind blow back her hair; she wore no hat for this journey. She fixed the figure of Raymond in her memory; the slim form bending over the pebbles, his thin hands seeking; they were the shape of her own.

He found a cowrie shell and came over and gave it to her shyly. She let it lie in her palm. It was iridescent, with faint rainbow hues. Sabrina closed her fingers over it. 'I will keep it always,' she said. She reached in the pocket of her cardigan with her other hand and drew out a letter. It was addressed to Fenfallow and she wondered if the name would come to mean anything to Raymond, later in life.

'Can you post this for me?' she asked him.

'Yes, there is a box by the door. I will put it in. We should go now; the tide is coming in fast.'

'You go, and post the letter, and I will follow,' she told

him. He turned obediently; like herself he was used to obeying orders; and went from her up the steps. She watched him climb until the turn took him out of sight. Then she opened her hand and looked at the shell, and again closed her fingers over it. The tide was racing now between the pebbles; soon it would smash against the near rocks. She began to walk towards it, hearing her small shoes crunch on the shingle. Soon the waves wrapped her ankles. It was growing dark. She thought of the short green sward they had traversed together, starred with tiny wild flowers; the true machair. The water here was not cold. Soon Roddy would come back with the carriage and find her no longer there, and in a day or two Henry would receive the letter she had written him. All these things were clear in her mind as she stood with the waves rising about her. Their strength was great and she was soon buffeted, losing balance at last, her hand still clasped tightly round the shell. Then the cross-current came and deepened the inshore water, and there was blackness. Soon there was nothing to be seen but the grey waves, pounding and foaming against the rocks.

My darling,

By the time you receive this you will be free. We could never have trusted one another fully again; in fact I can never have had your full trust, or you would have told me the truth about our son. I realise that in not doing so you thought you were being kind to me, but in fact you were treating me like a child, which makes me sad for both our sakes. I do not know why Raymond is as he is, perhaps in my mother's family there was Moorish blood. I shall have seen him before this letter is posted. It is very peaceful here, right out of the world.

My love to you, and, if you ever meet, to him. You should marry again; you are still young. Tell them nothing but that I met with an accident.

Your
Sabrina

The body was washed ashore further down the coast two days later. The face and breasts had been eaten at by fish, and one hand was clenched so fast that they could not prise open the fingers and sent it as it was to the mortuary.

Fenfallow, September 9th, 1900
From the Earl of Fenn to the Father Abbot, Inshmara
Sir,
*   When my late wife visited you she perhaps revealed his identity to my son. It is of no great consequence except that I do not wish to see him or to have him here. I will continue the arrangement we made until he is eighteen, after which he will no doubt decide whether or not to remain with you for himself. As you will already have heard from my wife's lawyers, he will be in no need of money of his own.*
*   I enclose the testament from my wife's father, which she never read but which you should give to Raymond when he comes of age.*
*   I am grateful to you for caring for and educating my son.*
*   Yours faithfully,*
*   Fenn*

Inshmara, September 15th
Dear Lord Fenn,
*   I received your letter and have noted its contents. Raymond had no idea that the visitor was his mother, as I discussed the matter with her before she saw him and we agreed that this would be best for him.*
*   However since her visit, and the sad news of her death, he has grown restless and says he would like to go to sea. We have persuaded him that he is not old enough meantime, and that he should finish his education. He also says, as he has done before, that he would like to visit his grandmother's people; whether this will be possible by then I do not know.*
*   I may say that although we profoundly regret what happened, we ourselves had no idea that Lady Fenn had not returned in the carriage until it came for her in the evening. By then a search was made, but it was too late to help and Raymond himself told us that he had discussed the tides with her, so that she knew.*

I trust that you are in good health and offer, once again, my profound condolences and those of my brothers here.
Yours sincerely,
Desmond O'Donnell, Abbot

The years passed at Fenfallow and the Earl became a legend, seldom seen except at church. He never remarried. When he drove out he used Sabrina's brass-lamped Bentley, which he took great pride in polishing and maintaining. When addressed he was correct and courteous, but one got no further; as the schoolmistress Helen Adderley found when she visited him, by arrangement, about a suggested memorial to Countess Sabrina.

'Kept me waiting like a servant, then came in and said there was nothing to discuss, but that we should arrange matters in our own way, and gave me a donation,' Helen said afterwards to the librarian, Miss Clarkson, with whom she was fairly well acquainted, though she had made no close friends since the death of Sabrina Fenn. 'The dear Countess was quite different,' she said now. 'Do you know, when I think of her I always remember the lines:

Sabrina fair,
Listen where thou art sitting
Under the glassy, cool, translucent wave —'

and then clapped her hand to her mouth; what had made her say that, of all things?

It was undecided for some time what form the memorial should take. Plaques and statues were no longer as popular as they had been, and charitable purposes of some kind in memory of the dead had become more fashionable, and certainly more useful. The two main suggestions, put to the committee which had raised itself, were for a new wing to be added to the hospital or else some modernisation of the almshouses. The former suggestion triumphed, and those who had helped to raise the money were invited afterwards to a little tea-party in Matron's room. Lord Fenn was present, to everyone's pleasure. Speeches were made, and Henry opened the wing – there were sixteen new beds – and then drove off in his car, alone.

The guard above the level crossing was on the alert. The five-fifteen from London would shortly come thundering through, and he himself must have the gates shut a clear five minutes before that, to be certain of no accidents. But the lever in the gate-house had stuck; he should maybe have oiled it; there was no time now. He pulled and pushed frantically, but it would not budge, and the white-painted gates stood open – and there was a motor now – *Gawd, it's his lordship's Bentley* –

The guard ran downstairs, waving to stop with all his might; but the driver took no notice, and sure as fate the express came through; mowing down both guard and driver, leaving the car a mass of twisted metal and shattered glass, among which the dead lay. The train's brakes screeched to a halt, but too late. Guy's vengeance, after almost a century, was complete.

At the Admiralty, 6th February 1920
To Rear-Admiral Sir John Larrifield, R.N., at Elmworth
My dear Larry,
   I have been sifting through various papers concerning the late struggle and I have found one which will interest you, as you were a friend of old Lord Fenn. Evidently he had after all an heir who declined the title, a coloured man; don't know how it happened. This man, Raymond Thomas, joined the ship at Tunis, worked his way through the Mediterranean and Turkish passages, and when we ran into trouble in the Dardanelles displayed conspicuous bravery at the guns. He was killed by a shell and later, as the rest were, buried at sea. It was proposed that he be mentioned in despatches but somehow this lapsed. We understand that he is the last of his family.
   I trust that you are in health and that the old wound does not trouble you too greatly ...